FALLING

THE BLACKHAWK BOYS

HARD

FALLING

THE BLACKHAWK BOYS

HARD

New York Times Bestselling Author

LEXI RYAN

Cover © 2017 by Sarah Hansen, Okay Creations
Interior design and formatting by:

www.emtippettsbookdesigns.com

For all the little girls who prayed God might make them a statue and for the women they became. It was never your fault.

About
FALLING HARD

An NFL player with a secret past, and the one woman with the power to turn his world inside out…

Former actress Emma Rothschild is partying in Vegas in disguise. But I'm not fooled. Five years ago, I knew that body better than my own, and I haven't forgotten a single detail.

When Emma's unexpectedly left alone in Sin City, I agree to spend the weekend with her. As *friends*. Why not? If I can knock down the toughest guys in the NFL, I'm strong enough to keep my hands to myself, even if she is the sexiest woman I've ever met.

Emma is part of my past—years so shrouded in secrets that not even my best friends know the truth about who I am. I'm a single dad now and not interested in revisiting my old ways or trying to win back the only woman I ever let close enough to break my heart.

But this is Vegas, where all bets are off, and with Emma, nothing ever goes as planned…

FALLING HARD is a sexy and emotional novel intended for mature readers. It's the fourth book in the world of the Blackhawk Boys, but can be enjoyed as a standalone.

Football. Secrets. Lies. Passion. These boys don't play fair. Which Blackhawk Boy will steal your heart?

CHAPTER 1

KEEGAN

The marble countertop is covered in red spaghetti sauce, but it's nothing compared to the face of my fourteen-month-old daughter. Both she and my kitchen look like they were involved in either a gruesome crime or a grade-school food fight. I pull a washcloth from the drawer and run it under warm water from the faucet. I bypass the messy counters and go around to the other side of the island, where Jazzy sits in her highchair.

"Here it comes." I reach for her with the wet rag and she grins, flashing her two tiny bottom front teeth. "Wishy, washy, wishy, washy, wishy, washy, wee!"

Giggling, Jasmine turns away from the washcloth, dodging my attempts to uncover her rosy cheeks. This isn't my first rodeo, so I make a sneak attack on the opposite side and wipe her face clean with two swipes.

"Look at that," I declare with mock shock. "There *is* a little girl underneath all that spaghetti sauce."

Jasmine giggles again, and I lift her from the highchair. All my friends say Jazzy is the happiest baby ever, and I might be a little biased, but she certainly is the coolest I've met. I keep her in my arms and take long strides toward her bedroom.

"Let's get you cleaned up before Mommy gets here." Olivia will be here to pick her up in the next five or ten minutes and she doesn't like Jazzy to get messy.

"If you let little girls eat spaghetti, suckers, or ice cream cones, they end up looking like they wandered out of the trailer park. No. Just no."

Mommy's a snob, I think, but I don't say it out loud. Olivia might not be perfect, but she's Jasmine's mother, and for that I owe her everything.

I lay Jazzy on the changing table, where I make quick work of putting on a fresh diaper and pulling her pink sundress over her head. She rolls over onto her stomach and tries to crawl away from me, and I use her little maneuver to my advantage and button the back of the dress before scooping her into my arms.

When the doorbell rings, I close my eyes for a beat, holding her and smelling her sweet baby shampoo from this morning's bath. "Daddy's gonna miss you this weekend."

She reaches up and puts her chubby little hands on either side of my jaw. "Da-da."

I'm six foot four and a wall of hard-earned muscle, but when she does that, I'm fucking helpless. "Okay, okay, I'll buy you the pony, the castle, and the Corvette when you're sixteen, and anything else you want."

Her grin stretches across her face as she smacks my cheeks. I swear, this kid knows she has me wrapped around her little finger.

"Mommy's here." I shift her to my hip as we leave the nursery and walk to the front door.

"Mama?" Jazzy says, clapping her hands. "Mama. Mama."

"That's right." I open the door for Olivia and wave her into the house. Her dark hair is down around her bare shoulders. The way she smiles at the sight of our daughter makes something pull hard in my chest—grief for the family we could've been. "You don't have to use the doorbell," I tell her. "That's why you have a key."

"I know. It just doesn't feel right to let myself in." She sweeps her hair over her shoulder and reaches both arms out for Jazzy. "How's my girl?"

"She just had dinner." I hand over our daughter but don't mention that I gave her spaghetti. That would be asking for an argument. "Another tooth broke through a couple nights ago. She's a much happier girl now."

"I bet she is."

"We went to the park this morning and she took a two-hour nap this afternoon, so she should be in good shape until bedtime."

Olivia beams at Jasmine as she snuggles her against her chest, and the sight makes my throat go thick. *Family.* That's what we should be. That's what Jazzy deserves.

Olivia Crowe is the mother of my child, and for a long time

I wanted her to be more. When the Gulf Gators signed me after graduation as an undrafted free agent, I moved Olivia to Florida so I wouldn't miss Jasmine growing up. Sometime during the last year, I've accepted that she's never going to see me the way I've always seen her, but acceptance doesn't mean the sting has gone away.

"She should have plenty of diapers in the bag." I nod toward the bag on the floor. "I packed enough outfits for the weekend, and a few extras too. I think she has a couple more teeth trying to break through, so if she gets cranky, go ahead and give her some Motrin."

"Keegan, I'm her mother." She sighs heavily. "Calm down. I can handle three nights with my baby."

"I wasn't trying to imply—"

"But you did." She shakes her head and reaches out to disentangle Jasmine's hand from her hair. "I don't want to fight. Just go be with your boys and have a good weekend. Tell the crew I said hi."

I frown. "You could come, you know. They invited you for a reason."

She waves away the suggestion and stoops to grab the diaper bag. "Have fun and relax. You deserve it."

I nod. "I will. Thanks."

"Hey, babe, are you coming?"

We both turn toward the door to see my quarterback, Dre Olsen. His face goes pale as he spots me. *Well, fuck. Isn't this awkward?*

I lift my chin. "Hey, Dre." I look to Olivia and, judging by the way she grimaces, I'm sure the question is in my eyes or—at the very least—*what the fuck?* is written all over my face.

"Sorry, man. I didn't know you'd be here. I thought she was picking her up from the nanny."

I smile, but my teeth grit together. Olivia started dating Dre shortly after I moved her down here. I was trying not to push her into a relationship she wasn't ready for, but I thought we were on the same page—that we'd live together and see if we could give our relationship a go. I rented this beachfront condo that stretched the limits of even my NFL salary, and though we weren't officially a couple, I thought our relationship was moving in the right direction.

Just like since the beginning of our relationship, she was doing just enough to keep me on the hook while keeping me at an arm's length. I found out—in the most awkward way possible—that she was fucking my quarterback. Let's just say the locker room isn't the only context in which I can say I've seen Dre's bare ass.

I turn to Dre—the quarterback, the dream man in Olivia's eyes. "Do you think you could give us a couple of minutes?"

"Sure, man." He turns to Olivia. "I'll be in the car."

She watches him go before turning back to me.

"You're keeping Jazzy at Dre's this weekend?"

"Where did you think I was keeping her?"

I turn up my palms. "I don't know. Maybe that fancy apartment I pay for?"

She frowns. "I didn't think it would be a big deal."

"It is a big deal. Anything that has to do with Jazz will *always* be a big deal to me. Okay, Liv?" I drag a hand through my hair. "You picked him. I can deal with that. I've had six months to deal with that. But she's my daughter, and I deserve to know who she's going to be spending her time with."

Olivia nods. "Okay. I'm sorry." She cuts her eyes away from mine, and I watch as they fill with tears. "I'm just trying to have a normal life."

I feel like an ass. A never-good-enough, discarded-for-the-better-guy-with-the-bigger-salary asshole. "Just keep me in the loop, okay?"

Nodding, she lifts onto her toes and presses a kiss to my cheek. "Okay. Thanks, Keeg. You know I love you, right?"

I'm too busy mentally dissecting those words to respond, so I open the door for her and watch her leave, wondering if she was right and *I* was the one who never gave us a chance. When she's gone, I go back inside and lean my head against the door.

"You say you want me, but you're so closed off. You say you want this to work, but being with you is lonelier than being alone."

The words felt like an excuse at the time—a way for her to justify going after her dream of marrying an NFL quarterback. But maybe she's right. Maybe I am closed off. Maybe I'm just one of those guys whose long-ago broken heart turned him cold.

Ten seconds later, my phone buzzes with a text.

Mason: *Are you as ready for this weekend as I am?*

A bachelor party in Vegas with my best friends? I look out the window and watch Dre pull away with the only two people in the world I'd call my family. Fuck yeah, I'm ready.

EMMA

A weekend in Vegas with my best friend—what more could a girl ask for?

I wander around the massive suite Becky booked for us and shake my head. I know she won't want me to pay her for this, but I'm going to have to find a way. This is too much.

"Should we come up with some sock-on-the-door system?" Becky asks as she follows me into the bedroom.

I turn to meet my friend's sparkling blue eyes. "Sock on the door?"

"So I don't interrupt your much-needed one-night stand."

I snort. "Yeah, right. As if I'd even know how to have one of those if I wanted to."

"I'll teach you everything you need to know." She holds out a black wig.

"What is that?"

"What does it look like?"

"Uma Thurman's wig from *Pulp Fiction*?" When she just stares at me, I sigh. Socks on doorknobs and disguises aren't what I had in mind when Becky suggested we indulge in a weekend in

Vegas. We got a suite at a fancy hotel, and I thought we'd spend our days at the spa and evenings by the pool, with maybe a couple of hours here and there for a game of blackjack or a round at the roulette table. "I get that it's supposed to be some sort of disguise, but why? What exactly do you have planned? Killing hookers and snorting blow?"

She laughs. "Look at the good girl who thinks there's nothing between a celibate monastery life and murder."

"I don't live in a monastery."

"Might as well, for all the action that goes down in your place."

I might be offended if there was any scorn in Becky's voice, but her evaluation of my sex life isn't too far from the truth, so I let it slide. "I didn't come to Vegas to screw a stranger. I came to spend time with *you*."

"Can't blame me for trying." She turns up her palms helplessly. "Okay, one-night stands aside, when was the last time you let loose? For that matter, when was the last time you were in public without worrying someone was watching?" We both know that's a rhetorical question, and she doesn't wait for my response. "You can't come to Vegas and not *do* Vegas. We're here to have fun, and do you really think you can tuck a buck into a stripper's G-string as *Emma Rothschild*, America's sweetheart?"

I make a face. "Strippers? Really? That doesn't seem a little skeevy and desperate to you?"

She shakes the wig. "It's called *fun*. Have some."

I sigh. Becky's my best friend. We aren't lifelong best friends like I hear people talking about—because spending your childhood in the spotlight and your adolescence in your mother's shadow makes it hard as hell to develop meaningful relationships. We met in college, and she has been there for me through some of the craziest decisions of my life, including the rollercoaster of the last year. "Fine, but if I wear this wig, you have to get out of bed and work out with me in the morning."

She slaps her butt. "And risk losing this?"

"You're the one who picked out the dress I have to squeeze into next week," I remind her. "If you're going to have me sucking down liquid calories all weekend, I need a minimum of sixty minutes of cardio every morning."

She wiggles her brows. "What kind of liquid are you planning to *suck* down?"

Rolling my eyes, I throw the wig at her chest. "Dear God, you're the worst."

"You love me."

"Therein lies the problem."

CHAPTER 2
KEEGAN

Bailey Green tosses her long blond hair over her shoulder as she hoists her glass in the air. "To Vegas," she says.

"To Vegas!" everyone seconds, clinking their glasses together.

"May our nights be epic and our memories be blurry." She gives me a pointed look before throwing back her shot while the rest of the group downs theirs.

Bachelor parties, for all their various manifestations, essentially fall into three categories. There's the "skeevy strip club" kind where you spend the whole damn thing watching girls flash their bits and pieces for tips while spending way too much money on watered-down alcohol. At a couple of these, the groom was so obsessed with lap dances that I seriously worried about the future of his union. Don't get me wrong. I've spent as much time enjoying strip clubs as the next guy, but Bailey is a former stripper and likes to regale me with tales of the things the dancers would do to the guys behind the scenes; let's just say the magic has died a little.

Other bachelor parties fall into the "poker night with the guys" category. These typically happen when the groom is afraid of his bride and wants to make sure she knows he was a good boy and didn't need the titillation of a dancer's tits in his face to have a good time. There are a lot of variations on this one, from paintball to golfing to a literal poker night in somebody's basement. Regardless of the location, the focus is on the cigars and bourbon and the groom gushing about how "lucky" he is until he gets drunk enough to bitch about how she won't let him shop for his own shoes, let alone live his own life.

And then there's the "anything-goes wild weekend," which really should go without explanation, because what happens in the anything-goes weekend stays in the anything-goes weekend.

This weekend's festivities were supposed to fall into the third category. I mean, *Vegas*. Need I say more? Or they were supposed to, until the bride and her entourage decided to join us. Honestly, I wouldn't have it any other way. These are my people, and what matters is what the groom thinks, and right now Arrow's smiling bigger than a teenage boy after receiving his first hummer. His would-be bachelor party has turned into more of a college friends' reunion than anything else, but since we haven't all been together in a year, nobody's complaining. Sebastian and Alex stayed home, opting for a quiet weekend with their new baby, but everyone else is here.

A week ago, the last three of our group graduated from Blackhawk Hills University, ringing in the end of an era. Before this, we haven't been together since the other half of us graduated last May.

"Would you look at that," Mason Dahl says. We're at the bar at the nightclub in our hotel, crowded into a big circular booth. Mason's opposite me and has been using his straight-shot view of the dance floor to scope out women and make Bailey jealous as hell. "Damn, she's beautiful."

The thing about Vegas is there are a *lot* of beautiful women. And the pretty women you might not notice anywhere else come to Vegas and vamp it up so much in short dresses and high heels that you can't help but pay attention.

"Go after her," Chris says, following Mason's gaze. "She keeps turning this way."

I shake my head but keep my mouth shut. There are four NFL players hanging out together in this booth. This isn't the first time tonight it's drawn female attention our way, and it won't be the last. The oddity is that Mason even cares.

"I don't think she's looking at me," Mason says. He raps his knuckles on the table in front of me. "She's got her eyes on you, Keller. Black hair, long legs, curves from here to Seattle."

"What can I say?" I ask, not bothering to turn. "My milkshake brings the girls to the yard."

Chris snorts. "He's cursed. The second he decided he didn't want casual hookups, they all came running."

"It's a burden to be this irresistible," I mutter before taking a long pull from my beer. A couple of years ago, I'd have been down for that, but now I'm a single dad who's spent the last year trying and failing to make things work with his baby's mother. I'm a business owner *and* an undrafted free agent who's thanking his lucky stars he got picked up by an NFL team. These days, I'm more interested in a full night's sleep than I am a hot piece of ass.

Mason grins. "You going after her or not?"

"And lose out on the first night with all my boys in eleven months? No way. You go over there if you're so interested."

Mason takes a long sip from his bourbon, and I don't miss the way his gaze skims over Bailey before he says, "Don't mind if I do."

I've had just enough to drink that I'm about to tell them both to get over themselves and just get together already. Not a single person at this table believes Mason is going over there for any reason other than to make Bailey jealous. But before I can speak, someone laughs behind me, and I spin in my seat toward the sound. It was a big laugh—full and bright and just like...

I stop breathing when I land on a pair of familiar icy-blue eyes. "Damn."

I'm faintly aware of Mason sliding out of the booth, but I can't take my eyes off the girl standing beside the dance floor. The dark hair I don't recognize, but the face I'll never forget.

My eyes are playing tricks on me. That's the only explanation. Being in Vegas for my buddy's bachelor party is fucking with my brain. Watching Arrow and Mia together is making me think about that intense love that turns you inside out and makes you forget everything else around you.

It can't really be her.

The woman in question bites the corner of her lip before sliding a pair of sunglasses onto her nose and covering her eyes. It's her. She's wearing a black wig, but I'd recognize that laugh anywhere. The eyes and the telltale nervous habit just confirmed what I already knew.

I instinctively look for her date, but she's talking to a brunette, and the only men around her don't seem to be *with* her.

Tearing my eyes away, I climb out of the booth to grab Mason before he can get any closer. "Don't."

He must see it on my face. "So she *was* looking at you."

"Probably."

Mason slides his gaze down to where my hand is still wrapped around his arm, and I release it. If he's wondering what was between us, he doesn't ask. "Understood." He takes his seat again, but this time he takes my old spot, giving me the side of the booth with the better view of Emma.

I take it without comment. Maybe I shouldn't, because it's masochistic as fuck to look at her, let alone watch her dance when I know she saw me, but I can't take my eyes off her. I haven't seen her in five years, and like a parched man after his first sip of water, I don't want to do anything but take her in.

"Who is she?" Bailey asks behind me.

She's Emma Rothschild, America's sweetheart, the daughter of Oscar winner Miranda Rothschild. She's the first woman I ever loved, and when I gave her my heart, she pulverized it. But I only reply, "Somebody I used to know."

EMMA

For the first time in five years, Keegan Keller is in the same room as me, but now, instead of being alone, we're in a dance club with hundreds of other people. Now instead of being a couple of lovesick kids, we're full-blown adults who've gotten on with their lives. He has a baby, a bar, and an NFL career, for Christ's sake. He's carried on just fine without me.

Not that I stalk him on social media or anything. That would be creepy. *God, I'm pathetic.*

When he turned around, I could have sworn he made eye contact with me, but the club's flashing lights make it so hard to tell for sure. Once he started talking with his friends, it was as if I didn't exist, so I made myself dance with Becky so I'd stop staring.

"I told you that wig looked hot on you," Becky says as she sways to the music.

I didn't want to wear this stupid thing, but I get the point. I can't go anywhere as Emma Rothschild and just have a good time. I haven't taken an acting role since I was sixteen years old, but according to last month's *People* magazine spread, I'm "Still America's Sweetheart." Not that America ever asked *me* if I was interested in that label. "The wig looks ridiculous."

"Tell that to the hottie giving you fuck-me eyes at nine o'clock,"

Becky says before her tongue returns to its lewd molestation of the penis straw in her drink.

I arch a brow and start to turn, but she stops me.

"Don't look *now*."

Sighing, I take a pull from my drink. We have been in Vegas less than two hours, and Becky is nearing "dance on the bar drunk," while I've not even touched buzzed yet. "At least tell me what he looks like." *Yes, tell me anything to distract me from the fact that Keegan is over there with a bunch of his football friends and may or may not know that I'm here. Tell me anything to distract me from the possibility that the only man I ever loved saw me again after five years and is choosing to pretend he didn't.*

"Tall, clean-cut, dark hair, shoulders that would make you think about being swept into his arms and carried through a doorway but would make *me* think about being pounded against the nearest wall. In other words, completely your type."

I groan, barely resisting the urge to turn and look for myself. He does sound like my type. I'd like to say I don't have a "type," that I'm not that predictable, but hell, isn't what Becky just described the "type" of most heterosexual females? "Nice smile?"

"I don't know yet. He's kind of got that broody thing going on. Oh, fuck, he's coming this way. Play it cool."

I shake my head. Not to worry. I haven't gotten nervous about a guy approaching me since I was eighteen, I'm certainly not going to start tonight. I turn toward the hottie in question, ready to paste on my confident, don't-you-wish-you-had-a-chance smile, but when I meet his eyes, my stomach lurches forward, flip-flops, and shimmies all at once.

His steps slow and then he drags his gaze over me, shakes his head, and closes the distance between us. "Emma."

Is it normal to get turned on by the sound of your name coming out of someone's mouth? I love the way he shapes his lips around the syllables and the way his gaze drops to my mouth as he says them. *Christ.* I'm pathetic. He steps closer—maybe because the bar is loud and we have to be this close to hear each other. Or maybe because, even five years later, he feels this pull between us as strongly as I feel it. "It's really you."

"Keegan." I run my gaze over his face. That strong jaw. Those dark eyes. His dress shirt is unbuttoned at the top, and he's rolled the sleeves up to his elbows. If there was better lighting, I'd totally take a minute to perv out over his forearms, because they're a thing of beauty. "What are you doing here?"

He cocks a brow and lifts his beer. He gestures over his shoulder toward the booth where I spotted him earlier. "It was supposed to be a bachelor party, but the bride and her friends crashed it." His lips quirk, as if he's mostly amused by this. Wouldn't most guys be annoyed to have their bachelor party usurped by a bunch of chicks? He drops his gaze to my skintight, low-cut tank, another Becky idea: *Want a wild weekend in Vegas? Dress the part.* "How are you?" He looks at my hand, inspecting my ring finger—or is that my imagination? "Did you and Harry ever…?"

Harry? As I stand here, I could recite his statistics from last season, the name of his bar, and tell him a half-dozen facts about his one-year-old daughter—*thank you, Instagram*—but he hasn't even paid enough attention to my life to know that I stay as far from Harry as possible? "I'm… No. I don't even live in California anymore."

Something passes over his face. I'd give an ovary for better lighting in this place right now, because I can't pinpoint the emotion and I want to know what he thinks about that—or if he even cares enough to think anything of it at all. "I just saw you and thought I'd say hello."

"I'm glad you did."

He's changed. He's more hard bulk and less softness than the summer we spent together, but it's not just his body that's changed. There's something in his eyes that tells me he's wiser now. He seems older than he is, and yet, for all he's matured, his effect on me hasn't changed at all. My stomach is a veritable flock of butterflies. Flock? Considering the ruckus they're making in there, *infestation* might be a better word. My stomach is going wild, and at the same time my chest tightens because I want to sit down and have him tell me everything that's happened in the last five years.

"Oh my God," Becky says, throwing her arms in the air. "This song! Let's dance!"

Without giving me a chance to respond, she grabs my arm and drags me to the center of the packed dance floor. I look over my shoulder toward Keegan, and he's watching us. Watching *me*. A waitress circles the floor selling test-tube shots, and I buy two— liquid courage time—down them, and give her the tubes back before she walks away. I'm not sure what was in those shots—

cheap vodka and some sweet stuff, I'm guessing—but I can feel it hit my system, and I dance. I dance because I'm supposed to be cutting loose this weekend, because it feels good to move my body to the beat and laugh with Becky. I dance because he's watching, and that feels as good as the vodka hitting my bloodstream. *Better.* Nothing feels as good as his hot gaze on me, and memories of our last nights together warm me from the inside out.

"Crap," Becky says, laughing when the song ends. "I totally pulled you away from that guy. Did he want to dance? You should totally dance with the hot stranger. He's looking at you like he'd like to do you against the nearest wall and then drop to his knees and use his mouth to clean up his mess."

I gasp and laugh at the same time. "Becky!"

"What? I'm just saying it how it is."

Is he looking at me like that? Do I want him to? That's crazy, crazy thinking. I let Keegan go five years ago, and when I did, I knew it had to be over. I needed to end things, and I did. With a man like Keegan, there is no going back.

"Should I get him for you?" she asks.

"What? Are you crazy?"

"Or maybe you want to do the honors. We're in Vegas, after all. Go over there and tell him you wanna be licked."

"You're insane!"

Laughing, she gives me a soft nudge in Keegan's direction. "Give me a break and let me live vicariously through you."

"You're an impossibly bad influence."

"If Zachary were here, he'd totally be on my side about this."

I smile hard at the mention of her brother, my other best friend, but then the smile falls away. I'm not sure Zachary would approve of anything that would complicate my life as much as Keegan returning to it.

"Oh shit, girl, he's coming over."

I stop dancing and watch as Keegan maneuvers his big frame through the throng of swaying bodies and comes to stand with us.

It's so crowded that he has to step close, and I can feel the heat rolling off his body as he lowers his mouth to my ear. Everything in me feels charged and ready for release. My body remembers him and instinctively sways into him. "I'm glad you're doing well. I—"

I put my fingers to his lips. I don't want to talk right now, because talking means rehashing sad crap I want to pretend never happened. Maybe because it's been so long since I've seen him or maybe because I'm drunk going on trashed, I step close and lock eyes with him as I move my hips to the beat.

CHAPTER 3
KEEGAN

I came out here to tell her goodnight, to tell her I was heading out and to remind her to be careful. But the words died on my tongue the second she put her fingers to my lips and started dancing in front of me. I've had too fucking much to drink, and maybe I'm hallucinating, because I can't believe what's happening right now. This can't be real. Emma Rothschild is close enough to touch, and she's even more beautiful than I remember. She's all curves and soft skin in that outfit, and even though it's nothing like the outfits she wore when I knew her, I love it, because it shows her off. She's relaxed and happy, her face tilted toward the ceiling as she rolls her hips to the beat.

I lower my head to inhale the scent of her hair, and fuck, she's so real. I've imagined this moment a hundred times—what I'd say if I saw her again, what I'd do. In the early months after we split, my reunion fantasies had me turning my back on her, walking away from her like she so easily walked away from me. I wanted her to feel my anger, but this is so fucking much better.

I'm forced to stop dancing when someone taps me on the shoulder. "We're all getting an Uber and heading to Rain. Are you coming?" Bailey shouts so I can hear.

I shake my head. "I'll catch up with you later."

Bailey's brow wrinkles. "Okay. But use protection, for Christ's sake. The last thing you need right now is more baby-mama drama."

Use protection. Those words snap me from this drugged haze I've been trapped in since Emma rolled her hips against mine. Fuck. What do I think I'm doing? This isn't some random beautiful woman in Vegas. This is *Emma*—the woman who held my heart in her hands and crushed it. Even if we could put the past behind us, I don't have time to start something up with anyone. My daughter is my first priority, and that's never going to change.

Emma steps away, following her friend to the waitress weaving her way through the crowd.

What the hell did I think I was doing out here? I wasn't thinking at all. I was operating completely on instinct and a need to touch her that's never gone away. If I'd been thinking, I wouldn't have let myself remember what it was like to have her close. Hell, if I'd been thinking, I wouldn't have come over here to begin with.

As the girls hand over cash for shots, I turn to Bailey. "Let's go."

At four a.m., just three hours after I fell into bed, I'm wide awake and sick of staring at the ceiling in my hotel room. It's seven at home and I'm up by five every morning, so this is sleeping in for me. Even with the time difference, it's too early to FaceTime Olivia so I can see Jasmine. But thankfully, the hotel gym is open twenty-four hours. I change into a pair of athletic shorts and a T-shirt, slide into my running shoes, and slip out of the room.

After seeing Emma last night, I need a good workout to clear my head. I slept like shit, tossing and turning. Remembering. Considering how she ended things, I should be pissed. I should give her a fucking piece of my mind. Or better yet, I shouldn't give her a second of my time. It's better that things ended when they did, right? I dodged a bullet. I got to walk away the good guy instead of being found out for what I really am. It's not like she was the only one with secrets. I just didn't expect hers to fuck me up so much.

Despite all that, after five years, my anger is gone and all that remains is the bittersweet nostalgia of first love. It'll fade in no time. And if it doesn't, I really need to see a doctor about this fist that's been wrapped around my heart since I heard her laugh last night.

I take the elevator up to the health center and find it dark. At four in the morning in Vegas, people are too busy stumbling half-drunk to their rooms to be worried about fitting in their workout. I use my keycard to let myself in and hit the lights.

The space isn't huge, but it has everything I need for a workout. A couple of treadmills, an elliptical trainer, a bench, and a bunch of dumbbells. I put on my headphones and climb on the treadmill. It might be the off-season, but I'm not going to be one of those guys who goes soft between seasons and pays for it at training camp. Hell, I only signed a two-year contract. I can't afford to go soft. I hit some intervals and am getting a good sweat started when the door swings open.

Emma's eyes go wide and she stares at me, her soft pink lips parting into a tiny O.

I hit the stop button on the treadmill and meet her gaze. She's not wearing that ridiculous black wig this morning. Instead, her curly red hair is piled on top of her head in a sloppy bun that reminds me of lazy Sunday mornings tangled in her sheets. I want to take out the hair tie just to watch it tumble down her shoulders. I want to remember how it feels in my hands as she straddles my hips.

Her eyes skim over me, slowly taking in my sweaty T-shirt before coming back up to my face. I see the same denial in her eyes that I felt when I saw her last night. "Keegan?" she asks with a squeak.

I pull out my earbuds, step off the treadmill, and grab a towel, trying to pretend seeing her doesn't fuck me up ten ways to Sunday. Last night was different. With the music, the dance floor, the crowd, and all the alcohol pumping through my blood, I could pretend the past didn't happen. I could pretend she didn't break promises and end everything with a note full of explanations that didn't make sense and apologies I didn't want. This morning, it's smacking me in the face. The good, the bad, and the ugly. "Good morning."

Her expression is a jumble of emotions, and I'd give all my pennies if it meant knowing her thoughts. Is she wishing she hadn't run into me? Is she feeling remorse for how things ended five years ago? Or is she just embarrassed to see me here? "You..." She shakes her head and blinks at me. "You didn't say goodbye last night."

"Funny. I thought that was the way things worked between us. You didn't say goodbye five years ago." Oh, *there it is*, that old anger back right when I need it the most. Being a dick sure beats the humiliation of taking her hand and begging for the answers she never had the courtesy to give me.

She frowns, a line forming between her brows. "I never..." She shakes her head and exhales heavily.

"I'll get out of here so you can work out."

"Don't go." She runs her eyes over me again. "I mean, you weren't done, were you?"

No. I wasn't done, but with her so close, my mind has fixated on a very different kind of workout. Since getting her naked and fucking her against the wall isn't in the cards for this morning or ever again, it's probably better that I leave.

"You were here first," she says. "If anyone is going to leave, it should be me."

The door swings open, and the brunette I saw with Emma last night bursts into the room. "Sorry I'm late, but holy hell, sister, why do we have to work out so early? Or at all? This is supposed to be a Vegas bachelorette party, not fat camp." She makes a face when her gaze settles on me. "Oh, hey. Hi. Hello. Sorry," she stammers. "I didn't expect anyone else to be in here at this obscene hour." She offers her hand. "I'm Becky. You're the guy from the club, aren't you?"

I shake it quickly before putting my hands back at my sides. "Keegan."

"Kee…*Keegan*?" She looks to Emma and back to me. "Well, what a coincidence. I've heard a lot about you."

"Becky," Emma says, warning in her tone.

Emma told her friend about me before last night? Well, that's interesting, but not as interesting as something else Becky said. "Bachelorette party?" My gaze drops to Emma's bare ring finger. I'm not proud to admit that I looked last night. Who'd blame me?

"Oh, yeah," Becky says. "It's my last weekend of freedom and I'm trying to make the most of it, but Emma's a fucking slave driver with the workouts, you know what I mean? And, yeah, I know I have a dress I have to fit into, but my man loves me, soft bits and all."

Emma flashes her friend a pained look. "Becky, could you give me and Keegan a minute?"

"Oh, crap!" Becky makes a face and points to the hall. "I'll be out there if you need me."

When the door swings closed and we're alone, the room seems too quiet. Silence is always heavier when it's loaded with the weight of years and secrets.

"Would you meet me for coffee or breakfast or something?" Her tongue darts out to wet her lips in that old nervous habit, and my stomach knots. "I know I don't have the right to ask, but I've always hated the way things ended and I…" She shakes her head. "Last night was crazy, but I'd love to catch up somewhere quieter."

"Do you really think that's a good idea?" My jaw aches as I remember sitting outside her complex for hours, waiting for her to come home so I could demand an explanation. She never came, and all I had was her letter in my pocket and a thread of unanswered text messages on my phone.

"I understand if you hate me."

Oh, hell. "I don't hate you." The words come out so softly I'm not sure she hears.

"You don't?"

"No." *I fucking miss you.* "Breakfast would be fine," I say before I can talk myself out of what has to be the worst idea in the history of bad ideas. "How about I meet you at the café by the gardens in two hours?"

Her whole face lights up with her smile. I decide right here and now that any heartache caused by having breakfast with her will be more than worth it if I can make her smile like that again.

CHAPTER 4
EMMA

I climb onto the treadmill as I watch Keegan go. If I'm looking for an elevated heart rate this morning, I don't need this equipment. God, I'm dying. My pulse races from being in the same room as him. Hearing his voice again does things to my insides that I'd rather not analyze.

I didn't think he left me last night. Not at first. I thought I'd just lost him in the crowd for a minute, but then he didn't come back after a few songs. When I checked the booth where he and his friends had been drinking, I found it filled with a bunch of giggling college girls. I told myself he'd return, that he'd never walk away without saying goodbye. I was wrong.

When Becky comes back in the room, she's wearing her biggest shit-eating grin. "You didn't tell me the hottie from last night was *Keegan*."

I roll my eyes and punch buttons on the treadmill until the

belt under my feet starts turning. "If you followed football, you would've known. He plays for the Gators."

"Yes, but unlike my family, I don't care about football. You know that, and I find your omission very interesting. Very interesting indeed."

"Stop right now." I crank up the incline for my warmup. I hate treadmills, but I've accepted them as a necessary evil in my life—like high heels during political dinners and weekly phone calls with my mother. "You're way off base if you think something's going to happen between us."

"Last night looked like something." She climbs onto the elliptical. "I say you go for it."

"He hates me."

She smirks. "So I guess that means angry sex is on the menu."

"Would you quit putting ideas into my head? Now when I see him, my hoo-ha is going to be all disappointed when nothing happens."

"Then *make* something happen," she says.

"Listen to you. Living in your fantasy world where eye contact with a good-looking man equates to an open invitation to his bedroom."

"If that fantasy world is wrong, I don't wanna be right. Was he good in bed?"

"He was…" I look away, trying to think of the word. He was good, but the word feels too cheap for what we had. It wasn't just about getting off. It was about connecting. It was about learning to make love. "Tender, I guess? We were young." I swallow hard as I compare sex with Keegan to my only other experience. It's not a fair comparison. "It was special."

She hums. "Time to find out if the old boy knows any new tricks. He's a fucking NFL player, girl. You know he's had some experience."

I sigh. "We both know that's not happening."

"Ah, but if it could." She shrugs. "My imagination runs away with me. I just want to see my friend happy."

I stop my treadmill, turn to her, and prop my hands on my hips. "I am happy. I know you don't necessarily agree with all my decisions, but I *am* happy." *And safe.* But I don't say that out loud. Becky might be my best friend, but even she doesn't need to know the full extent of the dark corners of my past. It would break her heart. It would keep her up at night. "Don't worry about me."

For the first time since she spotted Keegan this morning, her smile turns sad. "Ah, but I do. I worry about you enough for both of us."

I've auditioned for major motion pictures, given speeches at prestigious universities, and been interviewed by more media outlets than I can count, but I've never been so nervous in my life as I am about meeting Keegan this morning.

When I invited him to have breakfast with me, I didn't expect him to say yes. He should hate me. But here I am, staring at a cup of coffee and wishing it were something much, much stronger. Like vodka. Or a portal to a parallel universe where I didn't break the heart of the sweetest man I've ever met.

"Would mademoiselle like to order?"

I snap my head up to see the waiter looking at me expectantly. "Um, not yet. I'm expecting someone."

"Yes, of course." The waiter gives me a forced smile—one that tells me this is the end of his shift and he's running out of fake cheer. "A mimosa while you wait, perhaps?"

"No thank you, I..." That's when I see him. Keegan Keller strolls into the café and seems to suck half the oxygen from the room. He's gorgeous. His hard, defined jaw has the slightest bit of stubble. His dark hair, still wet from his shower, curls a bit at the nape of his neck, and his big hands are tucked in his pockets as he scans the room. Those hands... *Baby Jesus in a manger.* How can I eat a meal across from him when the sight of his hands makes me feel like I'm naked beneath him again, as if no time has passed since the summer he touched every inch of my skin and worshipped every curve of my flesh?

Regardless of what he thinks of me, I know I wouldn't be who I am today if it weren't for Keegan. He made me feel smart and clever. He made me believe I was beautiful. When he was gone, the confidence he gave me never left.

Keegan spots me and hesitates for a beat before heading my way. Is he disappointed that I showed, or was he hoping I might bring Becky along to ease the tension between us?

"Actually, I'll take two mimosas," I tell the waiter as Keegan approaches the table. "Thank you."

"Em," Keegan says softly. He sits across from me and fills his coffee cup from the stainless-steel pot at the center of the table.

"I ordered us mimosas. I hope that's okay." I reach for my coffee, but my hand is shaking so I put it back in my lap before he notices. Stupid nerves.

"Sure." He takes a sip of his coffee—he still takes it black—and studies me. "You put the wig back on."

"Easier that way," I say, but I'm actually not sure it was necessary this morning. Maybe it gives me a false sense of security.

He meets my eyes and draws in a deep breath. "I almost didn't come."

"I wouldn't have blamed you if you didn't. But I'm glad you're here." I meet his steady gaze for several beats before I realize I'm holding my breath and have to look away. It's like my heart is trying to beat so hard that it might reach out of my chest and grab him. I wonder if he feels the same. I wonder if I should feel guilty for hoping he does.

We study our menus in charged silence until the waiter returns with two champagne glasses fizzing with champagne and orange juice. "Two mimosas," he says, setting them before us. "And what to eat?"

"I'll have the waffles," Keegan says. "With a side of scrambled eggs and bacon, please."

"And for the lady?"

"I'll have the waffles too, but no sides for me."

"I'll have that right out," the waiter says.

Keegan smirks at me.

"What's that look for?" I ask.

"Waffles…" He shakes his head. "You probably don't remember."

But then I do. I haven't thought about that day in a long time. Keegan wanted to teach me to cook, and since I liked waffles so much, he decided to start with that. He had no idea what he was in for or just how clueless I was in the kitchen. Of course, it wasn't long before I was having so much fun witnessing his aggravation that I started breaking the egg shells into the bowl on purpose just to see if he would lose his cool.

I grin. "We made such a mess. There was flour everywhere." My smile falls away and my skin heats as the rest of the memory floods my mind. The way he stood behind me and licked batter off my shoulder, the feel of his flour-coated hands sliding under my shirt and across my belly. I swallow hard and meet his eyes as I remember the way he spun me around and lifted me onto the counter. He pulled off my T-shirt and stepped between my thighs, lowering his mouth to my collarbone and sliding his hand between my legs.

His pupils dilate as he holds my gaze. "We did have good times."

"The best." He turns away at my words, and I watch his jaw go hard. It's like watching someone erect a wall around their heart. "How have you been?" I ask. I want to know everything. I want him to bring down that wall and let me in. Just for one meal. For one hour, I want everything.

He runs a hand through his hair. "I've been good."

"You had an amazing rookie year. Are you ready for next season?" It's not the question I'm dying to ask, though. I want to know how he balances owning a bar in Indiana and playing football for a team in Florida. I want to know if he loves being a father and if that was planned or a total surprise. I want to know if he has a girlfriend and what she's like. When he props his forearms on the table, my gaze drifts to the ring finger on his left hand. His social media profiles are public, and I've creeped enough to know he's not married, but what about his baby's mother? Are they involved? He never posts anything about her.

"I'm getting there. I can't believe how fast the last few months have gone. What have you been up to?"

"Not much. I'm doing some charity work and trying to steer clear of my mom as much as possible."

"Things never improved between you two?"

I shrug. I don't want to talk about me. If I had my way, we'd spend this whole meal focusing on him. "You must be really busy." I take my mimosa and drink half of it in one long swallow. On the one hand, I wish he would sit here with me all day. On the other hand, I'm kicking myself for asking him to breakfast. What good did I think would come of this?

"Yeah. I have a little girl, and she keeps me busy. What about you? You said you aren't living in California anymore?"

"I sold my condo after..." I don't know if that sentence needs an ending or is complete just like that. *After Mom's wedding... After the letter... After you moved to Indiana...*

"Do you miss it?"

"In some ways I do, but it was time to move on." Every corner of that place was filled with memories of Keegan, and while it was hard to walk away from those, it was also hard to live with them. It might have been worth it, though, if other memories weren't there too—the kind I try not to think about, the kind I had to escape to stay sane. "I'm in Georgia now. My life has changed for the better since moving out there."

"Em!"

Keegan and I both turn toward the entrance to see Becky rushing toward our table, her soft-sided carry-on slung over one shoulder. "Em, I'm so sorry. Adam just called and told me the doctor admitted the baby to the hospital. She has pneumonia. I'm going to the airport to get the next flight home."

"Oh my goodness. I'm sorry, Becky." I put my napkin on the table and scoot out my chair to stand.

Becky shakes her head and puts a hand on my shoulder. "No. You stay put. Go to the spa, enjoy your weekend. I'm serious." She turns to Keegan. "Will you make sure she enjoys herself? She needs a break, and I'm afraid if I'm not here she'll be glued to her laptop working the whole time."

"My daughter had pneumonia over the winter," Keegan says. "It was terrifying, but they'll be able to keep an eye on it while she's in the hospital. I know it's scary. Remember she's where she needs to be."

"I know. She's my baby, is all."

Keegan nods. "You'll feel better when you're in the room with her."

Becky's eyes fill with tears. "I feel so bad leaving Em. We planned this months ago, and—"

"Stop it," Emma says. "Stop worrying about me, for goodness' sakes. Go home to your baby. I'll be just fine."

Keegan nods. "She will. I'll make sure she has a good time."

Becky gives him a watery smile. "You're the best. Thank you so much." She squats down to wrap me in an awkward one-armed hug and whispers, "I'll call later. Promise me you'll try to have fun. You *deserve* this."

CHAPTER 5
KEEGAN

I'm pretty sure I just agreed to spend my weekend in Vegas with Emma Rothschild. No, I just agreed to show Emma a "good time" in Vegas. To say this is a dangerous proposition is an understatement.

Our food is served shortly after Becky rushes from the restaurant, but Em just pushes her waffles around on her plate instead of eating.

Reaching across the table, I lay my hand on top of hers. "The baby will be okay."

She lifts her eyes to meet mine and nods weakly. "I know. And I'm glad she's going home to be with her. She wouldn't have had any fun worrying about the baby the whole time."

"Then what's wrong?"

She looks up at me through her lashes, and I'm rocketed back in time to our first date and the way she studied me with a combination of wonder and nerves, as if she'd never been on a date before. "I don't want you to feel like you have to make good on your promise. I'm a big girl and I can handle a weekend in Vegas alone. I'm sure you have your own plans. It's just…"

"Just what?"

Her lips are sweet pink, and I can't help but watch as her tongue darts out to wet them. "Doesn't it seem strange to you that we ran into each other this weekend? After all this time?"

"It's a small world, as they say."

"The right thing to do would be to say goodbye."

"Is that what you want?"

She blinks at me and her lips part before she releases a puff of air and drains the rest of her mimosa. "No."

I exhale a rush of relief. Saying goodbye might be the smartest move, but now that she's close, I don't want to let her walk away. The waiter returns with our bill, and I take it from him and scribble my name and room number on it before dropping it to the table. "Take a walk with me?"

Her face lights up and she nods. "I'd like that."

We're quiet as we leave the restaurant and stroll around the gardens. It's still early and the tourists from other hotels haven't descended upon this spot yet, but there are enough people milling around that the silence between us doesn't feel awkward.

"Do you know them?" Emma asks, pointing to the garden's entrance.

My friends are walking in our direction, led by Bailey and Mia.

"You ditched us for a girl?" Bailey says. "Of course you did."

Mia nudges her. "He's with us all weekend. He's entitled to a breakfast alone."

Mason arches a brow. "I don't think he ate *alone*, Mee. Are you going to introduce us to your friend?"

Right. "Everyone, this is Em—" I look at Emma, my eyes widening as I realize she probably wouldn't be wearing the wig if she wanted me to share her true identity with my friends.

"Emily Zimmerman," she says, covering my mistake without a hitch.

"She's an old friend from high school," I lie. I don't know Emma from high school, or from college. She was from the space between—that summer when I thought my life was already mapped out in one direction and a young actress made me believe I was good enough to turn the other way. "Em, this is Mason, Arrow, Mia, Chris, Grace, and Bailey."

"Wow," Emma says. "A bunch of NFL stars right here in front of me. It's great to meet you." Mason shakes her hand, and Em blushes hard. "That was a great catch you made in the fourth quarter in the game against the Patriots. For what it's worth, that offensive interference call in overtime was completely bogus."

Mason beams. "A Gators fan?" He looks to me and them back to Em. "It's always nice to meet a fan."

Mia and Grace wave, but Bailey crosses her arms over her chest and narrows her eyes at Em. "You look familiar."

Em smiles. "I get that a lot. I think I have one of those faces."

"Well, it's nice to meet you, Emily," Mia says.

"Mia and Arrow are the reason we're here," I tell Em.

"You're the ones getting married next weekend?" Em asks, directing the question to Mia.

Mia laughs. "In two weeks, actually, and our friends are the ones who made this happen. We haven't all been together in a long time, so it's pretty much the best wedding gift ever."

Emma turns to me. "See? You should be spending your time with them, not me."

"She was here for a bachelorette weekend, but the bride had to go home unexpectedly," I explain to my friends.

Emma shifts awkwardly. "And now Keegan thinks he's obligated to entertain me, but I'll be fine. I have an appointment at the spa this morning and plans to sit by the pool all afternoon. There's plenty to keep me busy."

Mia jumps in, as I knew she would. "You're welcome to hang with us this weekend." Arrow nudges her, and her eyes go wide. "What?"

"Maybe he wants to be *alone* with his old friend," he says in a whisper we can all hear, and the others laugh.

Bailey, who'd typically be in for ribbing me in any conversation that had to do with my sex life or love life, stays silent. As all our friends have paired off, Bailey and I have become close. When I bought the bar that would become The End Zone, I didn't think I had a chance to play in the NFL, but when the Gators signed me, Bailey stepped up to manage the bar during the football season. I know people suspect we're fooling around, but we really are just friends brought together by our crappy love lives.

Mia tilts her head and studies Emma. "No pressure on joining us, but if you two wanted *group* activities, my offer stands."

Emma shakes her head. "I don't want to impose."

"You can't do Vegas alone," Mia says. "Come on. A friend of Keegan's is a friend of ours. I don't see any reason you can't hang out with us. We have a VIP bungalow reserved at the Wet Republic pool at the MGM. We're going to spend the afternoon there and then go to dinner and a show before we hit some new club at Caesars."

Emma looks at me and then back to Mia. "You really are sweet to invite me."

"I mean it," she says. "The more the merrier, but your choice."

Bailey gestures toward the café. "We should go before they give away our table."

"Oh no," Emma says. "I didn't mean to keep you from breakfast."

"It's not a problem," Mia says, shooting Bailey a hard look. "I hope we see you at the pool this afternoon."

The idea of spending the entire afternoon with Emma in her bathing suit makes my gut warm and knot all at once. She's always been self-conscious about her body for no damn good reason. Her mom has that Hollywood-waif thing going on and always criticized Emma for not dieting and exercising her body to fit the same mold. You can't change your body type though, and Emma wasn't built to be a waif. Emma was built to be all curves and hips. She's femininity and softness in all the right places, and it's a fucking crime that she's spent most of her life feeling ashamed of that.

When my friends walk away toward the restaurant, Emma and I stroll through the hotel.

"You canceled your breakfast plans to eat with me?" she asks.

I shrug. "It wasn't a big deal."

She shakes her head. "You didn't come to Vegas alone. You're supposed to be with your friends. I'm ruining your weekend."

I smile at her. "You're not." I stop in front of a topiary that's been shaped to look like Harry Potter riding his broom and tuck my hands into my pockets. "I'm sorry I was such a dick last night, leaving you like that."

"I'm surprised you were even willing to speak to me. I shouldn't have expected you to dance."

I cut my eyes to her. "I was afraid if I stayed, something might happen between us."

"Oh." Her lips curve into a small O as her cheeks turn pink.

"But now that I have you next to me, I realize how stupid I was being last night. I want to spend the weekend with you. For old times' sake, hang out with me and my friends."

"Why do you want to do this?" She shakes her head, her brow creasing. "You don't know me anymore. My life is... It's complicated, Keegan." She frowns and tugs her bottom lip between her teeth. "You've been caught up in my problems before, and I don't want to do that to you again."

I wince at the reminder. Is that what Harry was to her? A "problem"? I push the thought aside to be filed under "shit that's not my business." I don't have a right to be hurt by what Emma did to me, not when my intentions going into our very first date were never what she believed. "I promise you I have a really fucking busy life waiting for me and I don't need romantic complications any more than you do. We're adults, and just because we used to be involved doesn't mean we can't be friends now. Right?"

She meets my gaze for a few long beats. "I'll think about it."

CHAPTER 6
EMMA

Five Years Ago...

Y ou know that bad feeling you get somewhere between the back of your neck and your spinal cord when you feel something terrible is going to happen? It's the feeling that makes you look over your shoulder to see if someone's following you. It's the feeling that makes you close your curtains at night because you're so sure someone's looking in your windows that you can practically feel them on the other side of the glass.

I know that feeling. I've known that feeling for more of my life than I care to think about. It's the feeling of being watched and never knowing if the person who's doing the watching is just curious or wants something from you.

"Small price to pay for a life in the spotlight," Mom would say. But if a life in the spotlight isn't what you want, then I'd argue the price is way too high.

People still want to know what's happening with the cute little girl from the popular family sitcom *Lucy Matters,* but it helps that I haven't taken a role of any kind in two years. Even though the paparazzi likes to follow me and try to catch me in a pose that best highlights my double chin, I don't have to put up with half of what Mom does.

On her good days, Mom just grins at the camera and positions herself so they get her best side. On her bad days, she'll flip them off, spit at them, and pay her security guard to go after the footage. Nevertheless, even the bad days she lets roll off her back.

For me, though, there's something about that level of privacy invasion that feels like a violation. Even if it's been weeks since the last paparazzo snapped a picture of me, I still feel like I'm always on display, and not in a good way. It's as if everyone's looking and waiting for their turn to point and laugh.

I know why Britney Spears lost her mind. I know why she shaved her head. I get it, and I don't even have Britney levels of fame. Far from it.

It's a beautiful day on Laguna Beach. One of those days that makes me forget, momentarily, to look over my shoulder. The air is warm, the sun hot on my skin, and the breeze off the ocean is the perfect combination of cool and salty that reminds me that, despite everything else I hate about California and being this close to LA, the ocean is part of who I am.

I'm walking Bigsy downtown when I see him. I have a hat on and my big sunglasses in place. I look like half the other people wandering around here. People here are either tourists or have more money than God. Shamefully, I fit in the second category.

I have Bigsy's leash in one hand and an ice cream cone in the other. I don't eat in public very often—nothing as incriminating as ice cream, at least—but I ran five miles on the beach this morning, and I felt like I earned this treat. Now I have a camera pointing at me as my punishment.

The man steps close, snapping pictures even as I hold my hand out, pressing him and his camera away.

A tall guy comes out of nowhere, stepping between me and the man with the camera. He's all broad shoulders and angry eyes as he takes a swing at the man with the camera.

The man collapses to the ground and holds his bloody nose. "What the *fuck*?"

The taller man puts a foot on his chest. "Give me the camera," he says, holding out his hand.

"Fuck you," the photographer says, and that's when I recognize him as the same man who took pictures of me on the beach last night. My gut twists. Someone taking the opportunity to get a quick picture of me is one thing, but I hate being followed. It makes me feel trapped in my own life.

"Give me the camera." The tall guy puts more pressure on the photographer's chest. "Do it or you and this concrete are gonna become real close."

The man throws his camera, and the mess of gratitude, relief, and residual fear tangle in my chest to keep me speechless.

My rescuer hands me the camera, and I take it with shaking

hands. It's a crappy little thing, too, and maybe that's what made the photographer good. He can sneak up easier with something so small and discreet. My rescuer kicks the man in the side with his boot. "Get out of here."

The photographer scrambles to his feet and mutters something before rushing away.

The guy turns to me. "Are you okay?"

I shake my head. "That was… I'm so embarrassed that you had to do that."

He smirks. "I kind of enjoyed it. Do you have that problem a lot?"

"Sometimes. I've taken self-defense classes before. It's not like I don't know what to do when men get too close." The irony of those words makes me flinch, but I shake my head and continue. "I froze. He took pictures of me on the beach last night, too." I shudder. I hate this feeling.

He looks me over as if scanning my body for injuries. "Some guys turn into complete lunatics when they see a pretty woman."

His words and his eyes on me nudge away the fear, pushing it from the center of my consciousness and replacing it with something warmer. "I don't think that's why he was taking my picture." I laugh.

He runs his eyes over me again and shrugs. "Why else would he take pictures of you? Are you some guy's cheating wife?"

"Hardly." My cheeks are hot from blushing so hard. This guy is so good looking and he saved me from the photographer, and now he's flirting with me. I know he's probably just trying to make me feel better. It's working. He's built, young—my age, if I had to guess—and his eyes are so sincere, I think that maybe he truly doesn't know why the jerk with the camera would want my picture.

"Thanks," I say, holding up the camera.

He points to my ice cream cone in its sad little puddle on the sidewalk. "Can I buy you another one?"

"I think I'll be okay without it."

"Nah. Let me buy you a new one. I'm about to buy some for myself, and I'd hate to eat it alone. We're *supposed* to eat ice cream on days like these." He points to the clear blue sky, and I like him so much in this moment. There's probably some psychology term for that—rapid infatuation with someone who's just rescued me. "I insist," he says. He turns and walks into the ice cream shop as if he has no doubt that I'll follow.

I look at Bigsy and think about taking him home and ignoring the guy's invitation. I don't. For one, that seems very rude after what he just did for me, and two, I'm curious about my hero and don't want to say goodbye yet. Or maybe it's less curiosity and more loneliness. Maybe I like the way he looks at me.

When I step inside, he's placing his order. He looks at me over his shoulder. "Do you mind if I get something for your dog?" Bigsy rushes forward as if he understands his words. "It's just a little cup of whipped cream."

"You're so sweet."

"Can't have your dog resenting me because I didn't get her anything."

"He's a boy," I say, laughing. "And I'm sure he'd love his own cup of whipped cream."

"What'd you have?" he asks.

"Just the peanut butter gelato in a cone."

"Two scoops?" he suggests.

"Just one, thanks."

He grunts. "Just as long as you don't judge me for eating two." We get our cones and head outside. "You wanna walk with me?" When I hesitate, he laughs and points at the public beach on the opposite side of the street. "Not into my dark secret lair or something. I mean walk over there on the brightly lit beach where everyone will be around to help in case I turn out to be a creep."

"Okay." It's probably not good that I like him so much when I know nothing about him, but usually I feel awkward and uncomfortable around guys, and this one makes me smile.

"My name's Keegan," he says when we step onto the beach.

"I'm Emma."

"It's nice to meet you, Emma. I'm sorry you've had such a shitty day."

I shrug. "I've had worse."

We wander down the boardwalk before we find an empty bench. Keegan stops and puts Bigsy's treat on the ground. On the beach beyond, they're setting up an inflatable screen for an outdoor movie.

"They're showing *Ghost* tonight," I tell him, nodding at the screen.

"Ever seen it?"

I press my hand to my chest. "Of course! What self-respecting woman hasn't cried her eyes out with Demi?" I sigh. "Only Patrick Swayze could make the word *ditto* seem so sexy and romantic."

His lips quirk. "He was dodging the L-word, but that's romantic?"

I shrug and lift my palms. "It's Swayze. What can I say?" Laughing, I shake my head. "Wait, that means you've seen it too."

"Guilty." He grins. "Thanks for having ice cream with me."

"I should be the one who's thanking *you*."

"How do you figure?"

"You stopped some jerk from taking pictures of me and then replaced my ruined ice cream. In my book, that practically makes you a knight in shining armor."

"I'm no knight." He looks me over again, but this time it's less like he's looking for injuries and more like he's…appreciating the view? Maybe?

My cheeks heat. "Ah, but here you are, helping me out for nothing."

He laughs. "Nothing, huh? Have you looked in a mirror lately? Spending time with a woman as pretty as you isn't exactly a hardship."

"Do you talk like that to all the girls you meet?"

"Only the pretty ones," he says.

"I should…" I reach for my purse. "Can I give you something? As a thank-you?"

"Like your number?"

I laugh, and my warm cheeks kick up into inferno. "No, like cash."

He rubs his chin as if pretending to think this over. "Mmm, I like cash, but I'd still rather have your number."

"That's probably not a good idea."

"Well, you can't blame a guy for trying."

"I'll be walking Bigsy again tomorrow morning if you'll be around." I'm embarrassed the second the invitation leaves my lips. All this talk about him thinking I'm pretty and him wanting my number is no more than a nice guy trying to make me feel better, and in return I offered to let him help me walk my dog? Yeah, I suck at guys.

"I can't tomorrow morning," he says. "I have work."

"Right." Of course. Because normal people work. "I'm sorry, it's no big deal. I just—"

"How about lunch?" He points down the beach. "I heard there's an awesome French café down that way, and the movie set I'm working on isn't too far from here."

"Lunch?" I ask lamely.

"Unless you'd prefer dinner?"

"Lunch sounds good."

His smile is perfect. I don't just mean that his teeth are straight and white—though they are—but the way he smiles and how it begins as a slow slide up his face and makes me feel warm. "Do you have a pen I could borrow?"

I fish one from my purse and hand it over. "Here."

He takes the pen then grabs my hand and slowly opens my

closed palm. "Now, I'm giving you this in case you need it." I watch as he carefully pens numbers onto my hand. "Say, for example, you develop a killer need to send a picture of yourself in your nightgown to someone tonight. That would be a time you should use this. But this number should absolutely not be used to cancel our date. My phone is weird and it just won't work for cancelations."

I laugh. "Oh really?"

He pulls the pen away and lifts my hand to his mouth. He blows a steady stream of cool air across the numbers on my palm, and my laughter falls away. My heart is pounding and I know I need to walk away now, but I don't want to. I want to stand here forever in this weirdly erotic tableau.

When he lowers my hand back to my side, he grins. "Noon?" I nod, and his eyes skim over me again. His tongue darts out to wet his bottom lip. "I don't think I've looked forward to anything this much in a very long time."

CHAPTER 7
EMMA

I never want this day to end.

I went straight to the spa after leaving Keegan, but I spent my entire massage and facial thinking about him and our summer together five years ago. When I got back to my room, it was pure impulse that made me put on my suit and cover-up and get a cab to meet them at the Wet Republic pool. By the time I found their cabana, reason was taking charge again, so I decided I'd make a polite appearance and then cut my visit short, but that was hours ago. This group is so easygoing and welcoming. I'm having a good time and don't want to leave.

They look perfect, like something off a TV show. I always wondered what it would be like to have friends who know you so well they know just how much they can tease, friends who just want to spend time with you and don't expect anything in return. I have Becky and Zachary, but I've never had a group like this.

The bride and groom, Mia and Arrow, are a beautiful couple, and they truly seem happiest when they're next to each other. Mia's a Latina with long, dark hair and an easy smile, and Arrow is one of the most lusted-after running backs in the NFL. "Women mail him their panties," Mia confessed after a couple drinks. I can believe it, but I bet that problem would be even worse if his intensity translated over the TV screen or if they had any idea how much he dotes on his bride-to-be.

Then there's Chris and Grace. Grace is cute—petite with lots of tattoos. She's quieter than the others but has a sharp wit and clearly adores Chris, who plays football in New York. Their first-string quarterback got hurt last year, and it's rumored that Chris is going to be their starter this season.

Then there's the curvy blonde, Bailey, the one who thought she recognized me. She's all curves and sass, and I get the feeling that she and Keegan are close. Then again, she spends most of her time talking to Mason Dahl. There's a weird sort of tension between them that makes me wonder about their relationship. Then again, maybe she's just looking at Mason the way any red-blooded single woman would. Mason's a wide receiver on Keegan's team, the Gulf Gators. Really, the beauty of the men in this group is too much, and Mason is over the top with his big hands, white smile, gorgeous green eyes, and dark skin.

Then there's Keegan—his dark hair, his eyes on me. When he took his shirt off, I almost choked on my tongue. That amount of muscle on one man shouldn't be legal, but there he is, a living specimen of strength and beauty just inches from my fingertips.

Since I've always been self-conscious about my weight, I've never been attracted to skinny guys, and Keegan's broad chest and thickly muscled arms make me feel small in comparison.

"Can I get you another drink?" he asks, smiling at me.

I've been sitting in one of the lounge chairs in the bungalow since I arrived. While Grace and I opted for the seats in shade, Bailey and Mia are soaking up rays in front of the bungalow. I'm warm from a fruity cocktail and just this side of tipsy. "I think I'm going to get in the pool."

His eyes skim over my body and the black cover-up I haven't taken off yet. I wore my wig, of course. I can't abandon that disguise now that we've told his friends I'm Emily Zimmerman, but it's pinned in my hair so securely that I think I can get away with a quick dip as long as I keep my head above water.

"I'll go with you." He drains the last of his beer and puts the glass on the table before offering his hand to help me out of the chair. I follow him to the stack of inner tubes the resort has piled by the entrance to the lazy river. We step into the water, and I pull my tube over my head and wrap my arms around the front of it to hold on. It's a beautiful day, and this pool complex is so gorgeous that you almost forget you're on the Vegas Strip. The sun is shining, the air is warm, and all my problems feel like they're locked up in Georgia, thousands of miles away.

Keegan slides into his own tube beside me, and we let the chlorinated river carry us slowly along its winding path through palm trees and bungalows. "Thanks for coming today," he says. "I hope you're having a good time."

I'm grateful that my sunglasses cover my eyes. I'm having more than a good time. This is exactly what I needed this weekend. It was exactly what Zachary and Becky had in mind when they ganged up on me and insisted I take this trip. "I should be thanking you. Your friends are nice. It's great that you've all stayed close."

He nods. "Yeah. I'm lucky. We're spread out all over the country since graduation, but I'm never alone. When the Gators picked me up, I knew I'd get to play with Mason, and when I go back to Blackhawk Valley for stuff with the bar, I have Bailey there."

"Oh. So, you…and Bailey?"

He shakes his head and laughs. "No, not like that. I bought a bar after we graduated. Arrow actually went in on it too, but he never intended to run it. I, on the other hand, thought my football days were behind me, and the bar gave me a job in Blackhawk Valley so I could stick around for my daughter. Then I got a call saying that the Gators wanted to pick me up as a defensive end. You don't walk away from that kind of opportunity, even if you did just make the biggest investment of your life. So I've got both."

"I already knew about your bar and football career," I admit, and when he arches a brow, I add, "Social media."

"Oh." He looks truly surprised.

"You never looked me up?"

He shakes his head, and something passes over his face before he looks away. "I've always been an all-or-nothing kind of person, Em. It was just easier not to look, and then eventually…"

"You forgot about me," I fill in. I try to sound nonchalant, even if it hurts.

"Hardly," he mutters. "I just didn't see the purpose of dwelling on the past."

"So you have the bar and football and Jasmine," I say, changing the subject. "That must be tough."

"Bailey runs the bar for me. She does a great job and I keep offering to sell it to her, but she says me owning that bar is the only thing that keeps me coming back to Blackhawk Valley. I think she's afraid we're all going to forget about her if there's no reason to come home."

"So she's not with you, and she's not with Mason?"

"I don't know what's going on between her and Mason. They have a history, but I'm not sure any of us knows the whole story." His brow wrinkles above his sunglasses, but then he shakes his head and that visible worry smooths away. "So are you coming tonight?"

I bite my lip. "You've all done too much already. I really don't want to be in the way."

He looks from me to our right as we float past our bungalow. The rest of the group is gathered there, but they're all paired off. Arrow and Mia are sharing a lounger, limbs tangled, fingers threaded and looking dangerously close to napping. Chris and Grace are talking and drinking, and Mason and Bailey are sitting close, staring into each other's eyes. "You'd be doing me a favor.

I'm like a seventh wheel in this group, and you and I are doing a fantastic job of being friends, if I do say so myself."

I laugh. He's right. It hasn't been awkward or anything weird all day. It's just been nice to spend time together. Any sexual tension I feel is probably one-sided. If Keegan was still attracted to me, would he have walked away so easily while we were dancing last night? "What's the plan tonight?"

"Dinner with the group, and then a show."

"What kind of show?"

"A bachelor- and bachelorette-party-appropriate show."

I grin. "Oh, one of *those*."

He laughs. "Yeah, I hear it's a little dirty, but it's a classier choice than going to a strip club and losing all our money to some random chicks rubbing their tits in our faces."

"I'm sure." My cheeks heat. I've never been to a burlesque show or anything like that, and to do it sitting next to Keegan sounds equal parts fun and dangerous. Then again, Keegan doesn't seem to have any trouble with us being buds and nothing more.

He sighs. "You don't have to come, but just so you know, Mia already made calls to make sure we had a ticket for you just in case you decided to."

"Why is she being so nice to me?"

He shrugs. "Why shouldn't she be? I think she likes you."

"I'd hate for her to have bought an extra ticket for no reason."

He pulls off his sunglasses and grins, his eyes crinkling at the corners. "Thatta girl."

KEEGAN

"Okay," Mia says, swinging her legs around to the side of her lounger so she's facing me. She props her elbows on her knees. "I'm sure she's heard this a thousand times so I didn't want to say anything to her, but did you notice that your Emily looks like Emma Rothschild? You know, that girl from *Lucy Matters*, the TV show?"

I smile and try to keep my face neutral. It's been a long time since I've made a habit of lying. I'm almost glad it doesn't come naturally anymore. "She does get that a lot."

"I mean, if she had red, curly hair, she could win look-alike contests."

"Don't say anything to her, okay? She hates that."

Mia shakes her head. "I wouldn't. She's so pretty, Keegan, and I think she likes you. Are you two…?"

I look at her. "Seriously, Mia, we just ran into each other this weekend after not seeing one another for years. We're just friends, and chances are, after we leave Vegas, we probably won't see each other for another five years. Maybe never." The word sticks in my throat. *Never.* Last week, I would have said I was okay with never seeing Emma again, but now I'm not so sure. Now, I hate the idea of saying goodbye and knowing it might be forever.

When I left Los Angeles for Blackhawk Valley five years ago,

I thought there was a good chance I'd never see her again. Emma Rothschild is a goddess among women. She's Hollywood royalty. And I was just a peasant who got close to her for reasons I'm too ashamed to admit.

I watch her standing at the bar, laughing at some guy next to her as she waits for her drink. She has a wide-brimmed hat pulled atop her wig, and she spent the day applying and reapplying sunblock. Despite her efforts, she has a fresh coat of freckles on her shoulders that remind me of the summer before I left LA. We spent days in the California sun lounging on her beachfront balcony. Those freckles remind me of slipping into the ocean with her in my arms and the way she wrapped her legs around my waist and clung to my neck as I stepped deeper. I taught the woman who lived on the sea that her fears of going into the water were unnecessary. And she taught me what it was like to love without expectation, what it was like to be loved by someone with a pure heart.

The memories are a dangerous place to go, and they don't do much to help me plant my feet into the friend zone. If we're careful, maybe I can get through tonight without screwing it up.

That makes my gut knot. What about tomorrow? Despite all my concern about what complications with Emma might mean, I absolutely hate the idea of tomorrow not including her. I hate the idea of leaving Vegas, sending her on her way, and never seeing her again.

She returns to the bungalow and takes the lounger next to me in the shade. "The guy at the bar told me I look just like Emma

Rothschild," she whispers.

I shrug. "Eh. I mean, your eyes are blue like hers, but she's *way* hotter."

Emma gapes at me then bursts into laughter, and the rest of the group turns to stare at us, and Emma ducks her head. "Tell me about your daughter," she says when everyone has gone back to their conversations. She slides her straw between her pink lips and sips as she waits for me to answer.

"You want me to be that guy who sits here and talks about his kid as if she's the coolest kid on earth?"

She smiles. "I do if that's how you feel."

"Good, because she is. She's so damn cool." I shake my head. "She's got these big eyes that always tell you exactly how she's feeling. She's just a happy kid, always giggling and clapping her hands as if the world as a whole amuses the hell out of her. I honestly never knew I could love another person as much as I love her."

"Your face lights up when you talk about her." She bites her bottom lip. "What about her mom? What's she like?"

Something knots in my stomach. It's not that I don't want to tell her. It's just odd. Here's Emma, a woman I wanted and couldn't fight for, asking about Olivia, the only woman I've ever fought for.

I take a breath. "Jazzy's mom is sweet. We weren't really together when she got pregnant, so our whole relationship has been a little screwed up."

"Are you together now?"

Maybe I'm just hearing what I want to, but it sounds like there's hope in her voice. As if maybe she wants me to be single, as if maybe she's hoping I'm available. "No. We're not." I take a long drink from my beer and rub my thumb over the condensation on the side of the glass. "When I found out she was pregnant, I hoped we might be able to make it work. Kids deserve both parents, ya know? It's complicated to be a family living in different homes and leading different lives."

"Why didn't it work out?"

I lift my eyes to meet hers and think, *Because I wasn't good enough. Because my heart already belonged to another woman I couldn't have, and Olivia knew it.* But it's too good of a day to ruin with a ride on the self-pity train, and I like the way she's looked at me today, as if I'm some sort of Greek god who can do anything. It's the way she looked at me when we first met and I bought her an ice cream cone. "It just didn't work out."

"Would you want to be with her if you could?"

I exhale heavily. "I don't think it'll ever be that simple, but yeah, I'd bend over backwards if I thought I could make it work with Olivia. Jazzy deserves to have a family."

"She does," she says, and her smile makes warmth bloom in my chest. "It might not look like what you'd imagined, but you've given her a family, and she's a lucky little girl."

"You should come to Seaside sometime and meet her." The words are out of my mouth before I think better of it, and when she flinches and looks away, I regret them.

When she turns back to me, stress has taken away her easy

smile. "I never thought I'd see you again."

The words don't seem out of context or take me by surprise, because I know exactly what she means. Two days ago, I thought Emma's only place in my life was in my past, and now we're talking about the future.

CHAPTER 8
EMMA

The group insists that I share a ride with them back to the hotel in the limo-bus they rented for the weekend. I've been in more than my share of limos, but never anything like this. Colorful lights race around the ceiling, and the seats curve around the interior in a big oval so they all face each other.

Everyone seems to be glowing from the time in the sun and maybe from the booze, and the ride back is relaxing and quiet. Mason plugs his phone into the sound system and plays some mellow tunes that make me wonder if he's consciously or unconsciously serenading Bailey.

It's such a relaxing ride that I'm almost sorry when we arrive at the hotel and I know it's time to leave the group.

"Em has decided to join us tonight," Keegan informs Mia when we all file into the hotel.

"That's great," Mia says. "I hope you don't mind if the show's a little risqué. It's just that I've never done Vegas before and we thought it'd be fun to do something a little different."

"I've never been to a show like that. I'm excited." I look to Keegan. "I'm going to take a shower. Should I meet you guys at the show?"

"No, you should come to dinner with us too. Let's just meet in the lounge," Mia says before Keegan can reply. She looks around the group, all circled around us in the lobby. "Will two hours be long enough for everyone to chill for a minute and get ready?"

Chris and Grace grin at each other before nodding their agreement. "Two hours should be good," Chris says.

"I'll meet you down here later," I say to Keegan, and he nods as he looks me over.

It feels so good to have his eyes on me again. I've never believed I was particularly beautiful. Intellectually, I know my weight doesn't make me less beautiful. I can look at plus-size models and believe they're gorgeous, but when it comes to me, I struggle with getting past the number on the scale and the size on my clothing tags.

When you've had an ideal body image hammered into your head your whole life, it's hard to let that go in order to embrace something else. But during my summer with Keegan, I felt lucky to have this body. He looks at my curves like they're the most beautiful composition of flesh, bone, fat, and muscle he's ever seen. I'd forgotten that little flutter I get in my belly every time he puts his eyes on me. I've missed that—the thrill it sends through my blood and the confidence it gives me.

"See you later," he says when he brings his gaze back up to mine.

"Later." I wave goodbye, reluctant to walk away.

When I get to my room, I grab my phone from my purse to call Becky. She picks up after one ring. "Is this an okay time?"

"It's perfect. Whitney's napping."

"How's she doing?"

"Okay. It was scary for a minute, but Keegan was right. She's where she needs to be. They think we might even get to go home tomorrow." I hear her yawn. "How about you? Did you have a good day?"

"Actually, yes," I admit. "I ended up spending it with Keegan after all."

"Do tell," she says. "A hot day in bed or…"

"Shut up. We're just friends and we agreed to spend time together as that and nothing more." I look around my suite, realizing how lonely it feels up here without the background noise of all of Keegan's crew. "The people he's here with are really nice. We just spent the day at the pool, and tonight we're going to go to dinner and a show. Maybe somewhere else after?"

She sighs and sounds relieved. "I'm so glad you're having a good time. For all my razzing, that's all I really want."

I bite my lip. "I haven't told him, Becky."

I can feel her hesitation across the line. "Do you think you should?"

"I'm afraid if I do, he'll ask questions." *And I'm afraid if I lie, he'll see through me and guess what no one else can know.* "I'm having a good time, and I don't want to ruin it. I'm not doing anything wrong."

"You could just tell him the truth. You can trust him, right? Maybe then he'd give you the wild weekend you really deserve."

I sigh. God, that sounds amazing. After spending the day next to Keegan, I love the idea of spending my *night* with him too—and not just dinner and a show. "Becky, you know it's complicated. The fewer people who know the truth, the better."

"I know," she says. "I like Keegan, though. I might have only talked to him for, like, two minutes, but he seems like a good guy. I've known you for four years, and in that time, every time he came up in conversation, you'd get that dreamy look in your eye. I can't help but want that for you."

"He is a good guy. But what we have here is *nice*. We get to be friends again. That's more than I ever dreamed, and I'm gonna take it." Something tugs in my chest at those words. Maybe even five years later, my heart hasn't given up on the possibility of being something more.

"Whatever you decide, just have fun tonight. You deserve it. You have to see the Motherbeast this week."

"Don't remind me."

"I still think you should switch her protein powder out with that weight-gain stuff. At least then the torture wouldn't be a total loss."

I laugh. "You're awful and I love you. I need to get in the shower. Give Whitney a kiss for me."

"I will tell her Auntie Emma sends her love," she says. "And you give Keegan a kiss for me."

"You wish. I'll see you in a few days, okay?" We end the call, and I strip out of my clothes and climb into the shower. I pay more attention to my body as I wash and shave, and take extra time moisturizing my skin after. I tell myself it's only because I want to feel confident tonight. It has nothing to do with wanting Keegan to look at me just so, or with wishing he could be more than my friend.

CHAPTER 9
EMMA

Five Years Ago...

The café is bustling at lunchtime, and I'm immediately overwhelmed with the cacophony of silverware scraping plates, people talking, and servers rushing around packed tables. I scan the dining area and don't see Keegan. My heart sinks, and I swallow hard, feeling foolish.

I *liked* him, and I wanted him to show up today. That's a first for me. He's not the only guy who's ever shown interest in me physically, but it's not common for guys who don't know who I am to give me any attention. Guys like my hair and they like my curves, but I don't fit a typical standard of beauty. My waist is too thick, my hips too wide, my breasts so full that if I'm not very careful in what clothing I choose, they can make me look even heavier than I am. I take that whole curvy thing over the top.

Big girls like to use Marilyn Monroe as evidence that bigger women can be sexy, but the truth is that Marilyn probably never had a thick waist. Even though everyone likes to cite that she wore a size fourteen, that'd probably be a heck of a lot smaller in today's sizes. Don't get me wrong. I think she was gorgeous, and it *is* nice to see a woman who isn't a waif admired for her figure. I just don't think she actually gives curvy girls hope for their chance of being someone's ideal body type.

"Can I help you?" the man behind the host stand asks.

Keegan stood me up.

"Um, no thank you." I lift my chin and brace myself to walk out of the restaurant. I'm a grown woman. I'm successful and beautiful, and I don't need to feel foolish about this.

I spin on my heel and step toward the door, and that's when I see him. He's standing in the waiting area watching me, his hands tucked into the pockets, his jeans hanging low on his hips. He's wearing a white, lightweight button-up shirt with the sleeves rolled to the elbows, exposing thick forearms that are tan from the summer sun.

"Why do you look so surprised to see me?" he asks.

"I thought you stood me up."

He arches a brow. "Then clearly you must think I'm an idiot."

All the worry and nerves tangle with this new warmth that's gathering in my belly.

"I got us a table outside because it's just a gorgeous day. I thought the fresh air might be nice, but if that's not okay, I can talk to the host."

I shake my head. "Fresh air sounds great."

His lips quirk and his nostrils flare as he runs his eyes over me. I took a chance on this outfit, and now I'm glad I did. The pink sundress shows my arms, though I usually cover them. It fits tight around my chest but loose around my waist and hips. I paired it with strappy sandals and a floppy-brimmed hat and let my red curls hang wild down my back.

"Your necklace is pretty." When his fingers brush the sapphire resting at the base of my neck, a warm buzz zips through me.

"Thanks. My father gave it to me before he died. It belonged to his mother. It was her *something blue* at her wedding, and he wanted it to be mine." Our eyes lock for a long beat, and my heart pounds with nervous energy. "Not that I'm planning on getting married anytime soon," I stammer. "I guess that's why I wear it sometimes. Seems a shame to hide it away until a day that may or may not come."

"Whenever you do get married, you'll look beautiful. It's easy to imagine you in white lace with that sapphire resting on your neck. But it's hard to imagine you looking any more beautiful than you do today."

My cheeks heat, and suddenly this morning's wardrobe angst seems worth every piece of discarded clothing scattered across my closet floor. "You didn't think I was going to show up in yoga pants and a tank top I was wearing yesterday, did you?"

"Hey, there's nothing wrong with yoga pants. In fact, you're welcome to wear them anytime you're around me."

Laughter bubbles through my lips and I shake my head. "You're something else."

He winks and steps past me to say something to the host, who leads us through the restaurant and outside. We're seated on the patio that overlooks the sandy beach and rolling waves beyond. The weather is perfect.

"Order anything you want," Keegan says when he leaves. "It's on me. We're celebrating."

"What are we celebrating?" I ask.

"Our anniversary."

I roll my eyes. "You're joking, right?"

"Not at all. In five years, today will be the fifth anniversary of our first date. You'll be giving me a sweet set of boudoir photos— and seriously, you shouldn't be so nervous about that, I'm going to *cherish* them, but it's okay because I'm going to be just as nervous about the gift I'm giving you. Don't you think such a special occasion is worth celebrating?"

I snort. "Are you always so over the top?"

His lips quirk up in a lopsided grin as his gaze drops to my mouth. "Nah. I just like seeing you smile."

And I like smiling—real ones, not the kind you give the camera or paste on your face when you know people are watching. I like that he makes me want to smile when I haven't wanted to in a long time.

Mom's voice echoes in my mind. *"You used to be such a happy girl. What happened to you?"*

With a smile on my lips and this handsome guy across from me, I relax a little as I scan the menu.

Keegan tells me about how he just graduated from high

school and came to Los Angeles to work as a stuntman for the summer and that he ended up getting on a film being shot here.

"So you're a stuntman? Is that what you want to do for a career?"

"I like it. It's fun. I'm not trained like most of these guys, so I can't do any of the cool stuff. As far as I can tell, I'm mostly here to be a punching bag."

"What about college? Are you—" I bite my tongue, embarrassed that the question came out so full of presumption. College isn't an option for everyone. "Sorry. It's not my business."

"No, I don't mind. I just haven't decided yet. I thought I'd come out here and earn some money and then decide."

"No rush, right?"

He shrugs. "I played football in high school and I've been offered a guaranteed walk-on spot at Blackhawk Hills University. I'm weighing the advantages of taking that opportunity with the difficulties that come along with making it happen."

"I guess I have two questions, then."

He holds up a finger. "Let me guess. Your questions are, when am I going to take you out again, and will I spend my evening with you? Because if so, my answers are as soon as possible and I'd love to."

I laugh, but my insides shimmy at the thought of another date with him and the idea of spending an evening with his attention on me. I like it too much. "Close, but not quite. Where's Blackhawk Hills University, and what's a guaranteed walk-on?"

"BHU's in Indiana. Middle of nowhere, really, but their team is up and coming, and it's a good college. I went to school in Blackhawk Valley when I was a kid, and I guess I just love the idea of getting back there. We moved a lot when I was growing up, and it's the only place that ever felt like home."

"And the walk-on thing?"

"It means they're not giving me any scholarship money but they'll let me on the team. Honestly, it probably means that I'd be trading work as a punching bag here for time as a punching bag for no pay. But at least I'd get to play ball."

"You like playing football?"

His eyes go wide. "Yeah. I love it. I played defensive end and offensive line in high school. Pretty much any position that requires you to be big and fast at the same time has been my forte. It's a special niche because most big guys aren't fast enough and most fast guys aren't big enough." His gaze drifts to the beach. "It might be the only thing I've ever done that I'm proud of."

"Then you should do it."

He grunts. "I wish it were that simple."

He looks down at his menu, and I wait for him to explain. When he doesn't, I prod. "What's holding you back?"

He lifts his gaze to mine. "Tuition, I guess, but if I can find a way to pay for the first year, I might be able to land an athletic scholarship for the next three." He waves a hand as if the subject is a waft of smoke he can fan away from the table. "What about you? Are you in college?"

"I start in the fall." I bite my bottom lip. "I'm nervous but excited. I want to learn as much as I can and eventually run a not-for-profit organization."

The waiter comes to our table and sets two glasses of ice water before us, but does a double take when he sees me. "Miss Rothschild? What a pleasure to serve you today. I'm a big fan!"

I try to cover my flinch with a smile. I guess my identity is going to be revealed sooner than I planned, which would be fine, but I was looking forward to getting to know Keegan without my childhood acting career coloring his impression of me. "Thank you."

"I loved *Lucy Matters*," the waiter says, and I can tell by his tone that he means it—he's not just some jerk blowing smoke to get in good with the most famous person in the room.

Keegan arches a brow at me in question but stays silent.

"Are you still acting?" the waiter asks.

I shake my head. "Not at the moment. I might go back someday if the opportunity is right." That's such bullshit. I don't want anything to do with Hollywood.

"Well, it's truly a pleasure to meet you. Please let me know if I can get you anything—anything at all. Your lunch is on us today."

My cheeks are burning by the time he leaves the table, and I'm scared to look at Keegan, scared he'll look at me differently now that he knows. But when I lift my eyes to his, he's grinning at me.

"Did you know your cheeks turn bright red when you're embarrassed?" he asks. "It's the cutest damn thing I've ever seen."

"Yeah. Been like that since I was a kid."

"I guess I should have remembered that from your sitcom."

He shakes his head and rubs the back of his neck. "I thought I recognized you but I couldn't place you. I kind of feel like a tool now, actually."

"Please don't. Don't do that."

"Listen..." He scans the faces on the patio before turning back to me. "I mean, should you really be having lunch with someone like me? Shouldn't you be hanging out with some actors or something? Or maybe with someone who could afford to take you someplace nicer than this?"

"I love this place," I blurt before taking a breath. He looks truly baffled, and I want to explain. "I guess I could be eating lunch with some actors. I know a few."

He laughs softly. "Yeah. I imagine."

"I *could*, but I'm not. I'm eating lunch with you because you asked me. I didn't come because I had to. I came because I wanted to."

"And I guess that makes me the luckiest guy here." His gaze drops to my mouth as he says it.

My insides turn to warm mush and my whole body gravitates toward him. I lick my lips, suddenly parched. "You said you were free tonight?"

CHAPTER 10
KEEGAN

"**M**eet me here in fifteen minutes." The blonde tucks a piece of paper into my hand and sinks her teeth into her red bottom lip. When she walks away, there's a calculated sway in her hips. She knows I'm watching. Hell, she's all surgically perfected curves and tanned skin in that hot pink dress. Most of the men at the bar have their eyes on her.

Next to me, Mason shakes his head and cocks a brow. "What just happened?"

I look at the piece of paper in my hand that tells me her room number. "I'm pretty sure the girl just invited him to her room," Bailey says on the other side of me.

"Something like that," I mutter.

Mason clears his throat. "Are you going to go?"

I make a face. "Are you fucking crazy? I know nothing about

that woman."

Bailey grunts. "Never stopped you before."

I look at my watch. "Everyone's going to be here in five minutes. We have plans, remember?"

Bailey shakes her head. "Suit yourself, but you know Chris and Grace and Mia and Arrow are upstairs getting off right this instant." She steps between mine and Mason's stools and drapes her arms over our shoulders. "Meanwhile, we three stooges are down here trying and failing to silence our libidos with alcohol."

Mason ignores her, but the fact that he drains his bourbon tells me he's more than aware of her touch. And his libido. I wonder what he thinks of the reminder of what they could be doing right now. I'd say I wish these two would fuck and get over it, but apparently they did a lot of that once. So much so that Mason assumed what he had with Bailey was going to become something much more serious than fucking. When Bailey wasn't on board with that, he cut her off. Fast-forward three years, and Mason and I play on the same NFL team while Bailey is back home in Blackhawk Valley running my bar, leaving me the monkey in the middle of these two fools who can't figure their shit out.

"Or maybe you're saving yourself for..." Bailey studies me, cocking her head. "What was her name? *Emily*? Maybe that's why you're not taking the blonde up on her offer."

"Oh, good point," Mason says, and I think he might be a little buzzed. "I forgot about the hot new girl."

"We're friends," I mutter. Lord knows that reminder didn't

do shit to keep my mind from locking on Emma while I was in the shower. Every thought that went through my brain was about her—memories of her body under mine, fantasies of taking her to my room tonight, undressing her, finding all her sweet spots and reminding her how good I can make her feel. I turned the water hot and let my mind run wild as I imagined, in vivid detail, the scenario that would end the night with her in my arms.

"Are you going to tell us how you know her?" Bailey asks. "And don't give me that high school bullshit. You two were obviously more than *classmates*."

"It's a long story."

Bailey says something in response, but I can't focus on her words because Emma just walked into the lobby bar. My jaw falls open and I think I stop breathing.

Just friends. You're spending your night together as friends.

The words might be true, but they don't help my response to her. No man wants to be *just friends* with a woman who looks like that in a red dress. I slide off the stool and go to her, and I can feel my friends' eyes on me but I don't fucking care. The dress cradles her curves and shows off everything. It stops mid-thigh—sweet, soft thighs that I remember too well having wrapped around my waist.

"I didn't even think about what I'd wear until I got out of the shower and realized this was my only option." Her hand flutters to her chest, covering her cleavage. "Becky packed for me."

"Remind me to thank her." Stepping closer, I let my gaze skim over her again, from that stupid fucking wig that I might not mind if I didn't have such a thing for her hair, to her shiny, dangling earrings that nearly brush her bare shoulders. My eyes slide over her exposed collarbone, down to her breasts cupped in the red fabric, to the curve of her ass hugged by the fitted dress, down her legs to her high heels. My thoughts rush past PG-13 and into X-rated. The things I want to do to her are firmly outside the friend zone. "You look amazing."

The pink in her cheeks blooms until she's flushed all the way across her face and down her neck. She used to get embarrassed about the way she blushed, as if it was something that made her less beautiful, but I always loved it. Emma's emotions show on her skin, and I loved that I could watch embarrassment or arousal bloom under her freckles and spread.

"Keegan," she says. "You're not looking at me like a friend."

I grunt, unable to find words for a moment. Forming a complete sentence is too difficult while I'm busy taking her all in and imprinting her on my memory. "Just give me a minute," I manage. I pull in one deep breath after another before I lift my eyes to hers, but that doesn't help. Her pupils are dilated and she's leaning toward me, as if she not only likes the way I'm looking at her but wants me to do it again.

"Try to behave," she whispers.

"Are you *sure* that's what you want?"

"Keegan," she says. I can't tell if the edge in her voice is a warning or a plea, but it doesn't matter, because the rest of the gang has joined us in the bar and is gathering around.

Our ride is waiting outside, ready to escort us around town.

We all pile into the limo, me on the inside, Emma squeezed between me and Mia. Mia has herself wrapped around Arrow and is turned away from us.

I give Emma a lopsided grin and drop my gaze to where the hem of her skirt meets the soft, bare flesh of her thigh. When I settle my palm there, she closes her eyes and her lips part for a moment.

I'm rethinking everything. I'm rethinking all of my reservations about touching her and forgetting all the reasons I need to keep my distance. Were there reasons? They're all fuzzy right now, and I can't blame the beer I just had at the bar. Everything's gone blurry because she's here and she's soft and she's warm. She's Emma.

When she opens her eyes, she draws in a ragged breath before gently lifting my hand and moving it to my own thigh. "Friends," she says, no real scorn in the reminder.

I nod. That's what I offered, and that's what she has to give. I'll take it. Even if I want so much more, my dick aches like a sonofabitch in my pants. "Sorry."

She shakes her head and presses her hand to her chest. "Don't be," she says so no one else can hear us. "I'd forgotten how it feels to have someone look at me the way you do. It's...been a long time."

That's just absurd. Maybe it's because I've always been more obvious with my flirtation. I've never been afraid to tell a beautiful woman that she's beautiful. But I haven't seen Emma in five years, and it's hard to believe she hasn't had anyone around to make her feel as beautiful as everyone else can see she is. She's the only one who could never see her beauty. Then again, she was always so quiet, damn near cloistered, and so she never gave men the opportunity to flirt with her.

"It's nice, but we just have to be careful to keep this"—she waves a hand between our bodies—"friendly."

"If it helps, my thoughts about you and this dress are very, very kind."

She laughs. "Are they?"

"Oh yeah. And as a friend, I think you should know when you look good enough to eat, which you do right now. Not that I'm going to do anything about it. I just thought you should know."

EMMA

"*The next morning* at practice, we're running routes and Keegan slams into Dre—knocks him to the ground like he weighs no more than fifty pounds." Mason grins as he recounts what he called his favorite story from their rookie year—namely the practice after Keegan walked in on his quarterback screwing his baby's mother. "He fucking deserved it, and it was so nice to see him go down."

"I bet your coach was pissed," Arrow says. "Gotta protect the pansy quarterbacks."

Chris tosses a napkin at Arrow. "Shut your mouth."

"I wasn't talking about you, Trigger Finger," Arrow says. "You can take a hit, but some of these boys can't without crying to Mom."

"I was fined within an inch of my life," Keegan says, "and as if *that* didn't hurt enough, I was on Coach's shit list for weeks."

Mason folds his arms and looks at him. "But it was worth it, wasn't it?"

He smirks. "Fuck yes."

I'm still stuck on the beginning of the story. "So she was living with you, but she was sleeping with him?"

"She had her own room. It's not like we were romantically involved."

Mason grunts. "Right. Like you would have moved her ass down to Florida and gone broke for such a nice place if you weren't thinking you two could make it work."

Keegan shrugs, but I can see the hurt on his face, and I file away the information. He made light of his relationship with Olivia when I asked earlier today, but the way the guys talk about it, Keegan was doing all he could to make his child's mother a permanent part of his life.

"I think I'd be pissed at Olivia too," Mia says. "I mean, she knew what she was doing. Why not fuck him at his house? That's just inconsiderate."

"Changing the subject," Keegan mutters.

Mia waves down the waiter and holds up her empty martini glass. "We're empty," she says, and I realize in horror that she's right—and that was my second.

"Another round?" the waiter asks.

"No more martinis," Bailey says.

"That's probably wise," I agree quietly so only Keegan can hear.

But Bailey's not done. "We need shots." She looks around the group. "Tequila seems appropriate, and the good stuff because the guys are paying. And bring a bowl of limes too?"

"You're my favorite," Grace says, then Chris whispers something into her ear and she blushes hard.

Moments later, little glasses are set before each of us along with bowls of limes, and I realize Keegan is watching me.

"Have you ever done a snakebite before?" he asks.

I shake my head. "Never."

"There's so much I never got the chance to teach you." When I shiver at all the various ways I could take those words, he grins. "Allow me to demonstrate." He unbuttons one shirt sleeve and rolls it halfway up his forearm before licking the inside of his wrist and sprinkling it with salt. Then in quick succession, he licks the salt away, throws back the shot and bites into the lime, puckering as he pulls the sour fruit from his lips. "Just like that."

I meet his eyes when I lick my wrist and immediately recognize my mistake. There is something deeply sensual about holding Keegan's darkening gaze as I lick my own skin. The sight of his flaring nostrils and the way his lips part remind me of the night five years ago when I mustered all of my courage and stripped for him. I watch him through every step of the shot, and I'm as buzzed by the look in his eyes as I am by the alcohol hitting my blood.

We're still friends. We're not crossing that dangerous line, just toeing at it.

What does it say about me that I want him to cross the line? What does it say about me that yesterday morning I was so sure of the direction my life was going, but now I wish Keegan would sweep me into another room and kiss me hard? That I want him to push us both so far over the line that there's no coming back? I want to remember what it's like to have my body come alive when it's touched. I want *him*.

I lick the sour juice from my lips. "What are you thinking right now?"

"I'm wondering if it would be within the boundaries of our friendship to tell you how much I want to kiss you." He wets his bottom lip and drops his gaze back to my cleavage before returning to meet my eyes. "Because *damn*. I do. Right now."

"We can't."

He nods and flashes a mischievous grin. "Yeah, I know that, but it's not gonna stop me from thinking about it."

And knowing he's thinking about it means that I won't be able to stop imagining it. My whole body hums in anticipation of a kiss I can't have. There are too many secrets—old and new. "I know things ended badly for us, and someday maybe we should talk about it. Maybe—"

He puts his fingers over my lips to silence me, and all I can think is that I can almost taste his skin. "Let's leave the past behind this weekend. I don't want to rehash everything we've done and everything we have planned." He drags a hand over his face. "I sound like an asshole. But we only get tonight, and I don't want to screw it up."

"You don't want to talk about the past because you'll remember how much you should hate me."

"Em?" He shifts in his chair, turning to face me before cupping my face in his hands. "I don't hate you. I wish things had ended differently, and you hurt me, but I've never hated you. I couldn't if I wanted to."

My breath catches. I guess I needed to hear that more than I realized. "Really?"

"Really." His Adam's apple bobs as he swallows. "But I can't look at you without feeling things, without wanting to touch you. That's always going to be there no matter how much we want to pretend the past didn't happen."

The icy determination holding up my willpower melts under the heat in his eyes.

CHAPTER 11

KEEGAN

The second round of shots was probably a mistake. I behaved all through dinner, keeping my hands to myself, keeping my glances in her direction a respectable length. I didn't allow myself to touch or stare or ogle, though I wanted to, and by the time we took our seats at the show, my world was blurry around the edges but my desire was laser sharp.

The whole show, I'm so distracted by her nearness and my buzz that I can hardly pay attention to what's happening on the stage. Somewhere in the middle of the performance, Emma places her hand on my thigh, and I don't know if she knows that as she rubs her pinky along the seam of my pants, it drifts higher and higher, making my cock stir, then harden, then ache.

She watches the show with wide eyes, occasionally leaning toward me and pointing at a particularly beautiful dancer or a sexy couple on the stage. Every time she leans close, I catch her scent and have to give myself a firm reminder of where we've drawn the lines on our night together.

During the show's final number, she leans toward me and her lips brush my ear as she asks, "Can you imagine having a job like this? Do you think they go home turned on every night?"

I know the question is innocent and not an invitation to discover whether or not the show has left *her* turned on, but I want to. I want to take her to the first dark corner I can find and slide my hand up that maddening dress and feel between her legs. I want to take her hand and press it against my pants so she can feel exactly what she does to me, remind her what she's *always* done to me.

There are more drinks after the show—also probably a bad idea, but I love that Emma stands closer with every drink, touches me a little more often. Then we go to Caesars, and someone orders another round of shots as we try our hands at roulette and find that we're all too drunk to focus on the game.

Bailey insists that we need to go dancing, and this time when we file back into the limo to dance at a club in our hotel, Emma ends up in my lap, her arms draped around my neck. I groan and she giggles and rubs her thumb along the edge of my jaw. "Thank you for tonight." Her eyes lock on mine, and we might as well be alone in the limo for how aware I am of the people around us. "I've never had so much fun, and it's almost perfect."

"You're welcome." I can hear the slur in my words and focus on each one. "Tell me what would make it perfect."

She leans her forehead against mine and draws in a long,

ragged breath. "If I were someone else," she whispers. "It would be perfect if I were anyone but me."

Those words take me back to another time, another dark night when desire stretched so thick between us it was hard to breathe unless I was touching her. She told me she wished she didn't have to be herself, that all she wanted was to be someone else. "Tonight you can be anyone you want. You're Emily Zimmerman, remember? Tell me about Emily. Who is she? What does she think about tonight?"

She closes her eyes as if she's imagining and smiles. "She's brave. She's not afraid of life and she likes to dance." She holds my gaze, her lips parted as the limo pulls to a stop in front of our hotel.

"Are you lovebirds coming?" Bailey asks from the door, and I realize while I've been focused on Emma's lips and the feel of her in my arms, everyone else has already climbed out.

Emma scrambles off my lap, her cheeks pink, and we make our way into the nightclub, where she pulls me onto the dance floor and slings her arms around my neck.

"I always loved dancing with you," she says, rocking her hips toward mine.

I hold on to her waist, letting my thumbs press into the soft flesh of her belly. "We're playing with fire here, Em," I warn her.

She shakes her head and presses her body closer as she lifts her mouth to my ear. "But Emily Zimmerman likes to play with fire. She's good at it, and no one gets hurt."

"You don't need to worry about hurting me." I swallow. Is that true? Will I believe that in the morning? But fuck, she already broke my heart—how much more damage could she do? "Right now, I can't imagine anything hurting as much as not being here with you."

If alcohol has made my world go blurry around the edges, it's made her come into sharper focus, and I want to memorize everything about her—the part of her red lips, the sway of her hips as we dance, the way her fingertips curl into my biceps as she holds on to me.

"You're too beautiful," I tell her. I run my thumb along her jaw. "Too fucking beautiful."

"I've missed you. You're the best man I've ever met."

My stomach clenches and I shake my head. "Don't think that. It's a lie. It's what I wanted you to believe. Don't bring that lie into tonight."

"How was it a lie?" She grins up at me, and I know a full confession would erase all the happiness from her face.

"When we were together before, I wasn't the man you thought I was. I wasn't good." It's the closest to the truth I've ever given anyone about my past.

"So you don't want me believing you're good?"

I pull her hips tightly against me as I exhale in frustration. She still thinks this is some kind of joke. "I'm different now, but then…"

She lifts onto her toes and flicks her tongue against my ear. "Don't be so different. I like you a little bad."

I groan and stop dancing. I don't know how much longer

I can do this without diving over the line. "Is that permission to stop being your friend?" I'm obsessed with knowing if she tastes as sweet as I remember. And if I swipe my tongue over the sensitive spot beneath her ear, will she gasp like she always did?

She shrugs and grins, and the dance floor tilts off balance. It's crowded, and we're surrounded by writhing bodies, cocooned in the crowd. I turn her in my arms so her back is to my front and settle my hand against the soft skin of her midriff. She arches her back and rubs against me.

I sweep her hair to the side, and when I press my lips to the long, smooth column of her neck, she trembles against me.

"Are you okay?" I ask against her ear. "Is this okay?"

"I—I'm not sure…"

"Tell me what you want. Not five years ago. Not tomorrow. What do you want right now?"

She reaches back and threads her fingers through my hair to guide my mouth back to her neck.

I don't hesitate. I kiss and suck on that tender skin while we move to the beat.

The rest of the room fades and one song blurs into the next. A waitress comes by selling shots, and I buy two, one for each of us, and we lock eyes as we throw them back. At some point, I'm vaguely aware of Bailey checking on me, but my focus is one hundred percent on Emma, on this night that takes me back to when I was eighteen and so fucking in love it hurt. Tonight, Emma isn't the woman who once broke my heart. She isn't the girl who wrote me off with a simple goodbye note and apologies

I didn't want. Tonight, she's a dream, my fantasy in the flesh, my reward for surviving the hardest year of my whole life.

When her face begins to blur, I realize I'm way more drunk than I ever intended. I need to sober up or I'm not going to remember a minute of this night. "Want to get out of here?"

She nods, takes my hand, and leads me out of the bar and down the hall to the elevators. My watch reads a quarter past two.

"Let's get some food," I suggest, but at the same moment, an elevator dings and the doors slide open.

Emma grabs my hand and drags me inside. "I don't want food," she says, punching a button.

I spin her around and press her against the wall. "What do you want, Em?" I drop my hand to her side to skim my knuckles over her skirt, and she widens her stance to part her thighs. "Fuck," I whisper. I shouldn't do this. Not here, not when any moment someone could join us on the elevator, not when we're both so damn drunk it's a wonder we can stand upright. But *shouldn't* is so much weaker than *want*, and I want to touch her more than I want anything right now.

I'm faintly aware of the soft beeping of the passing floors as I slide my hand up her skirt and cup her between her legs. She gasps, and I rub my fingers over the damp lace of her panties, teasing her swollen flesh.

When the elevator stops and the doors slide open, she grabs my wrist and holds me still. "Please," she whispers in my ear. "Please. Don't stop." Then she tilts her hips and rocks against my hand. I couldn't refuse her if every person in the hotel was watching us.

I squeeze my eyes shut and step closer, then I pull the lace of her panties to the side and slide a finger into her wet heat. I don't know what makes me harder—the sound of her gasp followed by her quick moan of pleasure, or the way her muscles squeeze my finger so damn tight. Suddenly, I'm desperate to taste her. I want to lay her out and strip her bare, want to spread her legs and use my lips and tongue on her until she's screaming for more. I'm a better lover than the kid she knew five years ago, and I want to prove it to her.

Slowly, I fuck her with my fingers, watching the pleasure move across her face as I move in and out of her. "You're so damn close," I whisper.

"I know." She bucks against me, half helpless, half desperate. "God, I'd forgotten how good…"

I move my hand faster. Rougher now. Demanding. "Were you wet for me the whole time we were dancing?"

"Yes."

"Were you thinking about this? Or were you hoping I'd make you come on the dance floor?"

"I…" She closes her eyes and shakes her head.

I take her chin in my free hand and tilt her head up so she has to look at me. "No, baby. You're not getting off the hook that easily. I want to hear you say it."

"I want you to make me come," she begs. "Keegan, please. I—"

I slide a second finger inside her, and her muscles clench,

squeezing me tight as her orgasm rocks through her. I'm so turned on that my cock aches, but I watch every second. I drink in the way her lashes look against her freckled cheeks, the way her teeth sink into her bottom lip as she shudders with the aftershocks of her pleasure.

And when she drunkenly stumbles away from me and pulls me into her penthouse suite, I blindly follow.

CHAPTER 12
EMMA

I wake up with a gasp and confusion hits me in the face with the intensity of my aching head.

Oh my God. What have I done?

Keegan is sleeping on his side facing me, one arm draped over my waist. The few times we slept together, this was his MO. His body always facing mine, at least one limb wrapped around me as if he's afraid I might run away while he sleeps. The gesture makes my pounding heart ache for something I haven't let myself want in five years.

Snippets from the night before come to me. The burlesque show, Keegan's hands on my hips as we danced, his mouth skimming down my neck, flashes of the elevator and being pressed against the wall. His hands. His mouth. My desperate pleas for more. *What have I done?*

My stomach heaves. I slide out from under his arm and run to the bathroom. I lose the contents of my stomach in the toilet, and I don't know if I'm sick from the alcohol or the horror ushered in by sobriety and the light of day.

Our safety net of "just friends" failed us. I lean my forehead on the cool porcelain of the toilet bowl and whimper. Maybe the night was a bad idea from the beginning. I drank too much and fucked up, but can I really blame the booze when it led me exactly where I wanted to be?

When I close my eyes, I'm bombarded with flashes of what happened in the room. Clothes coming off. Hands and mouths everywhere. My thighs spread, his body over mine as he whispered in my ear... *"Do you know how many times I've thought about this since you left me? Do you have any idea how many times I've gotten myself off by remembering the sounds you make when you come?"*

The memories are fragmented—delicious bites of a decadent dessert. I relish them while feeling guilty for wanting more. My body aches in that delicious, well-used way I haven't felt in five years.

What have I done? What have I done?

The words echo like a death knell in my pounding head. I think about scribbling a note and leaving before he wakes up, but I left him with nothing but a note once, and I can't stomach the thought of how much he'd hate me if I did it again.

I climb in the shower and hang my head as I let the water pour over me. I don't want to wash away last night. If I could choose, I'd keep those moments and hold them close. No, it's the oppressive weight of reality that has me turning the water hot. It's tomorrow that I want to wash away, not last night.

I screwed up, and no amount of hot water will change that.

When I get out of the shower, I grab my toothbrush and scrub the taste of too much alcohol from my enamel and tongue. I splash water on my face and stare at my reflection. Last night, I excused myself to the restroom after dinner, and I remember holding on to the vanity and staring in wonder at the stranger in the mirror. She looked younger than I've felt in years. She looked like she knew how to have a good time. Like she'd never known the loneliness that's haunted me most of my life. This morning, the girl in my reflection looks lost and terrified, and all too familiar.

"Emma?" Keegan calls from the bedroom. His voice is husky with sleep and laced with an edge of worry.

I squeeze my eyes shut and grip the edge of the bathroom counter.

"Emma?" he calls again, and the sound of my name on his tongue makes my throat go thick with sadness.

I have to tell him. I screwed up, and now I have to explain.

"I'm coming," I croak. I slip into one of the hotel's fluffy white robes before returning to the bedroom. He's sitting up in bed, his broad chest bare, his gaze running over me again and again. I give him a shaky smile. I don't want him to see how unsure I feel this morning. I don't want him to know about the guilt that's eating away at my gut.

"I thought you left," he says. "Are you okay?"

I shake my head. "Hungover. The shower helped."

He leans back against the headboard, and I stand stupidly beside the bed, not sure where to sit or stand or what to do with my hands. I have no idea how I'm supposed to explain what a mistake this was or why I let it happen. I wish I could choose not to explain at all. Instead, I'd straddle his waist and run my hands over the muscles in his chest. I'd soak in his warmth and his strength and forget everything but the lust in his eyes and the way I feel when he touches me. Suddenly, with every breath I take, the question weighs heavier on me, the question I wouldn't let myself think yesterday. *What would happen if I didn't go home? What would happen if I stayed with him?*

He cocks his head to the side. "Penny for your thoughts."

"I was thinking…" I snap my mouth shut and bite my bottom lip. I'm not brave enough for this.

Reaching out, he grabs my hand and tugs me onto the bed. I squeak as he rolls over me, and his weight on my body is so delicious that I close my eyes. When I open them, he's propped himself up on his elbow and he's looking down at me. "Tell me what's wrong." He snakes one hand between our bodies and inside my robe. His knuckles graze my belly then dip lower. "You can tell me anything."

He slides a hand between my legs, and I gasp. "I walked away from you once, Keegan. I forgot how hard that was. What if I'm not strong enough to do it again?"

His hand stills and he exhales heavily before lowering his mouth to mine and kissing me hard. The kiss is teeth and tongue and a hunger that I understand all too well. His tongue slides against mine and his hand resumes its intoxicating rhythm between my legs. "Then don't," he says against my mouth. "Don't fucking walk away. Not again."

"Vegas can't last forever." My voice betrays me, cracking like my heart in my chest. I know I have to go home, but right now the week ahead of me looms like a hell I don't deserve.

On the nightstand, the suite phone rings. I don't reach for it. I don't want Keegan's hands off me. I want to close my eyes and sink into the pleasure of his hand working between my legs. I want to relish the way he makes me feel—like I'm a woman again, brave and unafraid of life and love. I'm a greedy dreamer refusing to open her eyes and let the dream end. "It's probably just room service wanting to know what time they can bring up breakfast."

"Then I'll let them know it's going to have to wait." Keegan reaches for the phone with his free hand, and I hold the other between my legs, letting my hips arch into his touch, showing him with my body what I need. He squeezes his eyes shut as he places the receiver to his ear. "Hello?"

I rock my hips, working myself against his still hand.

"Can you say that again?" I wonder if the person on the other end can hear the arousal in his voice as clearly as I can. In this instant, it's as if tomorrow isn't real. My life in Georgia and my plans are nothing but a work of fiction I enjoyed once. *This.* This is real. This is everything.

All the color drains from Keegan's face as he takes the phone from his ear and his hand from between my legs. His jaw goes hard and his eyes icy as he hands the receiver to me. "It's the front desk. Your fiancé is here and asking to speak with you."

CHAPTER 13
KEEGAN

When you just spent the whole night kissing, tasting, touching, and fucking a woman, and you tell her that her fiancé is on the phone, the last thing you want her to do is take the receiver and talk to the man on the other line.

I held my breath as I waited for her to laugh and tell me that the guy on the phone must have the wrong number. Instead, she rolled out from under me, stood beside the bed, took the phone, and said she'd speak with him.

"Zachary?" she asks. "What are you doing in Vegas?"

That's all I needed to hear. Ten seconds ago, she was getting herself off on my hand, and now she's speaking to *Zachary*? Who's her fucking *fiancé*? I climb out of bed and leave the bedroom. My clothes are scattered all over the suite, but I gather them and pull them on one item at a time. I don't let myself think about what we did in these rooms last night. Nothing good will come of thinking about the way she unbuttoned my pants just inside the door or how she ran her nails down my chest after I pulled off my shirt. If I think about taking handfuls of her red hair as she drew me into her mouth, I'll lose my fucking mind.

Instead, I buckle my belt and button my shirt as I head to the door.

Before I can open it, Emma's in front of me, standing between me and my only choice: walking away. "I can explain," she says. Her eyes are so big and desperate that I want to believe her. I want to listen to anything she has to tell me.

"That's why you wanted to be someone else. And that's why you kept changing the subject when I asked about your life." I arch a brow. "Is that what you wanted to explain? Because I get it. I figured that much out myself. But frankly, I'd have liked to have the choice before I fucked another man's fiancé."

She opens her mouth and closes it again. She hangs her head before she says, "I should have told you."

"Yeah. You should have. But now you can tell *him*."

She lifts her head, and when I meet her eyes, I hear my dad's voice in my head. *Wake up and see that she's conning you, son.* "It isn't what it seems."

"What? Like you and Harry wasn't what it seemed?"

She flinches and backs against the door as if my words were a punch that landed right in her gut. "Yeah. Something like that." She shakes her head. "I'm sorry, Keegan. I didn't mean for this to happen."

I swallow hard. I'm being torn in twelve different directions and I'm paralyzed because I don't know what the fuck to do next. Part of me wants to storm out of here and never look back. Part of me wants to pin her against the door and kiss her until she comes to her senses and tells me she won't marry *Zachary*. Then there are all of the variations between those two extremes: the part of me that wants to hear her explanation, the part that wants to say fuck her fiancé, last night she was mine, and if he wants her he's going to have to prove he's the better man.

"Will you tell him?" As soon as I say the words, I regret them. I hold up a hand. "Never mind. Please don't answer that. It's none of my business, and I honestly don't care."

"Keegan—"

"Emma, get out of my way."

She lifts her hand to my cheek. The second her fingertips brush along my jaw, I flinch and turn my head the other way. She makes an awful choking sound. I tighten my jaw and refuse to let myself look at her.

"I will always care for you." She steps out of the way as I turn the knob and yank open the door, leaving before I can talk myself out of it.

EMMA

Five Years Ago…

"Emma!" My mother greets me at the door of her brand-new

house in Hollywood and wraps me into her arms. Apparently, she's playing the role of *adoring mother* today. "It's so good to see you, baby! Come into the living room. I have a visitor I think you might be excited to see." She grabs my hand and drags me into the living room, where a man is sitting on the couch, one leg crossed over the other. He's tall and lean in his expensive suit, and his neatly parted dark hair curls at his collar. The bits of silver at his temples have taken him from Hollywood stud to "silver fox."

Something sharp rips through my chest at the sight of him. Harry Evans was my costar on *Lucy Matters*, and my feelings upon seeing him are never simple and rarely painless. "What's Harry doing here?" Does she know? Did he tell her? He's wearing headphones and bopping his head to a beat we can't hear.

"Remember, I told you I was seeing someone."

I shake my head. That explanation doesn't make any sense. "Who?"

She grins. "*Harry*. It just happened. You know I've always admired him, and then a couple of months ago he called me up and, well, the connection was there. It's all happening so fast and I've never been happier."

"You and…Harry?" I sound like a child trying to comprehend a complex physics concept, and Mom looks one hundred percent blissed out.

"Yes. Can you believe it? He can't hear us," Mom says. "He loves those noise-canceling headphones."

My heart lurches as she steps around the couch and into his line of vision. She pulls the headphones from his ears. "Harry, my daughter is here."

Does she see it? The way his jaw goes slack and his face goes pale? He's too good, though, and it's only there for a fraction of a second before he replaces his shock with a smile. Harry Evans is a lifelong actor who works magic on stage; he's certainly not going to be bested in a living room.

He stands and offers his hand as if I'm a stranger. As if we didn't spend years secretly meeting in his trailer. Is this some sort of sick joke? My stomach churns. I can't even speak, and I certainly won't take his hand.

He covers my shock by pretending to be shocked himself. "What a lovely surprise to see you again. How long has it been? Months? Years?"

I look to my mom and back to Harry. "Are you kidding me?"

"He's here for me, Emma."

Harry's eyes bore into mine. I see the warning there. That was the agreement, right? He said we needed to keep our relationship quiet. He said he'd be crucified if anyone knew he was sleeping with such a young girl—and of course it would have destroyed the future of the show—but he couldn't stay away from me.

"What's your problem, Emma?" Mom asks. "You can relax. Not everything is about you. I promise this isn't some scheme to get you back on screen again." Mom puts her hand on Harry's arm. "She's so defensive about leaving her acting, but really, everyone knows it's better for her to get her weight in check before she takes on adult roles. Otherwise, she's doomed to a career of being typecast as the funny fat friend."

Normally, Mom's jab would burn, but right now I'm too shell-shocked by the return of Harry to my life to be bothered by another low blow at my body. Swallowing hard, I force a smile. "Sorry about my manners. I'm not feeling very well today."

"Well," Mom says. "I'm just glad you stopped by. Harry and I are going to the Diamond Room for dinner. Why don't you come with us? Surely you have some old boyfriend you can call and invite."

I blink. The only man I've ever been involved with is slinging an arm around my mother's shoulders and pressing a kiss to the top of her head. "I need to go. I really don't feel well." I turn to Harry and wince. "Good to see you again, Harry."

His shoulders sag—with relief, or something else? "You too."

I turn for the door and manage to make it to my car before I start crying.

The road floats before me in a haze of tears. I don't know how long I drive aimlessly along the coast, but when I get to my condo in Laguna Beach, the sun has long since set, and I've talked myself down from the panic I felt at my mother's. This doesn't change anything. I got Harry out of my life and left Hollywood for a reason. Mom can spend every waking minute with him, and in the scheme of things, it won't change my life in any remarkable way.

My calm disintegrates when I walk up to my oceanfront condo and find Harry waiting by my front door.

When I look at him now, my heart twists painfully with the confusing mix of emotions I've always associated with him.

Tenderness, love, and something darker. Something twisted that screwed with the way I saw myself until I walked away from him and *Lucy Matters* at sixteen. "What are you doing here?"

Shrugging, he looks me over. "I missed you. What was I supposed to do? I didn't want you to find out like that, but you changed your number." He steps forward, and I hold up a hand.

"Don't." I turn and unlock the door. He follows me inside.

"Em, your mom and I... I can't explain it. She and I are a better match, but my relationship with her doesn't change how I feel about you."

"You're disgusting." My voice shakes wildly. "How long has this been going on? Were you fucking us both?"

"My career is tied up with hers. It's easier if we're together." His jaw is hard. He hates it when I don't buy his shit. Normally, I'm happy to play along and listen to his skewed perception of reality, but I'm done accepting his fiction as truth to soothe his ego.

I shake my head. "This has nothing to do with me. Enjoy your life. If you want to live it with my mom, go for it, but if this is your sick way of being my *dad* in some capacity again—"

"Don't you see this could be good for us? We could be together again. Think of all the opportunities we'll have." He tilts his head to the side. "There's a reason you don't date. You miss it as much as I do."

My stomach heaves. "I miss nothing, and there is no *us*."

"You're letting this go? Just like that?" he asks. "After all we've been through together, it's that easy for you to walk away?"

I don't even know what *this* was. An affair that breathed only in dark corners? A secret that started as a dangerous and forbidden thrill and turned into something my teenage brain mistook for love?

I open the door. "You can leave now. Please don't come back."

"Don't do something stupid out of anger."

"Leave."

He sighs and stares at me for a long beat before he walks out the door. I slam it behind him and turn the deadbolt with shaking fingers. I sink to the floor, pull my phone from my purse, and pull up a number from the memory. He picks up on the first ring.

"Keegan? This is Emma."

"Hey. I thought you were busy tonight. What's going on?"

"My plans changed. Could you come over?"

CHAPTER 14
KEEGAN

I went back to my room and packed my shit in record time. I want to get away from here. Away from this hotel, away from Vegas, away from Emma and her fiancé. It's not time to head to the airport yet, but I can't sit in my room and stew, so I go downstairs.

"Keegan!" someone calls across the lobby.

My stomach goes icy with dread at the sound of the familiar voice. *Fuck no.*

"Hey, son!"

I turn to see my father walking toward me, a big, shit-eating grin on his face. Dad never had much time for me once I started college and stopped helping him on his most recent scheme, but that all changed a year ago when he learned I got signed by the Gators. Suddenly, dear old Dad was there again.

Not every NFL player is a millionaire, and though I have no

complaints about my league-minimum salary, Dad refuses to believe I don't have the disposable income to buy him Corvettes and beach houses and whatever the fuck else he pleases.

I lift my chin. "What are you doing here?"

"Can't a father come visit his son?"

The question I should've asked was *How did you find me here?* It's probably one of the worst things about my new life in the public eye—it's hard to elude my greedy conman father.

"I stopped by your condo in Seaside." He tucks his hands into the pockets of his dress pants. He's dressed sharp today in pressed pants and a button-up shirt, and his silver hair is combed back. "Bastards wouldn't let me up because, apparently, you've forgotten to put my name on some list with security? You need to remember to take care of that when you get back."

"I wouldn't count on it."

"But luckily," he continues, as if I didn't speak, "I saw your girlfriend. What's her name? Olivia?"

Olivia's not my girlfriend, but I don't correct him.

"She's such a sweet girl. Real pretty, too. She said you were in Vegas for the weekend and where you were staying. Real helpful, that girl. Anyway, I thought what the hell? I haven't been to Vegas in a while. I thought I should treat myself." He lifts his arms from his sides. "So here I am."

The man was absolutely no help when I needed him, and then when he thought I had money, he became like a parasite I can't shake. "Well, you found me. Sorry I can't spend time with you. I'm heading home today."

"You never have time for your dad." He looks around the lobby like he's trying to spot someone. "Too busy hanging out with fancy bigwig NFL players to do a damn thing for your father." Once, that guilt trip worked on me. Once, I believed almost all the bullshit that came out of his mouth, but we're way past that now. I might be an idiot in a lot of ways, but when it comes to my father, I'm fucking ancient in my wisdom.

"What do you need?"

"Why do you assume I need something? I just want to spend some time with my son, maybe meet his friends."

And have him con them out of everything he can? *Fuck to the no.* "That's not going to be possible." I reach for my wallet. "Do you have a room yet? A place to stay the night?"

He grins. "Some assistance with that would be fantastic."

I walk up to the desk with him by my side and tell the petite woman behind the counter that I need a room. "Two nights," I say.

"Two?" Dad says. "I don't fly out for four nights."

My jaw hardens and my eyes dart to the elevators as I pray Emma doesn't appear. If he knew what she and I did last night and thought he could get ahead with that information…

I don't want to think about it. I just need to get rid of him as fast as possible. "Four nights, then."

"Okay, a standard room for—"

"Son, don't I deserve a suite? I came all the way out here to see you, and you won't even introduce me to your friends. A little comfort doesn't seem like much to ask for."

The woman behind the counter stops typing and looks at me. I shake my head. "A standard room will be fine, thank you."

Dad nudges me. "I guess. I mean, beggars can't be choosers. What did I ever do to you but feed you and clothe you and make sure you had opportunities your mom wasn't around to give you? I got you through college too, but no thanks to me for that."

If the team doctor took my blood pressure right now, he wouldn't let me play the damn game. This man is full of so much shit, but I don't take the bait. Instead, I hand over my credit card.

"Can we charge incidentals to this card too?" the woman asks.

"No," I say sharply. I just want to be rid of him. When I get my card back, I slide it into my wallet and pull out a couple of hundreds to hand to my father. "It's all I've got."

"I didn't even ask for cash," he says as he tucks it into his pocket.

He hadn't asked *yet*. We both know I'm not usually this easy a target. I know better than to give in to him all the time, but I also know that as soon as I get him a room and some money, he'll get out of my face, at least temporarily. I don't want him anywhere near me in case Emma shows up. The possibility that he might see her with me and recognize her makes my hands shake. Fuck. He might even already know she's engaged, and wouldn't he have a field day with that information if he saw us together again?

"You've gotta quit doing this," I tell him. "I don't have tons of money. Most of my extra money goes into the bar." All of it, actually, and then some. For someone who used to fear debt above all else, I'm carrying a ton of it right now. I shake my head. There's no reasoning with him, so I don't know why I keep trying.

"You wanna have a drink with me?" he asks. He's happy now that he's gotten a piece of me.

"It's eight in the morning."

"Right. No time for your old man. Not even to introduce him to his only granddaughter. But don't worry. Met her while I was in Seaside too. Jasmine. She's really something special. Olivia invited me to visit any time I want, so I'm really looking forward to that."

My stomach cramps. I don't want him around Jazzy, and I'll need to talk to Olivia about that. "Enjoy your stay. Don't get into too much trouble."

"I'll be on my best behavior. When can I come stay with you in Seaside? Maybe you need me to stay at your place when you're staying in Blackhawk Valley? Can't be good to leave a place like that empty."

"It's fine," I mutter.

Dad's talking, saying something about family and obligation and loyalty—bullshit that I wouldn't believe even if I could get my brain to focus on his words instead of the woman walking out of the elevator. *There she is.*

My eyes are glued to Emma as she walks across the corridor to a tall, dark-haired man in a suit. She's not wearing her wig today. She's abandoned her Emily Zimmerman identity and is down here as Emma Rothschild, fiancée to whoever the fuck *that* is. She throws herself into his arms, and he slides a hand to the back of her neck and presses his lips to her forehead before whispering something into her ear.

I want so badly to go over there and tear them apart. It eats at my gut. How could she do that? How could she be with me last night when she's engaged to someone else? How could she have slept with Harry when she was supposed to be in love with me?

She steps out of the man's arms and turns my way as if she can sense me looking at her. When her soft eyes meet mine, the fury in my gut melts away, and I just want to protect her from all the shit I've ever brought into her life. I owe her that much and more.

I turn my attention to my dad. "Maybe I have time for one drink."

"Thatta boy."

I put my hand on his shoulder and lead him toward the café and away from Emma.

KEEGAN

Five Years Ago...

Emma Rothschild is sitting on the floor in the middle of her sun-washed living room, her legs folded under her as she rubs Bigsy's belly. We've just gotten back from a walk in the sand, and she's wearing shorts and a big T-shirt that's slipped off one freckled shoulder. When she looks up at me and grins, there's nothing in the world I want more than to be the man she thinks I am. She wouldn't look at me like that if she knew the real me.

By the time I was fourteen, I knew all there was to know about running a good con. I knew all about choosing the story and how to decide on the long game or the short game.

Dad was best at cons that involved women, and he taught me how to spot the best mark. I think that most people believe they'll never be victim to a conman, but the two biggest characteristics Dad taught me to look for were loneliness and insecurity. Once you learn how to read people, it's almost shocking how many women fit the bill.

When I met Emma, I knew she was exactly what I was looking for. For two weeks, I've been hanging out with her, taking her to dinner, walking with her on the beach, playing with her aging miniature poodle she loves so much. For two weeks, I've been trying to convince myself that I can carry on with my original plan.

My dad told me once that my heart was too soft, that he'd never guess the son of a conman would have turned out to possess the personality of an ideal mark. He said I gave people too much credit. You see, when he cons a rich old lady out of ten grand, he doesn't feel bad about it. He believes people like that would never get rich to begin with if they weren't selfish and greedy. He believes that he's owed more than life's handed him.

While I might not buy into that, I had a plan when I paid the man to take pictures of Emma. I had a plan when I set it up so I could come to her rescue, introduce myself, and pretend I had no idea how famous she was. But two weeks later, I've laid the groundwork, and everything is going according to plan. *Better than planned.*

There's a moment in a con when you *know* you've got it, and that moment came quickly and easily with Emma. But you can't rush it. Even if you could get your money and run, that's not a good con job. A good job leaves the mark feeling like a hero. It lets them look back on that time in their life when they knew that guy and did that great thing for him, and *hey, I wonder where he ended up.*

I haven't kissed her. I haven't touched her. Guilt eats at me every time she drops her gaze to my lips or sits a little closer to me on the couch. There's no place for guilt in a con, and I sure as fuck didn't come out to LA for the summer to earn nothing more than shitty pay for a B-grade film.

She hops up and steps toward me. "So what are we going to do tonight?" She smells so good, like her citrus shampoo. She always smells so fresh and clean. It's intoxicating and makes me imagine things can change, like a new beginning, a Monday morning, the first buds of spring.

My gaze drops to her mouth for a beat too long, and her smile falls away.

"You can kiss me if you want." Her tongue darts out and wets her lips, as if they weren't already inviting enough before. Every cell in my body pulls in her direction, fighting to be closer.

"I—" *Shit.* I don't want to use her. I don't want to take from her. I don't want to do any of the things I set out to do. "I should probably head out."

She flinches and steps back, and I feel like an ass. "Okay. Sure." Her smile is fake, like hardened plastic pasted on her soft features. I love that she's an actress by trade but when she's with me, she can't cover her emotions. "I'll see you around. Sorry about saying that. It was…silly. I mean, you're probably not attracted to me like that, and that's really fine. I mean, I understand. It's not a big deal."

"Jesus." With two long strides, I'm cupping her face in my hands and lowering my mouth to hers. She gasps against my lips, and she tastes so sweet that a soft brush of lips isn't going to be enough. I sweep my tongue across her mouth, and she parts her lips and lifts a hand to slide into my hair.

I'm trying to be gentle, but I've wanted to do this since the first time she smiled at me. These lips were made for kissing, full and soft, and her body was made to be pressed against mine. She slides her tongue against mine and tugs on my hair. My cock hardens, and I want *more*.

"How could you think I'm not attracted to you?" I whisper against her mouth. I force myself to release her, to step back. I have to remember who I am. "Attraction isn't the problem here. I want you so much It's all I think about."

She lifts her hand to her mouth and touches her lips as if she's trying to catch the remnants of my kiss before it evaporates. "You do?"

"The problem is *me*. I'm trying to do the right thing and keep my distance from you because—" I swallow. How do I explain?

Because I'm already falling hard? Because I'm afraid if I take her with me, she'll give me exactly what I set out to get and I don't deserve it? I don't even deserve a second to taste her lips. "But every time you look at me like that, I forget that I'm not good enough."

"Why? Being born to rich parents somehow makes me better?" Her blue eyes go wide and her nostrils flare. "Is this about money? Or is it the fame? You really believe that bullshit?" She shakes her head. "I thought you were smarter than that, Keegan."

"That's not it at all." I shake my head, wishing she could understand. "Not at all."

"Then what is it?"

I draw in a ragged breath and reach for her hand, toying with her fingers. "A guy like me could exploit a woman like you. I could take and take, and you'd never know how much you lost until I walked away."

"There's nothing you could take that I don't want to give you."

I squeeze her hand. *That's exactly what I'm afraid of.* "Ditto."

CHAPTER 15
KEEGAN

I canceled breakfast plans with the rest of the crew, using my father's appearance as an excuse. I was spared having to face any of them until I meet up with Mason at the airport for our flight back to Florida.

I must look as shitty as I feel, because when Mason sees me at the gate, he arches a brow, gives me a once-over, and says, "I expected you to be on cloud nine today. Did this morning's goodbye with your 'friend'"—he holds up his hands to put air quotes around the word—"not go so well?"

I sink into the chair beside him and run a hand through my hair. The pounding in my head and the burning in my gut have eased up since I left Emma's room this morning, but I still feel like I'm recovering from a bad case of the flu. Frankly, I'm not sure there is any recovery for my epically bad drunken decisions. "My morning was shit. Why did you let me drink so much last night?"

He frowns. "Is this one of those times where you fucked up so you want me to blame myself and/or the alcohol so you don't have to take personal responsibility for your actions?"

"Shut up," I mutter.

"No, no. I'm serious. Because I can play that game if that's what you need, especially if you'll return the favor." He nods sagely. "Poor Keegan fell victim to the lure of alcohol and climbed into bed with the woman he couldn't take his eyes off all weekend. Who could've seen that coming?"

"We were supposed to be hanging out as friends." I shake my head. "That was the plan."

Mason's mock-serious expression is replaced with a sympathetic one. "There are some people we can't be just friends with, no matter how much we want to be."

I drag a hand over my face. "Fucking tell me about it."

"It's easy to forget, and then the next thing you know, you're three sheets to the wind and taking off her clothes."

"Are we talking about me and Em, or you and Bailey?"

He shrugs. "Tomato, to-mah-to."

"Wanna talk about it?"

"What are you, a twelve-year-old girl?"

"Fuck you," I mutter. "I was trying to help."

Frowning, he shrugs and looks away. "You and your girl aren't the only ones who got drunk and made some impulsive decisions last night." He swallows. "I let her get close this weekend. I know better than that. It fucks with me every time." He pauses a beat before turning back to meet my gaze. I can see the question that he's not willing to ask in his eyes.

"Bail doesn't tell me anything." Bailey and I have gotten close, but not close enough that she'll explain what her hang-up about Mason is. I mean, I assume it's not a race thing. The idea that she won't have an actual relationship with him because he's a black man seems pretty out of character for someone like Bailey, but I can't come up with a reason why she is the way she is about him anymore than anyone else can. She obviously wants to be with him—or, at least, it seems obvious to me.

"It wouldn't matter if she did tell you," he says. "If she won't tell me, the rest is shit." He groans. "It's too bad I'm too hungover to have a drink, because I could really use one right now. I'm having some serious morning-after regrets."

Tell me about it. "Me too."

"Do you want to talk about Emily?" he asks.

I wince at his use of her fake name. Once, I spent my days dressed in lies. Once, there was nothing more comforting than pretending to be someone I wasn't. I thought I left that behind me. Maybe lying about Emma's identity isn't a big deal in the scheme of things, but it weighs on me. These are my friends. They're my family. I shake my head. "Nothing to talk about."

"We're both full of shit," Mason mutters.

I can only shrug because I have no interest in denying it. I pull up FaceTime on my phone and dial Olivia. She answers on my second try, hair mussed, eyes half closed. She drags a hand over her face and yawns. "Yeah?"

"Good morning," I say with false cheer. I look at my watch. It's noon in Vegas, which means it's three p.m. in Seaside. Why the fuck is she sleeping? "I just wanted to say hello to Jazzy."

"She's not here." She rubs her eyes.

I bite back a snarl. "Where is she?"

"The nanny took her last night. She's at your house."

Mason is watching me curiously, so I try to harness my frustration and school my expression. "Why?"

"I had plans. You're not the only one who gets to have a life, you know?"

Deciding not to reply to that, I take a deep breath. "Listen, I know my dad was there this weekend."

Her face lights up. "He was. Keegan, he's so kind. I think you're wrong about him."

I have to hand it to the old man. He hasn't lost his touch. "He seems to think you extended him an open invitation. Why would you do that? We've talked about this."

She sighs, finger-combs her dark hair to the nape of her neck, and wraps it in a hair tie. "Keegan, you should forgive him. Whatever happened between you two, he obviously loves you and wants to be part of your life. You should see the way he treats Jazzy. What would it hurt to have another grandparent who loves her?"

"You don't know shit about my relationship with my father, and I'm telling you now, like I told you before, that he's not to be a part of her life. Period." I really have Mason's attention now, and I shake my head at him. This is not a topic that's up for discussion.

Olivia looks away from her phone. "I'm afraid that's a mistake you might regret later. Do you really want your daughter resenting you for keeping her away from her grandfather?"

I close my eyes. "There are choices we have to make as parents, Olivia, and this is one I'm making."

"Her only other grandfather is in prison." I can hear the panic in her voice. It's been a year and a half since her father's sentencing, and Olivia's still not over it. Maybe that's not something you're supposed to get over, but Olivia's taken the whole damn thing so hard that it's fucked with her head and her ability to live a normal life. Even if things between us didn't work out like I'd hoped, getting her to move to Seaside with me was the best thing I've ever done for her. "I suppose you're going to want my father to stay away from her too, huh? I mean, he's an ex-con and he made some fucking big mistakes, so maybe he can't be in our daughter's life either."

Mason turns his eyes to his phone but is clearly listening. I sigh. "I never said that."

"People make mistakes. Your father told me that you two had a rough time, and he wants to make amends."

"I need you to trust me on this," I tell her softly. I rub the back of my neck, trying to smooth away the tension that's built there since I picked up that damn phone in Emma's room. "Let's talk about it when I get back."

"Talk, talk? As in, you'll actually let me into that vault where you keep the details of your life?"

I sigh. "Yes. We'll *talk, talk*," I say softly.

She smiles. "It's a deal, then," she says, her tone gentler now. "I hope you had fun this weekend. You work too hard, Keeg."

I soften a little. My daughter's mother may be far from perfect, and she might be carrying around a metric ton of issues, but she's still the person I fell for two years ago. Most of the time, she means well. "It's been a good time. It's nice to see everyone again."

Her face turns sad. "I got an invitation to the wedding."

"Of course you did. You're going to come, right?"

"I haven't decided yet. Probably. Maybe. I'm not sure."

"Think about it. I'm sure they'd all love to see you."

She huffs under her breath but doesn't argue. "I'll see you tonight?"

"Yeah. Our flight leaves in forty-five minutes. I'll be in Seaside until Friday then I'm driving back to Blackhawk Valley until after the wedding. I hope you'll come with us."

"We'll see," she says, and that's been her response about this trip since I started making plans. Living in two places is hard enough for a family when they're a single unit, but living in two places when Olivia and I aren't even a couple is complicated.

"Need anything?"

She smirks. "Twelve hours of sleep and a good screw?"

I laugh. "That's how we got into this situation to begin with," I remind her.

"I suppose Dre wouldn't care for that anyway, but that doesn't keep me from remembering those days fondly."

My life is fucking weird. "I'll see you tonight, Liv."

EMMA

It's ninety degrees in Savannah today, and the humidity is so thick it's like walking through melted butter, but in the town car driving us from the airport to Zach's, the air is cool as the blood pumping through my veins. I'm cold and empty. I feel like I spent the last twenty-four hours living life as Emily Zimmerman, a carefree, adventurous young woman, only to be jolted back into the life and body of the woman I've been for the last five years. Emily is gone, and now I'm Emma Rothschild again. Cold, sexless, and so fucking lonely that she's happy to marry a man for all the wrong reasons.

I'm angry at my life for being so unfair and at Keegan for bringing up Harry when I was trying to open up to him. I'm mad at myself for jeopardizing my future with Zachary. What if someone had seen Keegan and me in that elevator? What if someone had recognized me when we were all over each other on the dance floor?

"Who was he?" Zachary asks.

He was quiet on the flight, digesting the little I'd confessed, and I can't decide if he's hurt that I was so careless or worried that I might change my mind about our marriage. When he found out his sister had to go home early to be with her daughter, he flew to Vegas to surprise me. When I didn't answer my cell, he had the front desk call my room, thinking his bride-to-be would be thrilled to have company in Vegas. And I was in bed with another man.

"No one," I say. "Just a guy. You told me to cut loose, so I did." The lie makes my chest ache. Keegan isn't just a guy. He's *the* guy. He is everything. But he was never supposed to find out about Zach like he did. That wasn't the plan. We were supposed to have our fun as friends and move on. If he ever met my fiancé, it should have been civil. Maybe Keegan would have been glad to see me with such a good man. Instead, alcohol made me forget who I was and what promises I've made, and I hurt Keegan again. That was the last thing I wanted to do.

"Did anyone see you together?"

Half of Vegas. "I was wearing Becky's stupid flapper wig, so it shouldn't be a problem. No one cares about me anymore anyway."

"They'll care when you're married to a senator," he says, but his tone is gentle, not cruel. "I told you to be a little reckless, but I never thought you would…" He drags in a ragged breath, and guilt saws through my chest. "You took him into your room. What if he knows who you are? What if he tries to blackmail you when he realizes what he has on you?"

"He won't blackmail me. He's not like that."

Zach's soft brown eyes go big. "Please tell me you used a fake name. Tell me he doesn't know who you are."

"Stop it. He's an old friend." My eyes fill with tears, and I look out the window to hide them. "Keegan won't go telling some dirty journalist about our wild night. He doesn't want the press any more than I do."

"Did you say *Keegan*?"

Nodding, I close my eyes and feel a hot tear slide down my icy cold cheek.

"Shit," Zach breathes. "Keegan? You spent the weekend with Keegan Keller?" His warm hand squeezes my knee, and I am reminded why I agreed to marry him. Zachary is my best friend, a kind man whose passion for politics is only exceeded by his passion for his country. He needed me and I needed him. We had the perfect arrangement, and I risked everything just to feel alive in Keegan's arms again.

At thirty-one, Zach is the youngest United States senator. Becky introduced us a few years ago—her brother and her best friend—and Zach and I clicked almost instantly. In fact, other than Keegan, he's the only man I'm comfortable spending time alone with.

"I didn't know he'd be there." The memories from last night come back like pieces of an incomplete puzzle. The sound of my laughter and the grin on his face. I remember teasing Keegan. *"I think maybe you like* Emily, *the sexy flapper girl, more than you ever liked Emma."*

His smile fell away as he shook his head and pulled the pins from my hair. The wig dropped to the floor. *"I only want to be with you,"* he said. *"Emma, I've only ever wanted to be with you."*

"Are you okay?" Zach asks. "You're flushed."

I put my hands to my hot cheeks. "It all felt like a dream."

"Can I at least have some dirty details?" When I cut my eyes to him, he's grinning like a loon. "What? Do you have any idea how much *I* would enjoy a wild weekend in Vegas? If you did something reckless enough to risk taking my political career down in flames, you can at least let me live vicariously."

"It was…" I exhale heavily, close my eyes, and remember the way Keegan's hands felt on me. "I never thought I'd see him again, and then I got this magical night." I shake my head. "It wasn't enough."

CHAPTER 16
KEEGAN

I've managed to spend the last five years avoiding any and all news about Emma Rothschild, but the second I come home from seeing her again, it's like I see her everywhere I look.

Olivia, Mason, Jazzy, and I are in my living room. We ordered dinner in, and while we eat, Olivia's watching one of those gossipy entertainment shows, and there she is—the curly-haired vixen who dropped to her knees three nights ago and greedily took my cock into her mouth.

The commentator on the screen calls Emma's "the wedding of the decade" and it's apparently going down this weekend in Savannah, Georgia.

"I wish I could get an invitation to that wedding," Olivia says. "Can you imagine? Black ties, beautiful dresses, champagne everywhere you look."

"I'm sure Dre will give you a wedding that nice if you want

him to."

Both Olivia and Mason drop their forks and gape at me, probably because I don't typically want to talk about Olivia's relationship with Dre, let alone sit around imagining my quarterback marrying the mother of my child. That proves how much things changed last weekend. Right now, I'd rather talk about their hypothetical wedding than Emma's very real one.

"Who is that, anyway?" I ask, letting my curiosity get the better of me and pointing to the screen.

"Um, Emma Rothschild," Olivia says. "Come on, didn't you watch *Lucy Matters* growing up? She was that chubby-cheeked kid with the red curls? Freaking adorable. It's just too bad for her she didn't outgrow the pudge. It's a wonder she landed a guy like him."

Mason arches a brow and waves to the TV. "Seriously? You think he's complaining about having *her* in his bed?" He shakes his head. "I'll never understand what women think is beautiful."

"I don't mean *her*," I say, ignoring Olivia's jab at Emma's appearance. "I mean, who's the guy?" He's older, but then again, maybe Emma always did go for the older guys. That gem of a memory is like a knife to the gut.

"That is Senator Zachary Dellaconte, the only man who's the subject of more female political fantasies than Justin Trudeau. Most eligible bachelor marries America's sweetheart. Does it get any cuter than that?" She gives a dreamy sigh. "I wonder what her dress looks like. And the reception is supposed to be out of this world with celebrity A-listers. Some girls get to have it all."

"Liv," I say, my voice harsh. "Don't make yourself crazy assuming other people's lives are better than yours. I promise you, Em has her own issues."

Mason's jaw drops as he looks at the image of Emma on the TV and then back at me. "Holy shit." He covers his mouth and coughs his surprise.

I drag a hand over my face. *Fuck.* Cover. Blown.

"*Em?*" Olivia's eyes go wide. "On nickname terms with the young actress, are you?"

I lock eyes with Mason, wordlessly pleading with him to stay quiet. "I knew her once. When I was younger."

"You had a relationship with a bigshot Hollywood actress and never *mentioned* it?"

"If I did, it seems like it would be a little douchey of me to go around talking about it."

She gives me a hard look and her jaw tightens. "Just like everything else."

"What's that supposed to mean?"

"You have a famous playwright as an uncle and you never mentioned it until he came to town."

"He's my mom's brother. We're not close. Why does that upset you so much?"

"You don't let anybody in, Keegan. It's like you don't have a past or you don't want anyone knowing about it. We're raising Jazzy together, and I'm just now learning you had a relationship with this Hollywood starlet."

"First, I don't know why it would matter. Second, I didn't

say we had a *relationship*." On the TV, they roll a clip of Emma laughing with her fiancé. He takes her hand and presses a kiss to her knuckles, and she stares back at him with such adoration, I have to fist my hands to keep myself from throwing something at the screen.

Mason gathers his drink and plate and stands. "I think I'll excuse myself to the balcony for a minute."

Standing, Olivia props a hand on her hip and points the other at the TV. "Do you even see the way you're looking at that screen right now? You had something with her. God knows you never looked at me like that."

"How do you want me to look at you?" I ask helplessly. "I tried to make it work and you didn't want me, so I backed away. What do you want from me?"

She shakes her head and scoops Jazzy off the floor. "I'm going to go give Jazz her bath."

The woman on the TV asks Emma, "What do you love most about him?" and I reach for the remote and smash the power button, but the TV doesn't go silent until after she says, "His compassion and big heart."

I grab my beer off the coffee table and join Mason on the balcony.

"You okay?" he asks.

"This night just went from relaxing to shit-tastic in record time." I glare over my shoulder toward the empty living room. "I don't understand why she's so pissed at me."

Mason's eyes shift from side to side, avoiding mine before

he turns up his palms. "She's right, you know. You never tell us anything about your past. You're an open book about the last five years, but it's as if there was no Keegan before we met you a BHU."

That's truer than you realize. I prop my arms on the railing and lean forward as I look out at the rolling waves beyond. "I'm not proud of my past. I don't talk about it because I don't want it to infect my life."

"But, just to be clear here, your past included Emma Rothschild, a.k.a. Emily Zimmerman?"

I rub the back of my neck. "We met the summer before I started college. It didn't end well."

"Bailey kept asking if I thought she looked familiar. I didn't understand why she was so hung up on it, but now I'm guessing she knew, or at least suspected. Last weekend…you didn't know Em was engaged, did you?"

I shake my head. "I've intentionally avoided any news about her, and she failed to mention it when we were catching up." Who the fuck only brings one friend to her bachelorette party? What kind of party is that? It's not like Emma's family couldn't afford to fly her whole graduating class down to party with her if that's what she wanted. And what kind of friend tries to get her soon-to-be-married travel companion to hook up with an old flame? None of it makes any sense.

"She didn't think to tell you even when she was taking you to up to her room?" Mason says. When I turn to him, he's shaking his head. "That's fucked up."

"It's no more than I deserve," I mutter, and if Mason wants to know what I mean by that, he doesn't ask.

He claps a hand on my back. "Forgive yourself for the shit that happened when you were a kid. Those of us who know you now know the real you. The person you are now is all that matters."

I swallow hard. "I hope you're right." I listen to the scrape of the sliding door as he goes back inside.

I remain on the balcony, staring out at the sun setting over the gulf until after Mason says goodbye and Olivia comes out to tell me that she put Jazzy in bed and is leaving for the night.

When they're both gone, I go to my bedroom and pull open the top drawer of my dresser. I shift aside stacks of underwear and piles of folded socks to uncover the single sheet of folded notebook paper tucked away there. The paper is worn and tattered from years ago when I unfolded it and reread it countless times.

> *Keegan,*
>
> *I'm so sorry. I just can't do this anymore. We come from different worlds, and I belong here, not in Indiana. I wanted to believe I could leave with you, but I can't, and I can't let you stay to be with me. It guts me to think this news will hurt you, because you deserve better than some fickle girl who's been careless with your heart.*
>
> *Please know this: As much as I want you for myself, I want more for you to be happy. Do that for me.*
>
> *All my love,*
>
> *Emma*

Old hurt flares in my chest every time I read the letter, a sharp, lingering pain that makes it hard to breathe. I refold the letter and slide it into my pocket before digging deeper in the drawer for the velvet box I keep back there. I feel along the back of the dark drawer and find nothing.

"What the fuck?" I yank the drawer out of my dresser and dump the contents on the bed. I sift through them, my heart racing faster and faster with every passing second. Did I put it somewhere else? Did my father get to it somehow? But he didn't know I had it. How would he have even known to look? I tear apart my room looking for it, but I can't find it anywhere.

Emma's sapphire necklace is gone.

CHAPTER 17
EMMA

"There's the happy couple," my mom says as she opens the door for me and Zach.

Zachary wraps his arm around my waist and squeezes. A warning or true affection? Tonight, it might be a little of both.

I force a smile for Mom's benefit then follow her into the house.

"How was Vegas?" Mom asks. She stops suddenly and spins on us. "You didn't elope while you were there, did you?"

My stomach rolls. No, we didn't elope. And judging by the way Zach has been looking at me since I told him I spent a night with Keegan, he might be having second thoughts about our whole arrangement.

"It was tempting," Zach says. "I want to be married to your daughter yesterday, but you know that already."

Mom beams. "Not long now." Turning away, she leads us to the formal dining room. The table is set for three, and a maid stands at the ready by the bar.

"Will Mr. Evans be joining us tonight?" Zach asks. The arm he's had slung around my shoulders squeezes me tighter as he asks the question, as if he knows I'll need him to help me stand at the mention of my stepfather.

"Please, call him Harry." Mom shakes her head. "He won't be in town until the wedding, but I promise he wouldn't miss it." She purses her lips and gives me a hard look when she adds, "He only wants the best for Emma."

My stomach cramps as I meet Mom's gaze. Since what happened with Harry five years ago, my relationship with my mother has never been the same. I still think she blames me for most of it. For a while, I blamed myself too. Even with Mom's disapproval pointed in my direction, I relax a little with the reassurance that he won't be here, that I won't have to look him in the eye or feel Mom watching me like she's convinced I might try to seduce him if she turns her back.

Mom claps her hands together and pastes on that fake smile that's served her so well on screen. Nobody can see through her but me. "Dinner will be served in about thirty minutes." She grins, always comfortable as the hostess. "Who'd like a drink?"

My stomach roils at the mention of alcohol, and I shake my head. "I'll just have some sparkling water."

She turns to the bar and shoos the maid away, preparing my drink herself. She sent me pictures of this place online. It's this grand Savannah mansion that she's rented out for the week before and after my wedding. She said there's too much for the mother of the bride to do for her to not be in town, and if she's going to have out-of-town guests, she needs a place to welcome them. So here we are, in Mom's fake Southern home with her fake Southern hospitality, preparing for my very real wedding and very fake marriage.

"Excuse me for a minute," Mom says. "I need to pop in the kitchen and see how the cook's coming along."

Zachary watches her go before turning to me. "She makes me want to take up alcoholism," he mutters. "I'm not sure how you're going to get through tonight without a little liquid courage."

I laugh. "I think I had enough alcohol in Vegas to last me a lifetime."

He lifts his chin and studies me. "Has he contacted you?"

I shake my head. "I don't think he wants to talk to me ever again."

"And here I stand wondering how differently this week might end if he knew the truth about you and me." He rubs the back of his neck. "Are you sure you want to do this? Because Emma…"

I put my hand on his arm and squeeze. "I made you a promise. You can trust me."

Zach presses a kiss to the top of my head just as the doors swing open, and my mother rushes in behind a servant with a tray full of food.

"Oh!" my mom squeaks. "We didn't mean to interrupt a romantic moment."

"You didn't interrupt anything," I assure her with a smile.

"We can't leave them alone too long," Mom says to the woman holding the tray. "I'm sure they're getting anxious for Saturday night."

I grimace. Does she plan to pretend I'm a virgin even though she knows damn well I'm not? I ignore her. "Come on, let's eat," I say, offering my hand to Zachary. He takes it, and the warmth of his touch is the reassurance I need. I just have to get Keegan out of my head. This will be enough again. It has to be.

KEEGAN

Five Years Ago...

She lifts her arms over her head and sways her hips as she tilts her face to the sky. The setting sun paints the horizon in yellows, pinks, and oranges that look like something off a painting in one of the Laguna art galleries. Is this really my life?

I step forward and take the glass from her hand before setting it on the table and pulling her back into the house. I don't want her intoxicated tonight.

She smiles at me. "I swear I'm not drunk."

"I know," I say. "I want to keep it that way." My gaze drops to her mouth—her pink lips, her wide smile—and my blood pumps harder and hotter because I want her.

She locks her eyes with mine and slides her hands up the

back of my neck and into my hair. She lifts onto her toes and presses her mouth to mine. The first few times she kissed me, her movements were soft and hesitant, almost as if she was waiting for instructions, but she's grown bolder over the last two weeks and now she kisses me like she knows I want her. She kisses me like she knows the taste of her on my lips will make me hungry for more, like she relishes that power.

"What do you have against a little wine?" she asks.

I shake my head. "Nothing." Reaching behind her, I find the clasp to the zipper at the top of her dress. Slowly, I slide it down her back until her dress opens and hangs loose on her shoulders. Her breath catches and she steps back, holding the unzipped dress to her chest and looking at me like she's asking a question.

All I can do is meet her eyes and nod. It's a silent message. *I want this. I want you.*

She drops her arms to her sides and lets the dress fall to the floor.

I hold my breath. She's so beautiful I'm afraid she might disappear, that this moment might fade away like a passing dream. Her breasts are cradled in a pink lace bra and matching panties that are just a shade darker than her pale skin. I have to consciously think about dragging my breath in and letting it out.

"It does something to me when you look at me like that," she says.

"Something good, I hope."

She lifts a shaking hand.

"You do something to me too." I step forward and trail kisses down her neck and across her collarbone. I skim my lips over the swell of each breast, and through everything, she watches me with hooded eyes.

Soon, I'll say goodbye. I'll end this before it can go down the path I started. But tonight we're just two people who want each other. I'll let her go soon because she deserves better than me, and because I don't know how to be good enough for her. Tonight, I'll take this moment, unwrap it like a gift and savor every second.

"I'm so nervous," she whispers.

"That makes two of us," I say against her soft skin.

"Why would *you* be nervous?"

"Because I'm not good enough for you." It sounds like one of those ridiculous things guys say when they don't know how else to make a girl feel special, but for me it's just the simple truth. And yet I'm grateful I don't have the words to explain, because if she knew who I really was, she'd run, and right now I need her. In my arms. Under my hands. The taste of her skin on my tongue. "I should walk away, but I want you too much." I swallow hard as I meet her eyes. "I want to be worthy of this."

She trails her fingertips along my jaw and whispers, "Ditto," and my chest feels so tight that the only thing I can do is kiss her long and hard and with all the desperation I feel.

I trail my knuckles over her belly and down between her legs, and she gasps. I love the sounds she makes and the way she arches into my touch like she craves it. I can feel her wet heat through the lace of her panties, and I want to kiss her there. I want to stroke her and make her come apart like she never has before.

I turn my hand, cupping her between her legs as we lock eyes. Sweeping her hair to the side, I press my mouth against her neck, kissing my way up it and to her ear. "Let me make love to you tonight." I slide a finger under the lace of her panties and inside her, and she gasps, and I don't know if it's from my words or from this touch.

"Keegan," she whispers, her hands tightening in my hair, her body squeezing around my single finger inside her. She tilts her head to the side, and I suck at her neck until she moans and writhes against my hand, my palm rubbing her clit.

I planned to take this slow, but now all I want is to get her off and feel her come around my cock. Her hands are frantic as she unbuttons my shirt and peels it from my arms, and mine are greedy as I unclasp her bra and yank her panties from her hips.

Soon we're both naked in the center of her living room, and I need her so much that my hands are shaking.

"Come on," she says, grabbing my hand and tugging me toward the bedroom. I follow, helplessly and desperately, and she lays herself out on the bed, one arm behind her head, one leg bent at the knee. She cocks her finger for me to follow, and I don't think I've ever seen anything so beautiful as Emma Rothschild naked and inviting me into her bed.

CHAPTER 18
EMMA

We're getting married in Zachary's home church. He grew up coming here, and the congregation did all they could to support him in his run for the Senate. The space is beautiful, and when he suggested months ago that we do it here, I instantly agreed. I didn't want to get married in Los Angeles because it doesn't feel like home to me. But this space, with its arching stained glass windows and warm wood pews, seemed like it would be the perfect place to marry my best friend.

It's not decorated yet, but tomorrow there will be bushels of blue hydrangeas attached to the end of each pew and sweeping swaths of fine tulle draped along the center aisle. The pews will be filled with guests, most of whom I've only met once or twice and few of whom I'd call friends. We'll say our vows and be through step one in our master plan.

I walk down the aisle for the rehearsal and keep my gaze focused on Zach to avoid my mother's teary eyes. I'm not sure what makes her happier—my impending marriage to a good man, or the public spectacle of it all.

If I'd stayed with Keegan after our summer together, if I hadn't let the whole ordeal with Harry tear us apart, would I be marrying Keegan tomorrow? It's the question my mind circles back to as I do my practice march down the aisle. If we'd been madly in love for five years and he put a ring on my finger and told me he wanted me to be his wife, I'd be looking forward to a future of passion, of babies I could grow in my belly.

I reach the front of the aisle, and tears well in my eyes as I take a deep breath. Companionship and adoption are more than enough. My relationship with Zachary is stronger than a lot of the husbands and wives I know. Sex is overrated.

I believed those things a week ago.

The preacher goes through the motions, letting us know what to expect and what we'll do at each turn in the ceremony. When he says, "And then I'll ask you to kiss the bride," my mom calls out, "You'd better practice, Zachary!"

Zachary flashes her that charming grin before cocking an eyebrow at me. I smile my permission and tilt my face toward his. He carefully cups my face in his hands and lowers his lips to mine. He knows better than to give a chaste peck in front of this audience. He opens his lips softly over mine, brushing against first my top then bottom lip before pulling away.

It's the kind of kiss that plays great on TV because it's tender, sweet, and sexy all at once. I told him once that my very favorite thing was to have a guy hold my face like this. He called it cupping, and I told him I didn't care what it was called, only knew that it made me melt and made my insides go gooey as lips brushed against mine. He knew then that I didn't really mean *any* guy. I meant Keegan. Just as he knows now that when he holds me like this, when it's his mouth on mine, I feel nothing. There's no melting or fluttering stir low in my belly, no ache for more. I feel nothing but the tender affection for a friend I worry I may have let down.

My mom cheers and so does his, but when he breaks the kiss, I see a face over his shoulder that isn't cheering at all, not even faking a smile. When my eyes lock with the best man's, Charlie gives me a sad little nod, and my heart tugs.

I'm not the only one making compromises for this marriage. We all are.

"That should do just fine," the preacher says, and everyone laughs. We turn to follow the preacher's directions and walk down the aisle. Zachary slides his fingers through mine and squeezes. Once we hit the church vestibule, he doesn't stop. He tilts his head toward the back hallway, pulls me down it and through the doors to the back of the church.

The sun is blinding and the birds are singing. It's a beautiful weekend for a wedding.

"You don't have to," he says softly. He shakes his head. "I told you from the beginning that I didn't want you doing this just for me."

"And I told you I wasn't. I have my own reasons."

"But don't you feel differently now? After Vegas?"

"Nothing's changed."

He pulls me against his chest and holds me there in a tight hug. "You might be able to lie to your mom, but I know you, baby girl. Everything changed for you last weekend."

My throat feels thick, and I swallow hard. "It was an illusion." I pull away and lift my chin. "And, to be fair, a mistake."

Concern is all over his face, etched into the wrinkles in the corners of his eyes and tugging at the edges of his usually easy smile. "I worry about you."

"I'm marrying the country's most eligible bachelor. He's handsome and kind. He makes me laugh and is going to let me spend my life fighting for causes that matter most to me. Never mind our plans to get lots of fat, happy babies. What's there to worry about?"

"What if all that isn't enough?"

I truly believed it was until I saw Keegan. I haven't wanted more in a really long time. It's like I'd forgotten my body could want to be touched, but Keegan woke part of me that's been dormant for five years. The only problem is that I don't want passion with just any man. I only want Keegan, and he believes the worst of me. I let him believe the worst, because I was too ashamed of my past to tell him the truth. "Zachary, the life we have planned is more than I've dared to hope for in years."

KEEGAN

I pull my SUV into a metered parking spot in downtown Savannah and grip the steering wheel as I try to figure out what exactly I'm doing here.

A little before lunch, I dropped Olivia and Jazzy off at the airport and set off to drive myself home. They'll fly home because Olivia can't tolerate the long drive. I could have gotten myself a ticket too, but it saves me money to drive myself, and it's just easier to not have to mess with a rental car once I get there.

I hadn't even made it out of Florida before I realized I'd detoured toward Savannah, and now I'm parked in front of the church where Emma is supposed to marry her senator tomorrow.

It's a hot and sunny day, and the picture-perfect blue sky seems to taunt me as I climb out of my car and follow the sidewalk to the church. There are a couple of security guards out front, and I flash my best *I'm just a regular guy* smile. "Am I late?"

"Who are you, sir?"

"Keegan Keller, a friend of the bride." I pull out an envelope. "She asked me to bring this?"

"Keegan Keller?" The other security guard nudges the first. "He's that defensive end who plays for the Gators. Loved watching you take Brady down last season."

"Thanks. I enjoyed it too."

"The way you do that spin move and break away from everyone, you know who you remind me of?" He snaps his fingers and tilts his face toward the sky as if looking for the answer. He claps his hands and points at me. "Dwight Freeney, that's his name. You move like him, man."

"That means a lot," I say, trying to hold on to my patience. "He's an inspiration of mine."

I hold my breath as the first man flips through pages on his clipboard. "Your name's not on the list."

I make a show of pulling my phone from my pocket. "No problem, I'll just give Emma a call and—"

"That's not necessary," my fan says. "The Gators owner is a guest tomorrow night. Real good friend of the Dellacontes. I'm sure he wouldn't want us turning away one of his rising stars. Go on in. We'll get your name on the list for tomorrow."

Tomorrow. For her wedding. Fuck, that still burns. "Thanks. Sorry about the trouble."

"No trouble at all," he says. "It's a real pleasure to meet you, man."

I shake his hand and take a deep breath when they open the doors for me. When I step into the church, I'm nauseated. The chapel's empty except for a few people running around with tape measures and clipboards. I saw on Olivia's celebrity gossip show that this was where they were getting married, and I assumed they'd be doing their rehearsal here tonight. Have I missed her?

"Keegan?"

I spin around and find Emma's mom staring at me with wide,

surprised eyes.

She remembers me. How shocking. Back when Em and I were together, Miranda didn't make me feel like I was worth remembering. Since she wasn't too far off base, I never held it against her.

"What a surprise," she says, then her face grows serious. "What brings you here?"

"I needed to talk to Emma." My voice cracks like I'm a little boy, and I feel so lost and unsure that I might as well be.

She lifts her chin and studies me. Her blue eyes are the same color as her daughter's but so different. Emma's eyes are expressive and warm. They hold hope and wonder for the world around her. But Miranda Rothschild's eyes are hard and cold. "She's in the back with her *fiancé*," she says, emphasizing the word in a way that makes me think she might give me a definition if I gave her the opportunity.

"Thanks." I draw in a deep breath as I head to the back of the church. I stop at the back doors and lift my hand to the window. Emma's on the flagstone patio in the arms of Senator Zachary Dellaconte. He's as tall as I am but lean like a distance runner and dressed in an expensive suit, even though it's gotta be at least ninety degrees out there.

Neither of them looks in my direction, and she's curled into him with her cheek against his chest as he runs his fingers through her hair. When he steps back and cups her face, she looks up at him with something I could only describe as adoration.

He leans down and presses his lips gently to her forehead,

I want to hate him, but even from this distance I can see the tenderness in the way he touches her and sense the warmth in the way he looks into her eyes.

What happened in Vegas was a mistake. I don't know why her friend lied to me about whose bachelorette party it was or why Emma let the lie stand. But I do know that what happened in the elevator and in the hotel room wouldn't have happened if we hadn't been drinking. If I hadn't pushed her to cross the line she kept reminding me of, if I hadn't encouraged her to be whomever she wanted to be for one night, maybe we wouldn't have ended up where we did.

I didn't come here to ruin her wedding, but suddenly it's clear that my appearance alone could do just that. And then what? Do I ruin her future because she had secrets when I had secrets ten times worse? I turn around, headed back to the front of the church and my car. I stop when I spot Emma's mother in the church vestibule.

"They were busy," I say. "Do you happen to have a pen?"

Frowning, she pulls a black ballpoint from her purse.

I take Emma's old note out of its envelope and scribble on it without letting myself think too much about what I'm doing. Then I tuck it back in the envelope and seal it before handing it to Miranda with her pen. "Could you see that she gets that?" I force a smile. "She wanted my notes on her vows. I promised I'd give her some feedback."

She draws in a relieved breath. "Oh, how kind. Thank you.

Will you be at the ceremony tomorrow?"

I swallow hard. "Unfortunately, I can't make it. Tell the happy couple I said congratulations."

CHAPTER 19
KEEGAN

As much as I love my condo on the beach, I'm not sure there's a single place in the world that can compete with the rolling green hills of Blackhawk Valley in the spring. The drive from my house into town past pastures and farmland makes some of the ache from last weekend ease from my chest.

Jazzy babbles from the back seat, where she's looking out the window and pointing at the horses. She's happy to be back here too. When I pulled into town last night, Olivia and Jazzy were already settled in at Olivia's mom's, but I picked Jazzy up this morning to spend the day with her. Blackhawk Valley was the first place that ever felt like home to me. It's the first place I ever lived for more than a year, and the people who became my friends during my four years in school are the closest I've ever had to real family.

Maybe that's why I'm reluctant to give up the bar. Even if Bailey doesn't want to buy it, I can certainly sell it to someone else. But I have ties here that'll remain even when all my friends have moved on to homes across the country. I think I'll have a fondness for this place forever, and luckily for me, I'll always have an excuse to come back. This is where Jazzy's grandmother lives, after all. This was my life after falling in love with Emma. This was the gift she gave me by believing in me. I know I never would have had the courage to take the opportunity and make something of it if it hadn't been for her. As much as I want to be angry with her for how things ended five years ago, and as much as my chest burns every time I think about her marrying someone else this weekend, I know I owe her everything. I am who I am because she believed in me. If it hadn't been for Emma, I'd be running around with my dad and hopping town to town, never settling down, never trusting anyone, always looking for easy cash and the thrill of the con.

I park my SUV in the back lot of The End Zone and get Jazzy from the car seat to carry her inside. We walk through the back storage area and the kitchen and into the bar, where Bailey is pulling down chairs to get ready to open.

"Hey, bossman," she says. "How was the drive up yesterday?"

"It was good." I put Jazzy down, and she toddles over to the basket of toys I keep tucked in the corner. "I'm glad to be back."

"How long will you be here this time?"

"Until after Arrow and Mia's wedding, then I have to go."

"Did Mason say when he was coming?"

I arch a brow and give her a hard look. "Why don't you ask him, Bail? I'm sure he'd be happy to tell you. Hell, if you wanted him to come early so you could spend some time together, he'd probably be happy to do that too."

She looks away from me and pulls down a few more chairs. "Don't go poking at me just because you're in a shitty mood. I know this is a crappy weekend for you, but consider it a life lesson and move on."

"I don't know what you mean." I've been brooding since Vegas and even more since I drove away from Emma and Savannah last night. I know it. Bailey knows it. Anyone who knows anything about me can tell I'm off.

"You don't want to talk about anything?"

"Nothing to talk about."

"You don't need to get what happened with *Emily* off your chest?"

I frown at the way she said *Emily*, as if she knows it's a bullshit name. Mason warned me that he thought Bailey already knew who Emma was. "Not a thing."

She grumbles something under her breath. "You know, friends tell each other things."

"What do you want from me, Bailey? I saw an old friend in Vegas, we spent some time together, and now I'm home. I've got Olivia's drama to deal with. I don't need any other drama to pile on."

She reaches under the bar and pulls out a magazine that

she plops on the counter in front of me. "Not even America's sweetheart drama?"

When I look down, my gut tightens and my breath catches in my throat. On the cover of the magazine, Emma and her fiancé mock me. She has her arms wrapped around his neck and she's looking up into his eyes as he gazes down into hers. They are so perfect they might as well be one of those happy couples in wedding advertisements.

I wonder if he knows she slept with me in Vegas. I wonder if he even cares.

I look up at Bailey. "What does this have to do with anything?"

"Come *on*," she says. Reaching across the bar, she flips the magazine open to an article about the happy couple. I scan the pages before I can stop myself, seeing bold headings introducing sections about how they met, their plans for the future, and their wedding.

"I recognized her," Bailey says, and I realize I'm still studying the article. "God, those cheekbones? That face? Those eyes? That wig wasn't fooling anyone." She shakes her head. "I cannot believe no one else saw it." She points to the glossy pages in front of me as she unlocks the front door and flips on the *Open* sign. "That's who you were with last weekend, and I don't know what happened when we weren't around, but I saw the way you looked at her, and it was really fucking clear what you *wanted* to happen."

"You can't tell anyone," I tell her softly. Because even now, all these years later, despite all the secrets between us and mistakes made on both sides, Emma's future is more important to me than petty shit like my feelings.

"What happened between you two in Vegas?" Bailey asks. "Hell, what happened between you *before* Vegas? How long have you known her?"

"I'm not talking about this, Bailey."

"I don't like this. I don't like *her*. You deserve better than some bitch who's going to use you for a weekend of fun before she marries some pretty-boy politician. Don't get me wrong—if I thought she was just a screw to you, I wouldn't say a word, but the way you looked at her broke my heart, Keegan. At least do yourself a favor and let it out for a minute. Call her on being a cheating bitch. Then I promise I won't tell a soul."

"Are you sure this is really about me? Are you sure you aren't just projecting because of what happened between you and *Mason* in Vegas?"

She goes pale. "He *told* you?"

I frown. "No details, just that you two got drunk and made some bad decisions."

"You can say that again," she mutters.

I give Bailey a hard look. "I've made a lot of those myself. Especially when it comes to Emma."

She flips her long hair over her shoulder, folds her arms, and stares at me. "Name one."

I fell in love with her. I fold my arms to match her stance. "I'll tell you my secrets if you tell me yours."

The humor drains for her face and she looks away. "Pass."

KEEGAN

Five Years Ago...

"When are you gonna close this deal?"

I jump at the sound of my father's voice then instinctively turn to make sure the door to Emma's condo is closed behind me. I straighten and set my jaw as I turn my attention to him. "How'd you get in here?"

The corner of his mouth twitches up into a mischievous grin. "Made a copy of your key. Let myself in the front."

Jesus. I hold out a hand. "Hand it over."

He pouts and plops a key into my hand. "Fine. But you ruin all my fun."

I tuck the key into my pocket and head for the stairs. Someone in the elevator might see me with him and ask Emma about it. I can't risk that.

"When are you closing the deal?" he asks again when we're in the stairwell.

I heard him the first time. "I'm not," I say. "There's no deal to close. I don't want any money from her."

"*Jesus,*" he says. "I thought I taught you better than to fall in love with a mark."

Stopping, I grip the handrail and try to calm my temper. "Don't call her that."

He shakes his head. "She's got you fooled. You think she's so great and so into you."

I release the handrail and continue down the stairs. "I'm not talking to you about this."

"Do you really believe a man like you can have a girl like that? You think you don't need to finish the job because what you two have is better. She's gonna let you live the high life with her, am I right? And fuck your old man. You don't need him anyway. That little cunt gave up the pussy and now she has you by the balls."

Spinning, I slam him against the wall and press my forearm against his neck.

His eyes go wide but then he smiles. "See what I mean?"

"Leave her alone. Take your pick of anyone else in this goddamn town, but leave Emma alone or I will make you fucking sorry you didn't." I force myself to step back, and I'm shaking, as if the anger and resentment I've felt toward him for the past ten years has coalesced into one violent ball of energy that's ready to tear out of me.

He chuckles softly. "You've got another think coming, son. Just wait until she's done playing around then you'll see I was right all along."

CHAPTER 20
EMMA

I'm getting married in two hours.

Becky zips up my dress and my mom gasps. "You look so beautiful, sweetheart."

Married. In. Two. Hours.

All day long, I've held it together. I made it through breakfast with my mom. When she had me walk through the ballroom to make sure everything was as it should be, I nodded and kept my smile in place even though I wasn't registering anything around me.

It wasn't until we started getting dressed that panic clawed at my chest.

I turn to the mirror and study myself in the strapless lace dress. My hair is pinned on top of my head in fat curls, and my makeup is flawless. But my eyes don't look like the exhilarated blue eyes of an excited bride. They look empty.

"It's missing something, isn't it?" Mom says. She moves to stand beside me, and I meet her eyes in the mirror.

"What?"

She hands me a jewelry box I didn't realize she was holding.

"What's this?" I open it, and for a moment, I think she's found my grandmother's sapphire necklace. It went missing five years ago, and I never found it. When I look closer, I realize it's a replacement. It's still beautiful, but the stone's setting and the white-gold filigree on either side are completely different than my beloved, lost heirloom. "Thank you, Mom. It's beautiful."

"It's actually more valuable than your grandmother's," she says. "I know you dreamed of wearing that old necklace on your wedding day, so I wanted to make sure you had something even better."

The idea that this necklace could be "better" because of its appraised value rather than its sentimental value says a lot about my mom, but I force a smile and let her fasten it around my neck.

"Beautiful," she says. "Oops! I can't believe I almost forgot." She fishes an envelope from her purse. "Your vows," she says as she hands it to me.

"My vows?"

"Your friend Keegan brought them to the church last night," she says. "I'd forgotten about him. I didn't realize you two were still in touch. It was nice of him to look over them for you, though I admit I'm a little jealous that you didn't ask me."

I turn to her but can't find the words to ask all the questions that are suddenly filling my chest and throat and threatening to flood out onto the cold tile floor at my feet.

Becky looks at me and then my mom. "Are you sure it was Keegan? Keegan Keller?" she asks, as if we know some other Keegan.

"Well, sure." Mom looks at me. "I remember that summer you used to run around with him. I'm sure he'd have given them to you himself, but he said you and Zachary were busy."

I open my mouth to reply, but I'm too afraid of what I might say. *Keegan was here? With my vows.* I snap my mouth shut again and turn to Becky.

She pats my back and turns to the other ladies in the room. "Could we have a minute? To finalize the *vows*?"

My mom gives her a stern, disapproving glare before she and the other bridesmaids leave the room.

"What's going on?" Becky asks when we're alone. "You've been acting funny all week, and today…" She bites her lip. I know this is Becky trying very hard not to say, *"I told you marrying my brother was a bad idea."*

I'm so grateful to have her here with me in this moment that the tears in my eyes spill over, not out of self-pity but out of gratitude. "He came. I can't believe he came."

"What aren't you telling me?"

I hold the blank, sealed envelope in two hands as if it weighs a hundred pounds instead of an ounce. "I slept with him," I whisper.

"I know, but—" Her jaw drops. "Wait. When are we talking about here? And how? And do you mean like *dreaming* sleeping together or the kind of sleeping together that doesn't involve much sleep?"

"In Vegas. We'd been drinking and…honestly, I don't even remember much. But there was definitely not much sleeping involved. It was stupid. I know it was stupid. I just—"

"It was not." She balls her hands into fists and spins in a little frustrated circle as she stamps her feet. The reaction might be funny if I weren't in the middle of a legit personal crisis.

Keegan came here. To the church. Where I'm getting married in two hours.

"It's not stupid. It's possibly the only thing you've done for yourself in five years."

"I shouldn't have let it happen, but first it was dinner, and then that sexy show, and then the dancing, and that seemed harmless, and then touching and then…more. I mean, he was bound to find out, right? I thought I'd have a chance to explain everything before I left him. Then your brother showed up because he was worried about me being in Vegas alone. The front desk called up to the room to tell me my fiancé was there, and Keegan answered." More tears roll from my eyes as I remember the look on Keegan's face. "He was so angry when he left. I can't believe he came here last night." I lift the envelope. "With this?"

"Okay. That's a lot of information." She draws in a deep breath and exhales slowly. "Will you please open it already?" When I just stare at her, she says, "Come on, we both know that's not your vows. Open. It."

With shaking hands, I tear the seal and pull the paper from

the envelope. It's worn thin and almost ripped along its folds.

"I'm dying here," Becky says. "What does it say?"

I unfold it as delicately as I can. After hours of staying calm and keeping it together, it's the sight of the letter I wrote to Keegan five years ago that brings more tears to my eyes and makes my heart ache so much I feel like it might burst.

"It's the letter I wrote him when we broke up." I wrote this letter on the way to the airport on my mother's wedding day. While we were stuck in traffic, I reread it so many times it feels like I wrote it yesterday and not five years ago. Keegan gave me back my letter, but not before writing on it himself.

I press my hand to my chest. I'm pretty sure my heart is breaking in there, but maybe this ache is the painful work of a broken heart mending itself.

Becky stands behind me, and she must be reading the note, because she mutters a curse. She squeezes my shoulder, and I turn to face her. "Emma, I need to know what I'm supposed to be doing here. I need to know if you need me to tell you everything is going to be okay. Do you want me to tell you this crazy marriage is the right decision, or am I allowed to tell you what I really think?"

"I already know what you really think." I sniffle and grab a tissue from the vanity. "You're smarter than me for seeing it so clearly."

She shakes her head. "I'm not smarter than you. Em, I just have perspective because I'm not the one locked into your life. I can see it. You're too close."

"I want to have babies," I tell her. Her face crumples and she wraps me in her arms. "I don't want to spend my life alone, and Zachary is my best friend. He needed me, and I needed him."

"Are you kidding me? Isn't this the twenty-first century? You can both have what you want without compromising your life like this."

"I'm not kidding, and you know it's true. If his constituency knew about him and Charlie... If he tried to run for president with a man on his arm instead of a woman..." I shake my head. "Don't be naïve. You know this country isn't ready for that yet."

She wipes a tear from my cheek. "So you're both supposed to spend the rest of your lives pretending you're someone you're not?"

"You make it sound so awful. Your brother is my best friend."

She gently wipes away my tears with the back of her hand. "It was different when this was what you wanted, but you've spent the entire week looking like a deer in the headlights of an oncoming big rig. Don't do it."

"You just want me to walk away and pretend I wasn't supposed to get married today? *Sorry, Mom. Your flaky daughter is at it again.*"

"Yes," she says. "Yes, I think that if there's any part of you that wants to walk away then you shouldn't just walk, you should *run.*" She picks her purse up off the floor. "He came last night. That means something."

My breath catches as I realize what I'm really about to do. I spin around the room, looking for my clothes before remembering that Mom already sent them to the hotel where Zach and I are supposed to spend our wedding night. "I don't have any clothes."

She fishes her keys from her purse, tucks them into my hand, and closes her palm around them. "Go as you are. Out the back. I'll buy you some time." She smiles. "You get a head start."

"What about you?" I squeeze her keys so hard they bite into my palm. "How will you get around?"

She grins. "I'll have to use my husband's precious Benz. It needs to get a little fresh air anyway. He keeps it cooped up like a princess in a castle."

I almost laugh, but my breath catches before the sound can fully form. "What about Zachary?"

"Like you said, he's your best friend." She turns up her palms. "I think he's going to be proud of you."

"When my mom finds out I'm gone, she's going to raise hell."

She grins. "I can handle it. Now get out of here and text me when you get there."

"Get where?" I say with a hysterical burst of laughter.

"You'll figure it out."

I rush out the door with nothing but my purse, Becky's keys, and my old letter to Keegan. He circled the last paragraph.

> *Please know this: As much as I want you for myself, I want more for you to be happy. Do that for me.*

Next to it, he wrote, *Ditto.*

CHAPTER 21
KEEGAN

Thunder booms outside and the lights flicker. Crappy weather is bad for business, but tonight's weather is such a perfect match for my mood that I don't even mind. She's getting married tonight. Hell, it's after midnight. By now, it's done and she's in some fancy suite with her perfect groom. By now, he's probably made her forget all about Vegas, all about me, all about the life we once planned to have together.

"A bride walks into a bar in a soaking-wet wedding dress," Bailey says over her beer.

I look up at her from where I'm wiping down the bar and arch a brow, waiting for the punch line. Ever since I bought this bar last year, Bailey has been all over the bad "walked into a bar" jokes. I haven't heard this one yet. I don't bother to fake a smile. She knows today is shit for me. "And?"

"No, seriously." She swivels on her stool and nods toward the door. "A bride just walked into your bar."

I turn and my stomach falls through the floor. Because Bailey wasn't joking, and there's nothing funny about this.

I've spent my entire day forcing myself to stop imagining Emma Rothschild in a wedding dress, Emma walking down the aisle, Emma in another man's arms. But more torturous than imagining her wedding were the fantasies of her not going through with it. I've been watching my phone as if she might use my number for the first time in five years. Every time it buzzed, I practically jumped out of my skin.

But there she is: in my bar, in her wedding dress, soaked to the bone from the storm raging outside.

Emma meets my eyes, and I'm yanked back to her suite in Vegas—to the feel of her skin under my hands, to the smell of her hair, and the sounds she made when she came, to the next morning's cruel gut punch of finding out she was engaged.

"Emma?" My voice cracks on her name, like a pubescent boy who's finally found the courage to speak the name of his crush. She makes me feel a little bit like that—always has. I see her and I'm filled with so much longing that it twists everything up inside me. It's a wonder I can ever speak clearly when she's close.

She glances over her shoulder at the door she just entered before turning back to me. "I didn't know where else to go."

I turn to Bailey. She nods at me, drains her beer, and comes behind the counter to mind my post without me saying what I need. "Get her out of here. I've got this."

"Thank you." I throw my rag down and retrieve my keys before motioning to Emma to follow me into the kitchen. In addition to a random reporter who may appear at any moment, there are a half-dozen sets of curious eyes pointed in her direction. They're probably all too drunk to recognize her, but staying out here is asking for trouble.

When we're tucked into the back corner of the kitchen, I turn to her and turn up my palms, waiting for an explanation.

She looks down at herself, as if just realizing she's wearing a fucking wedding gown. "I couldn't do it. I couldn't marry him."

Fuck. Those words rattle something deep inside me, and I swallow hard. At least I'm not hiding some rich, powerful man's new wife. *Only his runaway bride.* I drag a hand through my hair then squeeze at the tension in the back of my neck. "Did anyone see you?"

"Other than the handful of people who watched me walk into your bar?" She shakes her head. "I don't think so."

"We're going to leave your car here. I can come back for it later," I tell her. "If you wait here, I'll run out and get your things."

She looks up at me with those big blue eyes. "Things?"

"Luggage? Clothes? Stuff you brought from home?"

She shakes her head. "I don't have anything. I kind of left in a rush. This was unexpected."

"No shit," I mutter. "Fine. Let's get out of here, then." I lead her out to the back lot, welcoming the pounding rain on my hot skin and trying not to stare at the wedding dress, trying harder to tamp down the chaotic swarm of emotions in my chest—especially the sympathy and the longing, and the *just fucking tell me what you need and I'll give it to you.* Under all that, anger simmers, and I hold on to that as she climbs into the front seat of my SUV.

I live less than ten minutes from the bar, but there's so much tension twisting me in knots, the drive feels like it takes forty. I park in the drive, kill the engine, and squeeze my eyes shut. "Does he know where you are?"

"Who?"

I snap my head around and scrape my gaze over her wedding dress, ignoring the way she flinches under my scrutiny. "Your *fiancé?*"

She stares down at her hands. "I'm sure you have a lot of questions."

That's the understatement of the century. I'm drowning in questions. I exhale heavily. There are the questions that need to be answered: *Are you okay? Are you in trouble? How can I help?* Then there are the questions I'm not sure I want her to answer: *Why didn't you marry him? What did last weekend mean to you? Why did you come to me?*

"Let's get you inside and into some dry clothes." I swing my door open and head around to help her. Given other circumstances, this might be comical—the bride climbing from my Explorer in a waterlogged dress, her makeup smeared, her movements awkward. I offer her my hand, and she takes it. The feel of her shaking hand in mine makes something squeeze in my chest.

The house is empty. I wish it weren't. I wish Olivia's mom

was here with Jazzy or that Sebastian and Alex were hanging out with their new baby. Fuck, I'd even take a visit from Olivia and Dre right now. I don't trust myself with Emma and I'm suddenly questioning my judgment in bringing her here. Why was that my first instinct? She's not mine to protect. She's in her *wedding dress*, for God's sake.

But she came to you.

I lead her to my bedroom and pull a pair of cotton sleep pants and a T-shirt from the drawer. "The bathroom's in there. There are towels in the cabinet under the sink and some new toothbrushes in the cabinet." She's shaking when I hand over the clothes, her skin covered in goosebumps. "Take a shower, get warmed up, and put these on. You'll feel better when you're out of that dress."

As I listen to the old pipes squeak as the shower turns on, I pace my kitchen. When my phone rings, Bailey's name is on the display.

"Hey," I say, hoping I can keep my voice calm.

"For a man who claims he doesn't want any drama in his life, you sure know how to bring it."

I blow out a breath, but it does nothing to release the tension in my shoulders. "No kidding."

"You made good hustle, though. They're talking about it on the late night shows, but no mention of Blackhawk Valley." She makes a tsking sound, and in the background, I can hear the clanking of glasses and running water. I promised Bailey I'd close tonight, and now she's stuck doing it. "You can't run from such a high-profile wedding without creating buzz."

I drag a hand over my face and realize I'm shaking. I grab a beer from the fridge and open it. "I'm sorry I had to bail on you."

"Pfft. You had a damsel in distress to rescue. Don't even worry about it."

"I need to figure out what's going on with Emma and make sure she's okay."

"Has it crossed your mind that maybe she ran from her wedding and came to you because she wants to be with you instead of him?"

What if running away is just her MO? "Something tells me it's not that simple."

"Give me a call tomorrow and let me know if you need me here more than we planned this week. I'll help."

As Mia's maid of honor, she's busier this week than I am, but I know the offer is sincere. "You're the best, Bailey. Thank you."

"Someday, you'll pay me back. Don't worry."

We hang up, and I collapse into my recliner. I'm nursing my beer when Emma comes out of the bathroom. She has the pants rolled at the waist and they still sag around her hips under the big T-shirt. Her hair is down, hanging in wet curls past her shoulders, and her face is scrubbed clean of all her makeup.

"Thank you." She sits on the couch and pulls her legs under her.

"Do you want to tell me what happened today?"

"I panicked." She draws in a ragged breath. "I just couldn't go through with it."

"So, you're pretty much saying that nothing's changed." When she snaps her gaze to mine, there's so much hurt in her blue eyes that I want to take it back, but I can't. "You've spent your whole life without a single person calling you on your bullshit. But guess what? You came to me, and I'm not going to sit here and tell you what you want to hear. What you did last weekend was shitty. What you did to your fiancé tonight, also shitty."

"I know." She wraps her arms around her stomach as if she's trying to protect herself. *From me.* Fuck, that burns, but what do I expect when I'm acting like an asshole? "I'm not asking you to sugarcoat anything."

Leaning forward, I prop my elbows on my knees and cradle my head in my hands.

"I know you probably hate me right now." She's quiet for a few beats—maybe she's waiting for me to deny it. and I'm tempted to look up and see the expression on her face. The thing is, I know how I'll feel when I see the hurt in her eyes. Emma has never been able to hide her emotions from me, and by being a hard ass now, I know I'm breaking her heart. But fuck that. She's not the only one who's struggling with this. "I didn't expect you to take me in with open arms. I'm so sorry. I know what I did to you last weekend was unforgivable—"

"Are you sure I'm the one you owe an apology?" I shake my head then finally lift it to look at her. I was right. She looks broken. I hold up my hands, stopping her. "Forget I said that. Your relationship with the senator isn't any of my business." I meet her gaze for a beat, wanting her to contradict me, to tell me she is here because of us. She doesn't speak. "You can stay in my spare room tonight, and tomorrow we'll figure out what's next."

"Thank you." A tear slips out of the corner of one eye and rolls down her cheek. "I'm not here to ruin your life. I know you're happy and you have your life how you want it. I know I'm a complication."

Standing, I tuck my hands into my back pockets. "Don't presume to know anything about my life, Emma. We all publish our highlight reel online. No one's life is as simple as it appears." I turn and walk to my bedroom. When I shut the door behind me, I lean my head against it and squeeze my eyes shut.

I stretch out on my bed without bothering to change out of my jeans and End Zone T-shirt. Closing my eyes, I listen to the sounds of her getting ready for bed. The soft pad of her feet across the wood floor, the running of the tap as she pours herself a glass of water, the quiet swish of her brushing her teeth.

It's not long before I can't hear anything on the other side of the door, and I force myself to go through my own nighttime routine. I brush my teeth, wash my face, stare in the mirror, and wonder who the hell I've become. I can't decide if I'm more disgusted with myself for letting her stay or for the way I treated her just now. She was supposed to get married today. There were probably hundreds of cameras trained on her in the church, and instead of walking down the aisle, she ran the other way. She had to have a good reason. But regardless of what she was running from, by coming here, she's running right into trouble.

KEEGAN

Five Years Ago...

"Come with me."

We're on the beach soaking up the midmorning sun off the water, and everything seems perfect. But I know better than anyone that you can't judge a situation by how it seems on the surface. Beneath this picturesque morning, a shit storm in the form of my father is angry and brewing.

She rolls to her side and pulls her sunglasses down her nose so she can meet my eyes. "Where are you going?"

I swallow hard. I've been thinking about this, trying to convince myself that I should let her go and walk away, but I can't. "To Indiana. For college?"

What started as a cover for a con has slowly started to shape into a plan. When I told Emma I had an acceptance letter from Blackhawk Hills University and an invitation to be an "official walk-on" on their football team, I wasn't lying, but it was all part of the con. I didn't have any plans to go to BHU. I didn't believe college was for guys like me, but I saw the opportunity to go as the perfect way to convince some rich girl to hand over a bunch of cash.

I loved playing football in high school, but I wouldn't have dreamed of playing at a higher level. You see, if you're a conman who was raised by a conman, you believe everyone else is a conman too. Even though scouts had approached me about playing college ball on their team, I always believed there was a catch. They didn't *really* want me on their team. They just wanted me to sign my name on the dotted line so I'd be stuck at some college across the country and forced to pay tuition once they cut me from the team.

But after a few weeks with Emma, I've started to do something I haven't allowed myself to do in years. *Hope.* Time with her has planted the seeds of a belief in something better than this life, something better than living for one con after the next. Something bigger and more rewarding than being a social parasite. More than anything, I want a chance to start over. With Emma.

"What would I do in Indiana?" She smiles, but I can tell by the way she drags her bottom lip between her teeth that she's thinking about it.

"You could go to college at BHU. They have a great nonprofit administration program, and that's what you want to do, right?" I reach across the sand and grab her hand, threading my fingers with hers. "I know it's crazy, but I don't want to leave you."

"That is crazy." She squeezes my hand. "Probably the craziest thing I've ever heard, but I really like the idea."

I smile, and something lightens in my chest. "Think about it."

CHAPTER 22
KEEGAN

I toss and turn and force my eyes to close but I can't get to sleep. When I roll over to check the clock, it's two a.m. I have a long day tomorrow, and I know I need to get some rest, but I can't stop thinking about the woman in the next room. About what brought her here and why she slept with me when she was supposed to marry someone else. About why she ran away from her wedding while the whole world was watching.

"Fuck it," I mutter, climbing out of bed. I might as well go watch some TV. Anything would be less frustrating than lying here trying to find sleep that won't come.

When I walk out to the living room, I instantly sense I'm not alone. I click on a lamp and find Emma's sitting on the couch, her knees drawn to her chest, her head bowed, her body shaking. "Em?" I ask.

Her head snaps up, and she wipes away her tears as she looks away. "Did I wake you up? I'm sorry." Her voice hitches on a hiccup from her silent sobs.

"Shit. Are you okay?" What a stupid question to ask a woman who came to me in her wedding dress.

She gives a watery smile. "I'm the punch line of every late night comedian's joke. My mom hates me, I don't know what I'm going to do with my life or where I'm going to be tomorrow, and I just let down one of the best men I know." She wipes at her cheeks again and looks away from me. "I'm *great*."

Striding over to the couch, I sink into the spot next to her, but I lean my head back and focus on the ceiling because it tears me up too much to watch her cry. "I've been a dick to you since you showed up here, and I'm sorry."

"What were you supposed to do?" she asks. "Welcome me with open arms?"

I cut my eyes to her. "You thought I would, or you wouldn't have come."

She lifts a shoulder in a lopsided shrug. "It wasn't fair of me to come here. It's not your job to rescue me."

Her words make me think of what Bailey said. Is this a rescue? "This guy you were supposed to marry? Senator Dellaconte? Did he hurt you?"

She meets my eyes and stares for too long, because I can already see the answer there. She wasn't running away from some abusive man. She was just running. I can see the guilt in her eyes. "Zachary is my best friend. He's an amazing man, and I know that might sound crazy, considering what I just did, but he's one of the best people I know." She shrugs. "What I did today…I don't know if he'll be able to forgive me."

I look away. I really can't handle listening to her wax poetic about her fiancé or ex-fiancé or whatever he is to her now. I was her best friend once too, and maybe I didn't put a ring on her finger or plan a million-dollar wedding, but we planned a future together. "So this is my fault, then? You feel guilty about what we did last weekend, so you couldn't marry your best friend and live happily ever after?"

"I just decided I wanted…more."

"More what?" My voice cracks. When I met Emma, I was happy with my life. I didn't think there was much better than moving from one con job to the next. Then she smiled at me, and that was the beginning of the end of that life. She smiled at me, and I wanted *more*. I get wanting more. I just want to know what *her* more is.

She shrugs and drops her gaze to her hands. "I wish I could explain."

I draw one leg up onto the couch and turn so I'm facing her. I cup her face in my hands and swipe at her wet cheeks with my thumbs. It feels so good to have her here. Despite the anger and the confusion and how betrayed I felt in Vegas. Despite the fact that hearing her call him one of the best men she knows still makes me want to punch someone. "Why didn't you tell me you were engaged?"

"That was a mistake, but I was afraid to tell you."

I squeeze my eyes shut. "But if I'd known—"

"I was afraid you'd see through me and try to talk me out of marrying him. It was stupid. I know it was stupid. How many times can dumb Emma fuck everything up and run from her mess?"

"You're not dumb. But I'm still the man you walked away from five years ago." I cut myself off. I'm not talking about her marriage anymore, but I stop myself before I explain. I don't want her to see the vulnerability sure to show itself when I confess that I don't understand why, five years ago, she threw away what we had. How could she, in a heartbeat, go from planning to move across the country with me to telling me she couldn't do it and she didn't want to be with me anymore. I can't bring myself to ask any questions that I think might involve Harry as the answer, so I drop my hands and back away. "I'm going to bed. Try to get some sleep."

EMMA

I hear the front door click closed and the deadbolt sliding into place. I've been lying here awake for the last half-hour, listening to Keegan making coffee and getting ready for his day. The clock reads a quarter after five. Where the heck is he off to at this hour?

I grab my phone off the bedside table and check for messages from Zachary. What I did wasn't fair to him. But Becky's right—everyone deserves more than a life with a man who's in love with someone else. And it's not just that I want better for myself. I refuse to believe that Zach has to settle for life with me when he wants to be with Charlie.

I type a quick text to him.

> *Lying low for a while. I understand if you don't want to talk to me.*

I'm still in the sweatpants and T-shirt Keegan gave me last night. I tuck my phone into the pocket while I brush my teeth and wash my face. My eyes are gritty with lack of sleep, and I feel like I walked away from my wedding three weeks ago, when it's been less than twenty-four hours.

In the kitchen, I find a note on the counter in Keegan's neat print.

Coffee in the pot. Eggs in the fridge. I'll be gone all day. Make yourself at home.

I'm suddenly starving. Yesterday, the only thing I ate—if you can call it that—was the three mimosas I had while getting into my dress and getting my hair done. I didn't have an appetite. I was like the death row inmate who couldn't muster the enthusiasm to eat her last meal.

I pour myself a cup of black coffee and open the fridge, looking for some cream. Keegan's refrigerator is a study of healthy eating. Orange juice, eggs, vegetables, ground turkey, and a package of chicken breasts. He doesn't have any cream, so I settle for the milk from the door and add a splash to my coffee.

I stare at the carton of eggs. During the summer we spent together, Keegan cooked for me a lot. I remember him making eggs a few times. It didn't look that hard. Biting my lip, I pull the carton from the fridge, find a bowl from the cabinet, and start cracking.

I never intended to turn out a spoiled little rich girl who doesn't even know how to make her own breakfast. It just happened. My mom always had servants around, and when I moved out on my own, I hired a maid to prepare meals for me. When the food is there when you need it, you stop thinking about where it comes from.

I'm pouring eggs into a warm pan when my phone rings. I scramble to get it, using my dry hand to accept the call, and then place the phone between my shoulder and elbow. "Hello?"

"Emma?" It's Zachary. My heart sinks and surges all at once. Relief that he's calling me. Guilt that he had to.

"Zach? How are you?"

He clears his throat. I can imagine him sitting in his Savannah home, reclined on the couch, his feet stretched onto the ottoman in front of him and crossed at the ankle, a cup of hot coffee by his side. "You made a mess."

"I know." I find the paper towels and tear one off to dry my hands. "I'm so sorry, but I just couldn't do it. We both deserve more."

He draws in a deep breath. "Still an idealist at heart, I see."

I sigh. "Sorry."

"Don't apologize. It's one of the million reasons why I love you so much. I just wish you could have made this decision before I was in my tux and getting pictures taken."

I wince. "I'm the worst, aren't I?"

"You know how to make a splash, I'll give you that." He pauses for a beat. "Are you with him?"

He knows me so well. Or maybe we both know I didn't have anywhere else to go. For a girl the media declares is loved by everyone, I sure don't have many friends. "Yes, but I don't think he wants me here."

"To be fair, you slept with him while engaged to someone else. It does put a damper on the whole reunited-lovers thing."

"And it wasn't exactly without baggage *before* Vegas." I pace the living room while we talk, suddenly full of nervous energy I'm not sure what to do with.

"The media is swarming," he says, a note of warning in his voice. "I'll have to prepare a statement today."

"The reporters will get off on the fact that you and Keegan have a past. Add his minor celebrity status because of his NFL career, and they're gonna have a field day. Is he prepared for that level of scrutiny?"

"I don't know." I didn't think through how this might affect Keegan. I just ran. *Just like you always do.* "I hope this doesn't screw with his life. After the way he looked at me last night, I think it might be best if I leave before it can."

"Don't do that. You can't give up on him. Just because he didn't welcome you with open arms doesn't mean you should throw this away. He's important enough to you that you ran out on our wedding—"

"I didn't run out because of him."

"Bullshit. If you hadn't seen him last weekend, we'd be on our way to our honeymoon right now."

Yes, our honeymoon, where we'd be sitting on the beach each fantasizing about different people. "Can you honestly say that's what you want?"

Zach groans. "It's complicated, Em. I want to be me, but I also want my career. My point isn't about me, though. I know walking away last night was scary, and I know it wasn't easy. Don't give up on him and make it all for nothing."

"You're a good friend, Zachary. You're going to make this country a great president someday."

He makes a sound that's somewhere between groan and laugh. "I hadn't been selfish enough to want to make that happen."

"We both wanted it." Zachary was going to give me a life I once thought I could never have. Kids, love, a home filled with family instead of just servants. I want to panic at the thought of giving that up, at the possibility of a life alone.

"Listen, I might not be able to have everything I want in life, but you're too young to give up—" He pauses for a beat. "Shit, turn on the news."

I turn to the dark TV in the living room and shake my head as if he can see me. "I don't want to see what they're saying about me on the news."

"Your mom is giving an interview on *Good Morning America* this morning. They just announced the teaser."

"She's not." I close my eyes, imagining what she might have to say about her flaky daughter's decision to cancel her own wedding at the last minute. I can imagine she'll bring up my last-minute decision to back out of the *Lucy Matters* reunion. She *won't* mention that I was a last-minute no-show to her wedding to Harry, though I'm sure she'll be thinking it. "That'll show me."

"She's just doing damage control. You know she has to."

"She'd better leave Keegan out of it."

"You can't have it both ways, Emma. You went to him. He's in it, whether you want him to be or not."

I don't like that. When Becky handed me the keys yesterday, everything seemed so simple. *Get in the car and go to Keegan.* But it's just a mess. "Thank you for calling. I should go. I'm cooking." On the other end of the line, I hear coughing and sputtering, as if he's choking on his coffee. "Zach, it's not funny."

"Not funny to you." He sighs and chuckles quietly. "Just let me get the humor I can out of this mess of a situation. I love you, baby girl."

The old nickname releases a knot from my chest. I let Zach down, but he doesn't hate me. Relief makes me lighter. "I love you too, pretty boy." I end the call and put the phone down on the counter. When I turn back to the stove, there's a cloud of smoke over my pan of eggs. "Shit. Shit. Shit!" I grab the pan off the stove and throw it in the sink, turning on the faucet. More smoke billows up from the pan, and the smoke alarm overhead screeches.

I click off the stove before spinning in circles, looking for something to do about the smoke. There are big sliding doors at the back of the dining area, and I rush forward to open them and let the smoke out.

I leave them open as I take a chair from the table and climb onto it to reach the button on the smoke alarm. My ears breathe a sigh of relief when I silence it. Slowly, I lower myself back to the floor and rest my forehead on the counter.

Eggs in the fridge, he said. Like it was so simple. As if I'm not completely useless when it comes to the most basic life skills. *Make yourself at home.* And I almost burnt his house down.

Quit feeling sorry for yourself, Emma. Cut it out, right now.

I draw in a deep breath and lift my chin. Yesterday, I took a chance on a different life. A *better* life. If this is day one, I won't let burnt eggs get me down.

CHAPTER 23
KEEGAN

Bailey storms into the storeroom and slams the door shut behind her. "What the fuck do you think you're doing?"

I look up from my clipboard and frown. I had the office over the bar converted into an apartment while we were doing the other renovations, and Bailey's been living there. Judging by her sweatpants, tank top, and messy bun, I'm guessing she's spent her morning off catching up on sleep. "Adding this morning's delivery to the inventory?"

"You know that's not what I mean. Patsy texted and said you sent her home. What are you doing spending all your time here when your pretty actress ran away from her wedding and straight to you? Have you two even talked about what that means yet?"

Sighing, I put the clipboard down. I've stayed away from my house for three days. The first day, I went to the gym and went heavier and harder than I have since the season ended. Anything to get my mind off Emma. After a shower at the gym, Bailey met me at the bar to help me get Emma's car to my place. After that, I cleaned up the storeroom at the bar, had lunch with Jazzy, Olivia, and Olivia's mom, and pulled a couple of shifts working alongside Bailey. Yesterday, I spent a few hours at the park with Jazzy, had dinner with the guys who have already trickled in for Arrow's wedding, and reorganized the files in the back office. Today has been more of the same, and I'm planning to work behind the bar tonight whether Bailey needs me here or not.

"I don't know what you mean."

"I mean I'm going to lose my mind if one of us doesn't deal with their problems, and since I am currently unable to deal with mine, I would really like you to stop avoiding yours."

"I'm not avoiding anything." *When did I become such an awful liar?* "Things are complicated right now." Not to mention all the unanswered questions I have. I'm forcing myself to be patient and to trust that she wouldn't be here if this wasn't where she needed to be.

"And where's America's favorite runaway bride today?"

"Don't call her that."

She grunts. "Sorry. Would you rather I call her *Emily*?" I give her a hard look, and she sighs. "Why is she so precious? Why do you need to take care of her, to protect her like she's a child? She's a grown damn woman. And she slept with you when she was engaged to someone else."

"Yes, someone she didn't marry." There it is. The reason why I'm having trouble holding on to my anger. I needed Emma to run away from that wedding. My pride needed it and my heart needed it. That's what she did, and I'm glad even if she would've been better off with him. I'm glad even if that makes me an asshole. I told her I wanted her to be happy more than I wanted her for myself, but the selfish part of me is glad she ran and glad she spent the last two nights under my roof.

"She was supposed to marry someone else. This doesn't bother you? Maybe make you question her character?"

"There's always more to a situation than it appears, Bail."

"She ripped your heart out with her teeth, threw it on the ground, and pulverized it with her heels—"

"That's descriptive."

"—and now you've scraped it off the pavement and you're handing it back to her and saying *more, please*."

I close my eyes. Bailey is just trying to be a good friend. "Don't paint me as the victim here, okay? I'm a big boy. I know what I'm doing." I'm not sure that's true, though. I don't know what I'm doing with Emma right now. I don't know what she wants from me or how long she plans to stay.

She studies me for a beat. "How did you two meet, anyway?"

I set my jaw and cut my eyes away. "I had a summer job in Laguna Beach." I grab my clipboard and scan the list, trying to drop the subject and get back to work.

"And you just happened to hook up with a famous actress?"

I shrug but don't look at her.

"You've told me about your father, remember?" she says softly. "I know all about him dragging you through cons when you were a kid."

"That's not something I want everyone knowing." I glare at her. "I told you that for your own protection. He'll come around here, try to get money from you and the bar..."

She props her hands on her hips. "You told me because you needed a *friend*. That's what I am, Keegan. I'm your friend, and I've spent the last year watching you put yourself back together after Olivia rejected you. I hate to see you go through that again, especially if it's all rooted in guilt around an old con that went bad."

"I fell in love with her," I say softly. God, it's almost a relief to talk about it—to have a real friend I can confess my ugly deeds to without recrimination. "I thought it was just another job, but then I fell hard. She made me believe I could be as good as the man I was pretending to be. Better, even. I'm not going to let her break my heart again, but even if she did..." I shrug. I don't know how to say it without sounding sappy. She made me a better man. That's all there is to it.

Bailey nods solemnly then surprises me by wrapping her arms around me and hugging me. She's at least a foot shorter than me and makes me feel like a giant, but mostly it feels awkward because Bailey isn't often physically affectionate with me. "Don't get hurt," she whispers.

My phone rings, and she releases me as I pull it from my pocket. My dad's name lights up the display. *Fuck me.* I turn the screen to show her. "See what happens when you speak of the devil?"

She laughs. "Have fun with that."

I think about rejecting the call, but then dread crawls up my spine as I imagine Dad showing up on my doorstep and seeing Emma in my house. I swipe a finger across the screen to answer it. "Hey, Dad."

"You'd never guess what I just saw on the TV." He pauses a beat, but I don't bother guessing. "That old friend of yours— Emma Whatchamacallit?—she canceled her wedding." When he cackles, he sounds more like the Wicked Witch of the West than a seasoned conman. "Wonder what that's about. Do you think it has anything to do with that actor? The stepdad? You know who I mean. Harry Evans?"

"I wouldn't know, Dad." At least I'm not lying about that, but the possibility of Harry having more to do with her canceled wedding than I did turns my stomach sour.

She came to you.

"Not too late to make some cash from that waste of a summer," he says.

I pinch the bridge of my nose. "I don't want Emma's money, and I don't want you bothering her. You know how I feel about this."

He grunts and mumbles something that I suspect is *pussy,* but I don't care enough to call him on it. "Whatever, I'm clean these days anyway. Living on the straight and narrow, trying to be a better man."

Bullshit. "That's great, Dad. Hey, you need anything else? I'm at the bar trying to wrap up a delivery."

"Oh, then I'll let you go. I need to get back to winning my money back from this crooked casino."

"You're still in Vegas?" I guess he had money for a room after all.

"For now. But put a beer aside for your dear old dad. I'm gonna come visit my grandbaby here real soon."

"Don't fly all the way to Blackhawk Valley," I say, a little too quickly. "That'd be a waste when Jazzy and I are headed back to Florida on Monday."

"Does this mean you've changed your mind about me seeing her?"

No, it means I don't want you to know that Emma's here. "It means I might be willing to talk about it. If you really have gone straight, that is."

"Of course I have. Have I ever lied to you?"

I bite my tongue so hard, I grimace.

"I'll let you go," he says. "Talk soon."

I end the call and take a deep breath. Emma Rothschild ran from her wedding and is hiding out at my house, my dad's up my ass and looking in Emma's direction for easy money, and Bailey's convinced I'm on the fast track to heartbreak. Can my life get any more interesting?

Despite Bailey's objections, I stay for the nonexistent Tuesday night rush, opting for the easier path of work over facing my problems. When I pull into the garage, I've been going for eighteen hours, but my exhaustion is more from the effort to stay away from her than from what I've filled my day with. I dread going to bed because I know my mind won't let me sleep.

Last night when I got home, she was asleep, and tonight it's even later. The house is already dark except for a lamp she left on in the living room. I head straight to the bathroom, where I plan to take a long, hot shower. I need hot water to wash off the grime from the day and hopefully some of the tension from my shoulders.

It's just as I step into the bathroom and reach to turn on the light that I realize it's not completely dark in here. Emma is in the tub, candles lit all around her, her head leaned back as she soaks in the bubbly water.

Before I can back out of the room, she turns and blinks at me as though she fell asleep in the tub. "Hi," she whispers. "Do you need the bathroom? I can be out of your way in just a minute." She looks around and then back to me, and I realize that's my cue to leave, but I really don't want to. Her cheeks are pink from the warm water, her hair wet and wrapped in a sloppy bun on top of her head. The outline of her body under the bubbles is just visible enough in the flickering candlelight that my cock aches in my jeans.

Turning quickly, I force myself out of the bathroom and pull the door shut behind me. I close my eyes and take one deep breath after another. *Holy shit.* I've been working so hard to stay away from her, because no matter what I think about her and her decision to run from her wedding, her decision to keep her marriage a secret from me, or her decision to leave me five years ago, I know she didn't come here to fuck around. That's not

Emma. And hell, if she did, I'd be disappointed. I want more from her than sex.

I go to the kitchen and grab myself a beer. This is becoming a nightly habit, and Vegas aside, I don't typically drink much. When she comes out of the bathroom, she's dressed in the same flannel pants and T-shirt I gave her three nights ago. Of course she is. What else would she wear? She doesn't have any clothes with her other than her wedding dress, and I'm the dickhead who was so caught up in his own internal drama that he didn't even think to run to the store to buy her something to wear. *God, I'm a fucking asshole.*

She takes a seat on the couch and wraps her arms around her knees.

I want to pull her into my arms and hold her. I want to brush her hair back from her face and look into her eyes until she forgets about her senator. I can't do any of that. "I'm sorry I was gone all day."

She shakes her head. "You had to work. You have a life. I don't expect you to cater to me."

"I should have stopped by. I should have checked in on you." I cut my eyes away from her.

"I understand if you want me to leave. You can't keep avoiding your own house because I'm here."

I set my jaw. It's ridiculous, but I don't want her to leave. I want her to stay. She came here because she needed something, and is it so far-fetched to think that something might be *me*?

I draw in a ragged breath. Maybe Bailey's right and I'm

setting myself up for heartache, but I can't help it. "Tomorrow I'll take you shopping for whatever you need. Then, if you want to get out of the house, maybe we can hang out at The End Zone for a while." I flinch, realizing that the invitation might not be appealing if she only came here to hide. "It's up to you, though."

"No, I'd like that. I think it might do me some good." She bites her bottom lip before giving me the closest thing to a smile I've seen since she arrived. "And I'd like to spend the time with you."

EMMA

Up before the sun seems to be Keegan's habit. Since he promised to spend the day with me, I decide that means I don't need to pretend I'm sleeping when I hear him in the kitchen on Wednesday morning. I climb out of bed and rush to the bathroom, wanting to brush my teeth and tame my bedhead before facing him.

When I feel presentable—or at least the best I can manage, considering the circumstances—I find him in the kitchen making a pot of coffee. I love seeing him so domestic, padding barefoot around the kitchen in jeans and a T-shirt that stretches across his shoulders. His hands seem to be too big for everything he touches. I've always loved watching his hands, and I swallow hard looking at them now. I thought I saw desire in his eyes when he walked in on me in the tub last night.

I haven't cared about or tended to my body's sexual needs in five years. I went on a few dates before Zach and I hatched our plans, but every time a man would try to touch me, the moment would be invaded by something dark and sick, and I'd push him away. I thought I was broken forever, but ever since my weekend with Keegan in Vegas, it's like all that darkness has been washed away and replaced with snippets of memory, images of his hands and mouth, pieces to an incomplete puzzle that I desperately want to complete. Even if we never touch again, to have the memories from our night together, as foolish as all of that may have been, that would be something to cherish.

He smiles when he sees me. "Coffee?" He pours me a cup even as he asks, and I move into the kitchen with my arms wrapped around myself. "I found an old dress of Olivia's. She left it here months ago." He clears his throat and hands me a handful of folded black cotton from the other end of the counter.

I hold it up nervously, afraid his girlfriend was some tiny thing and it won't fit me. But it's a cotton sundress, and it looks like it might. I don't want to think too much about why his baby's mother has clothes in his closet. He said they were never a real couple, but if they weren't together, wouldn't her clothes be in the guest room and not his?

"Is it okay?" he asks.

I push away my worry and smile. "Do you think she'll mind?"

He shrugs. "I honestly don't think she remembers she owns it. Clothes are kind of disposable to Liv." He sighs heavily, and I feel like there might be more he's not saying. "I'll buy you some new stuff when I'm at the store today."

"I can buy them myself." I hold the dress to my chest. "I'm going to go put this on."

"Sure."

I run to the bathroom and quickly pull off Keegan's sleep pants and T-shirt. I washed them yesterday while he was gone, feeling more comfortable using his washing machine than I did digging into his drawers for another set of clothes, but I'll feel better dressed in something a little less sloppy.

I pull the dress over my head and look in the mirror. It's tight around the chest, but around the waist it's looser than I expected. The baby doll look isn't very flattering on me—and can even make me look like an expectant mother if I stand at the wrong angle— but it'll do for this morning and a trip to the store to buy clothes of my own. I had Becky pack me a few things and ship them, and they should be here tomorrow, but I want to have something that doesn't belong to Olivia to wear to the bar tonight.

When I step out of the bathroom, I feel self-conscious. Is he going to see me in this and compare me to her? I shouldn't be jealous of her if they aren't together, but I can't help it. She's the mother of his child. That's a connection that'll always be there.

Keegan's sipping coffee and, in typical male fashion, doesn't seem to even notice the dress. His eyes drop to my mouth and linger there for a long beat.

For a minute, I think he might feel it too—this constant pull that I'm always fighting when he's close, that need to be as near to him as possible. But then he blinks, his smile returns, and any temptation I saw in his features disappears as if it was never there.

My heart races. I want him to kiss me, and I know it's not fair, but I want him to forgive me for all the shit I've done to him that he doesn't understand.

I didn't grow up in a home where honesty was valued. I grew up in a home where you pick and choose what information you give to people, and you hide the unpleasant parts. While I was with Keegan, I thought I'd outgrown that and become a more mature woman than my mother. But the end of the summer proved me wrong.

"Do you still like omelets?" he asks. "I was about to make myself breakfast."

I nod. "Sure. Do you want some help?"

He arches a brow. "This from the girl who burnt eggs the other day?"

"You knew about that?"

"I saw the charred remains in the trash can."

I make a face. "I was hoping to keep my continuing ineptitude in the kitchen a secret."

He bites back a smile. "Come here, and I'll show you what to do."

I pad around to the other side of the island as Keegan pulls eggs from the fridge, bowls from the cabinets, and a cutting board and a couple of knives from the drawers.

He pulls fixings from the fridge and says, "Pick your poison."

"I like spinach, bell peppers, and feta cheese," I say, pointing at the items.

"Easy enough," he says. He slides a bowl across the counter to rest in front of me. "First, let's crack the eggs."

"That, I can do." I crack an egg on the side of the bowl and use both hands to open it. I wrinkle my nose when I see I lost a piece of shell. "Dang it."

"Here," he says. He steps behind me and wraps his arms around me to put one hand on each of mine. "Take the shell," he says, guiding it into the bowl, "and use it to scoop out the bit that dropped in with the egg. It comes out easier that way than trying to fish it out with your fingers."

He guides my hand into the bowl and scoops out the shell. I close my eyes at the feel of his hard body behind me. His heat, the breadth of him, his strength. My body buzzes with his nearness, but he must not feel it like I do, because he stays where he is and moves on to the next egg, showing me how to crack it harder—but not too hard—against the side of the bowl to get a cleaner break.

When we've broken eight eggs, he finally steps away to wash his hands in the sink. I follow after him, and after I dry my hands, he gives me a whisk.

"Got it?" he asks.

I nod, whisking the eggs in the bowl like I've seen him do before. I like parts of cooking I can't screw up. There's nothing to burn with a whisk and no danger of over-whipping the eggs. While I work, he washes a bunch of spinach and a green pepper and sets them on the cutting board.

"Those look good," he says. "Now how about cutting up the

veggies?"

He stands behind me again, this time showing me how to curl my fingers in so I don't cut my fingertips off while I'm chopping. I want the moment to last longer than it will—his body against mine, his breath in my hair, his hands guiding mine. If I could just slow down time, maybe I'd have time to mentally catalogue everything his nearness does to me, the buzz along my nerve endings amplifying every brush of his thumb against mine, the heat of his chest at my back reminding me of lazy Sunday mornings in Laguna and stretching out between cool cotton sheets.

Sooner than I want to be, I'm finished and sliding the vegetables into a second bowl.

"We'll just throw all this stuff in the skillet to sauté it before we add it to the eggs."

I nod and watch him do this part, enjoying the way his hands deftly move the ingredients into the pan and toss them around with a flick of his wrist.

I've watched Keegan on the football field over the last year, gotten to see him excel at the sport that he loves. As much as I enjoyed seeing him in pads and a helmet throwing guys around like they weigh twenty pounds, it's nothing compared to how he moves in the kitchen. On the spectrum of things that make him completely irresistible to me, there's nothing that compares to his abilities in the kitchen or the pictures on Instagram where he's holding his baby like she's the most precious gift he's ever received.

He's the full package. A kind father and a caring friend, with a mind for business and a work ethic that put him on the field when most men in his position wouldn't have seen game time for at least another year. As far as I'm concerned, he's the real modern Superman.

"So you're telling me no one picked up where I left off with your cooking lessons?" he asks as he stirs the contents of the pan.

"No offense to your teaching skills, but the things I learned last time you tried to give me cooking lessons had nothing to do with food."

His grin falls away as his gaze drops to my lips and his eyes grow darker. He doesn't look away, and I hold my breath. Suddenly, there's nothing I want more than to feel his kiss again. Did our night in Vegas really happen less than two weeks ago? It feels like a lifetime. I was reckless and careless, but being with him was one of the most honest things I've ever done.

He cups the side of my face in one big hand and my lips tingle in anticipation of his kiss.

There's a sharp knock on the front door, followed by the scrape of a key in the lock, and Keegan jerks back as if I've burnt him. He blinks at me and draws in a ragged breath.

"Keegan, I know you're in there. Would you come here and help me with the freaking door?" It's a woman's voice.

Keegan gives me one last long look before heading to the front door, where a girl my age with long, dark hair and pretty brown eyes is pushing into the living room with a baby in her arms. "I hope you have some extra binkies, because I forgot them. What do you say we put this kid down for a nap and climb into bed together for a little midmorning stress relief?"

She drops a bag by the door and looks at me for the first time. She frowns. "Who are you?"

If I knew the answer to that question, I might not be here right now. Or maybe I would. Maybe I'd have moved here with Keegan five years ago. I turn to Keegan, who looks as baffled as I feel.

"Oh my God!" The girl's eyes go wide and her jaw goes slack. "You're *Lucy*. I mean, Emma Rothschild." She glances over each shoulder—hoping someone else might be there to confirm who I am or thinking there might be a camera, I'm not sure. "Holy shit. You ran away from your wedding and came to *Keegan*?"

"Um..." That's the moment it clicks. I take in the baby's face and realize who she is. That's Keegan's baby. I lift my gaze to meet hers. "You must be—"

"Olivia." She stalks toward Keegan, her face angry. "You don't tell me *anything*."

CHAPTER 24
KEEGAN

Emma frowns as her gaze darts between me and Olivia. Her tongue darts out to wet her lips, and I think about how close I was to kissing that mouth, how jealous I am that she gets to taste her lips and I don't.

My life is officially off the rails. I was about to kiss a woman who's supposed to be married to a United States senator, and my baby's mother just walked into my house and offered a booty call. Seven or eight months ago, climbing into bed with Olivia just because she was down to fuck was nothing unusual, but I put a stop to that when she started dating Dre.

What the hell is going on?

I take Jazzy from Olivia's arms. "I thought you were staying with your mom this trip."

Jazzy reaches up to smack my cheeks, and I press a kiss to the top of her head. I catch a whiff of strawberry baby shampoo.

Something about the smell helps me stay calm despite the fact that my life feels like it's a disaster.

"We're fighting," Liv says. Her eyes skim over Emma. "Is that my *maternity* dress? Oh my God, are you pregnant? Does Zachary know?"

Emma winces and her cheeks turn pink. "I…" She squeezes her eyes shut, and when she opens them and looks at me, they're full of hurt, as if I've played some nasty trick on her. "You two probably need to talk. I'll get out of your way." She turns and quietly retreats to the guest bedroom, closing the door behind her.

Olivia pours herself a cup of coffee and leans against the counter, casual as fuck, as if she didn't just blow in here like a tornado and make a bigger mess of my life. "Keegan, you've got some explaining to do."

"I told you Emma's an old friend. I told her she could stay here until she gets some things sorted out in her life."

She arches a brow. "Sure. And what does her fiancé think of her staying with her ex-boyfriend or whatever the hell you are to her?"

I don't have a clue. "What are you and your mom fighting about?"

She rolls her eyes. "Not a subtle change of subject, Kee. You are such a hypocrite! You freaked out when I was taking Jazzy to Dre's without telling you, but now you've brought your ex-girlfriend—*whatever*—into our daughter's life without giving me the slightest warning."

I fold my arms. "Jazzy has been with you since Emma got here, so that really doesn't apply."

"She's staying in my daughter's home," she says, her eyes scanning the kitchen and living room as if she's looking for evidence that Emma's made it unfit for her baby. "I had a right to know."

"It all happened really fast, Liv." I put Jazzy down, and she half runs, half stumbles to her baby dolls in the living room. With a doll under one arm, she happily shoves a rubber giraffe in her mouth and gnaws on it, and I grin at her before standing and returning to my conversation with Olivia. "I'm sorry I haven't talked to you about it, but I honestly wouldn't have known what to tell you. I didn't know she was coming. I don't even know how long she's staying."

"Fine." Sighing, she steps forward and slides a hand under my shirt and around my back. "What do you say about my naptime plans? Jazzy should be ready for her nap soon."

I step away from her touch. Everyone thinks Olivia is Little Miss Innocence because she's got this girl-next-door look about her, but she's much more than meets the eye. "Liv…"

"You're *no fun* anymore, Keegan. I remember when you couldn't keep your hands off me."

"I told you I'm not fucking you as long as you're with Dre."

She smacks her lips and grins. "Then it's my lucky day, because I'm not with Dre anymore. So there."

I blink at her. "What happened? As of when?"

"I don't know. I've been thinking about it for a while, and

then he told me he was going to fly here with his kids to spend time with me and Jazzy, and I freaked out. The more he tries to make us like a family, the more I realize..." She looks away.

"The more you realize what?"

"It's just not what I want from him, okay? I thought it was, but if I'm his family, I can't be yours."

Jesus Christ. How long have I wanted Liv? How hard did I try to make her give us a chance? And now that Emma's shown up and thrown a giant, confusing, and complicated wrench in my life, Liv is going to play this game again. Since I found out Olivia was pregnant a couple of summers ago, she has done a fantastic job of keeping me on the hook. One day, she makes it clear she doesn't want me. The next, she gives me just enough to hold on to hope that we might be a family. I thought we'd moved past that when I caught her fucking Dre in my bed. "Here we go again," I mutter.

"What?" She squeezes my arm. "I know I always got frustrated with you. I felt like you didn't open up to me, but I can be patient." She sweeps the back of her hand up my arm and back down. "Come on. Let's put the baby down and have some fun. It's been so long."

"Emma's in the other room, Liv."

She stiffens. "The actress who just ran away from her wedding to a guy who's way out of her league and who's currently wearing my *maternity* dress? *She* is the reason you're not going to fuck me?"

I set my jaw. "You've always expected me to be there whenever it was convenient for you. I always have been, but..." I shake my head. "You and me, on and off? That's not good for either of us, and it's definitely not good for Jazzy. You've never been interested in giving me more than sex."

"You don't know that." Her eyes fill with tears, and I feel like a grade-A asshole. "Can't you just be honest with me? Are you and Emma together?"

"You said it yourself. She was supposed to marry someone else this weekend."

"You didn't answer my question."

"We aren't together. We're friends. She needed a favor, somewhere to go."

"Are you fucking her?"

"No." I clench my teeth, frustrated that I have to have this conversation. It would be one thing if I were evading, but I don't have the answers. I don't know what's happening, and instead of waiting until Emma can explain herself, Liv is going to push the issue.

"You wanna be, though." She turns and stares at the closed bedroom door before turning back to me. "What does she have that I don't?"

"Don't. Don't pull this on me. That's not fair. For two years, I tried to be with you. I did everything I could for you to take me seriously, and—"

"Bullshit. You did everything except open up to me. How am I supposed to be with a guy who can't even talk about his past, who doesn't trust me enough to tell me why he hates his mother or why he won't introduce me to his own father?"

"My father's a piece of shit. Don't make this about him when you couldn't handle that I was never going to be pulling seven figures."

"I was immature." She folds her arms. "But so were you. Did you even realize that until your dad told me, I didn't know he wasn't your biological father? *That's* always been our problem, Keegan. You wanted me, but not really. Do you know how lonely it is to be with someone who doesn't share themselves?"

"I'm sorry."

She looks to the bedroom door. "When you two were together, did you love her?" Her voice is a bare whisper now, and it cracks on the word *love*.

I nod. Olivia's right. I never did open up to her, and I owe her this much truth. "Yeah. I did. Completely."

"And now?"

"When you love someone completely," I say softly, "it doesn't go away with time or because they move on." I meet her watery eyes, and her tears cut me in two. I let out a long breath. "Everything's just really complicated right now."

"Are you cool with me staying here?" She takes a breath. "I kind of made a big deal about storming out of my mom's, and I'd rather not go back yet if I don't have to. But if you and *Emma Rothschild* need some privacy—"

"Liv, it's fine. You know you and Jazzy are always welcome. Since Emma's in the guest bedroom, you can use the extra bed in the nursery." I spent a lot of nights sleeping on the twin bed in there when Jazzy was a newborn and waking every two hours. It was easier to be close.

"Okay." She reaches out and trails her fingertips down my chest. "You know where to find me if you change your mind about the rest. We always had fun together."

Maybe nothing will happen between me and Emma, but even if her coming to me doesn't mean anything, every ounce of desire in my blood in this moment is directed at the redhead in my guest bedroom. Olivia deserves better than that.

EMMA

I'm so mortified that I feel like I want to crawl into the closet and hide. I'm so embarrassed that my cheeks may be stained this vibrant red for the rest of my life. His daughter's mother is picture-perfect gorgeous, and I'm wearing her *maternity* dress.

There's a knock on my bedroom door. "Em?" Keegan's voice, low and gravelly. An hour ago, if he'd knocked on my door and said my name like that, I would've tripped over myself trying to open it as fast as I could. Right now, I want to tell him to go away.

Unfortunately, this is his house, and I don't feel like I can ignore him. I climb off the bed. "Come on in."

He comes in and closes the door behind him. It's a nice-size bedroom, but now that he's in here with the door closed and there's nothing but this bed between us, it feels much smaller.

"Are you okay?"

"I thought you said you and Olivia weren't together."

He leans against the door and sighs. "We're not."

"You just sleep together sometimes?"

He draws in a ragged breath and drags a hand through his hair. God, he's so handsome. *Out of my league.* I tried not to listen, and I couldn't hear everything they said, but I heard her describe Zachary as out of my league. She's right. And if Zachary is out of my league, then Keegan is too—by leaps and bounds.

"We used to," he says. "We weren't *together*, together when she moved to Florida with me, but..." He shrugs. "The bedroom was one place we always got along."

"Casual sex." I feel like I'm testing the words on my tongue, trying to make myself wrap my mind around the idea of Keegan consistently engaging in sex without emotional attachment. Maybe if I can do that, I'll stop imagining our weekend in Vegas meant more to him than it did.

You were both trashed, Em. Stop putting meaning where there is none.

"It wasn't healthy," he says. "I'm not saying it was. I wanted more from her; she wanted me to expect less." He shakes his head. "It's probably for the best that Dre came along and I put a stop to it."

"*You* put a stop to it?"

He arches a brow. "Yeah."

"Oh." I frown. "She would've kept sleeping with you even though she was with him?"

"Probably." He leans his head back and stares at the ceiling. "I can't judge. The first time Olivia and I slept together, she was with Chris."

I frown. "Chris Montgomery? Grace's Chris?"

He chuckles. "Yeah. That one. He didn't like me much. I never meant for it to happen, but…" He looks me over. "I guess I have a habit of being attracted to emotionally unavailable women."

I don't know if he means to aim so low, but that hurts. He's not just referencing Zachary and Vegas. He's talking about five years ago when he thought there was something between me and Harry. Five years ago, when he saw what no one else could see.

"I'm completely in the way by being here." My gaze darts to my phone on the bedside table, where I was searching local hotels while he and Olivia talked.

"It's fine," he says.

"No. It's not. And to make matters worse, I never stopped to think about how showing up on your doorstep would affect your life." I fold my arms and pace the length of the bedroom. "You told me in Vegas how much you wanted things to work between you and Jasmine's mother."

He shakes his head. "*Wanted*. Past tense. It's not that simple anymore." He drops his gaze to the floor and mutters what I think is, "It never was," but his words are so soft I can't be sure. When he lifts his gaze, his eyes search my face. "Why did you come to me? Of everywhere you could have gone, why me?"

"Where else would I go? My best friends are Becky and her brother, the man I was supposed to marry."

"Yes, Zachary," he says, voice tight. "You've mentioned a couple of times now that he's your best friend. He's so fucking amazing and kind. And yet here you are." He draws in another deep breath as if searching for patience. "Listen, I'm sorry about all this. I just wanted you to know that I told Liv she can stay here, but that doesn't change anything. You're still welcome to stay as long as you need."

Were you about to kiss me when she came to the door? Would you be kissing me now if she hadn't?

I stop pacing. "I could just get a hotel room."

"Did you really drive here all the way from Savannah so you could sleep in a hotel room?"

"No, Keegan. I didn't. I drove all the way here from Savannah because you left that note for me."

"Fuck." He rubs the back of his neck. "I didn't mean to screw up your life. Vegas and then the note. That note was my way of telling you that I was okay with it all. That I just wanted you to be happy."

"I know." I swallow. "Listen, if you have a ball cap I could borrow, I think I'll go to the store."

"Sure. Of course." He waves toward the kitchen. "We never finished making breakfast."

"I'll be okay. I want to grab a few things so I don't have to keep wearing this maternity dress."

"I didn't realize that's what it was." He frowns. "That really bothers you, doesn't it?"

"It would bother any girl."

Shrugging, he drags his gaze down to my toes and slowly back up. "I think you look amazing." The corner of his mouth quirks into a lopsided grin. "Then again, I thought you looked amazing in my T-shirt."

My cheeks heat all over again, but this time it's not from embarrassment.

"Do you want me to go with you?"

"No, I think some time alone might be good for me. I can clear my head."

He nods. "Call me if you need anything? Then tonight we can hang out if you want."

"If you need to be with Jazzy...or if you and Olivia wanted to..."

He arches a brow, but if he's waiting for me to finish one of those sentences, he's out of luck. "It's a plan, then." He turns on his heel and leaves the room.

CHAPTER 25
EMMA

"I need to tell Keegan the truth." They're the words that were running through my head the whole time I was shopping, and they're the first words I say when I get Zach on the phone after lunch.

The house is quiet. The baby and Olivia are napping, and there's a note on the counter from Keegan saying he went out for a run.

Zachary's silent on the other end of the line. I know that I'm asking a lot. In all the years I've known Zach, I've never told anyone his secret. I haven't ever asked him if I could tell someone, either. It was an understanding. No one knows, and no one can know. It's fine to believe you can trust the people around you, but the more people who know a secret, the less of a secret it is. And Zachary's is career-ending huge.

"He needs to understand why what happened in Vegas

happened. He needs to understand why—"

"You slept with him again, didn't you?" I hear the smile in his voice—a cocky smirk that says he's impressed.

"No, but I…"

"Want to?"

So, so much. "It's not just about sex. I shouldn't have ever pushed him away."

"Hey now, you had reasons."

I wander into the kitchen and see that Keegan cleaned up our mess from this morning. The counters are shining and dishes are drying in the rack. "I panicked."

Zach sighs. "Mine isn't the only secret you need to confide in him."

"Yeah, I know. I'm ready." There's something about having distance from a trauma and a couple of amazing friends who believe your side of the story that gives you a little courage. Or that's what I keep telling myself.

"You're sure we can trust him?"

"I'd trust him with anything."

"Okay then." He sighs. "Just make sure he knows that it's not for public consumption. The last thing we need is for the media to glom on to this when we need their focus on the healthcare bill I'm co-sponsoring next month."

"I know. I'll explain." I breathe deeply, already feeling the relief of the secret lifting off my shoulders. "How's Charlie?"

"He's good. Really good. I think you did the right thing for both of us, Em."

"I hope so. I know it was right for me, but it still feels terribly selfish."

"I'm pretty sure I was the selfish one for letting you do it to begin with," he says. "Charlie is letting me make it up to him, though."

I burst out laughing and then bite my lip to silence myself. "I'm sure he is."

"I love you, baby girl."

"I love you too, pretty boy." When I hang up the phone and turn around, I jump because I thought I was alone. Keegan's in the living room and staring at me, his jaw hard. "What's wrong?"

He shrugs. "I don't know. You were just on the phone with your almost-husband, telling him you love him, but here you are in my house. I'm just a little lost. If you love him so much and if he's so damn perfect, why didn't you marry him? Why not confess that you got drunk and fucked an idiot from your past and then find a way to work it out? Why come back to me and then get on the phone with him and tell him you love him?"

I smile, so damn relieved that I finally get to tell him the truth. "It's okay. He's my best friend. I *do* love him."

"And you almost married him, Emma. I think you need to figure out exactly what it is you want. From him, from me..." He waves a hand, indicating the house. "From staying here. I keep trying to figure it out, but I can't read your mind."

"You need to let me explain."

"Explain? Every time I ask you questions, you evade." He steps toward me then stops, as if thinking better of it. He sinks into the chair and turns up his palms. "Go ahead. Explain. I'm all ears."

"Zachary and I love each other because we're best friends, but our marriage wasn't about *sex*. He needed a wife, not someone to warm his bed."

"*Bullshit*," he spits through clenched teeth. "I know you don't think much of yourself, but Emma, when you look in the mirror you don't see what men see when they look at you. I don't know what he told you or how he convinced you that your marriage was purely platonic, but I swear to you no heterosexual male is going to marry you and not want you in his bed."

I hold his gaze for a long beat.

He narrows his eyes, and I watch as the understanding dawns there. "He's not…" I nod. "Holy shit," he mutters, leaning back and rubbing his forehead. "Jesus." He bows his head and mutters a curse. "Then why were you doing it?"

"He needed a wife if he wants to stay in office, if he wants a chance at the presidency. His constituency…hell, this whole country." I wait a beat, hoping he can understand what even Becky never did. "He needed me."

"I get what was in it for him. Why were *you* doing it?"

How many times did Zachary ask me that question? "I didn't have any reason not to." Even though it's true, it's a half-assed answer. The full truth is raw to the point of embarrassing.

"That doesn't make any sense," Keegan says. He pushes out of his chair and stalks toward me, raking his gaze over me in my new dress. "What? You were going to have affairs the rest of your life?"

I shift under his scrutiny, simultaneously hating the judgment in his tone and loving the way he drinks me in with his eyes. "I had no intention of having affairs."

"Right. You're twenty-three years old and were going to happily be celibate the rest of your life?"

This is it. The part where I tell my secret. My shame. But the words won't come. I needed a minute to prepare. To figure out how to begin. We got here too fast and I'm not ready. "I didn't care about that."

"Emma…" He drags a hand through his hair. "What the fuck did you want from a marriage to a man who would never love you the way you deserve to be loved?"

"I didn't want to be alone anymore." The words come out sharper than I intended, as if they're pieced together with the shards of my broken heart. My eyes fill with tears without warning. I have to look away. "Maybe Zachary couldn't give me everything a husband should give his wife, but he could give me friendship, companionship, and the family I've never had. It wasn't perfect, but it seemed like my best choice."

When I blink away my tears and turn back to Keegan, he's staring at me like he's trying to piece together a puzzle. It's not that I thought he'd pull me into his arms at this news, but I thought he'd be relieved. Instead, he seems more frustrated with me than he did when he thought I'd cheated on my fiancé. Maybe I wanted him to hear this much and piece the rest of the truth together—Harry and me five years ago, the daisies in the trash can, and the wine stain on the carpet—but he didn't, and I can only blame myself.

He draws in a ragged breath. "I'm going to take a shower. If you still want to go to The End Zone tonight, we'll leave in an hour." He turns on his heel and walks away.

"Keegan?"

He stops, his hand on the doorframe to his bedroom.

"You can't tell anyone about Zachary. His career…"

His shoulders stiffen but he doesn't look at me. "I promise your secret is safe," he says softly. Then he steps into the bedroom and closes the door behind him.

KEEGAN

We drive to the bar in tense silence. In addition to my Gators cap and a pair of oversized sunglasses, she's wearing a new dress she must have picked up at the store today. Her bare thigh is so close I could reach out and touch the tender skin there. I could easily slide my hand under the soft cotton and remind her exactly what she would have been giving up if she'd gone through with her ridiculous marriage of convenience. The thought is so damn tempting, and I'm half hard just remembering the sounds she made in the elevator in Vegas, remembering the way she felt on my fingers when I touched her the next morning.

By the time I park behind The End Zone, I'm gripping the

steering wheel so hard, my knuckles are white.

"Why are you doing this?" she asks when I park the car.

"What?"

She studies me, her big blue eyes searching my face. "Why are you bringing me here tonight when you don't want to be with me?"

For the last hour, my mind has been flooded with the implications of what Emma told me about her marriage. On the one hand, it seems exactly like something she would do—enter a passionless marriage for the sake of someone else's goals and aspirations. But on the other hand, it fucking *burns*. I was eighteen and ready to push my father out of my life forever if it meant keeping her. Maybe we were too young for something so drastic, but I thought we were good together. More than that. I thought what we had was priceless. Was I not enough for her? And her senator and the half-marriage he was offering was?

I turn off the car and pull the keys from the ignition. I should probably ask her those questions, but I'm not sure I want to hear her answers. "I'm sorry if I'm being quiet. I want you here. It's just a lot to process." She has her hands folded in her lap, and I take one. "Come on. I want to show you my bar."

I lead Emma around the block to the front entrance. It's a quiet night at The End Zone. Wednesdays are never hopping anyway, but since half the town's population clears out after the close of spring semester, it's slowed down even more. Whereas on a typical Friday or Saturday during the semester, Bailey would have three or four waitstaff working the floor while she busted her ass behind the bar, tonight it's only her and one other tending to a room that's filled mostly with our friends.

"Hey, bossman!" Bailey calls from behind the counter. "We've been waiting for you!"

I grin when I realize Arrow, Mia, Chris, and Grace are here and sitting at the bar. After the day I've had, it's a relief to walk into my bar and be surrounded by my favorite people. It's even better knowing that this weekend, everyone will be together again, even if it's temporary.

"You didn't tell me your friends would be here." Emma's voice is small and quiet, but there's no accusation in the words, only nerves.

"I didn't think about it, honestly, but I should have guessed they'd come here." Is she worried they won't forgive her for lying about her identity in Vegas? "They'll understand," I say, though it's kind of a ridiculous thing to promise when I have more information than they ever will, and *I* don't understand. Not really. Not why she didn't tell me she was getting married or why she ran from her wedding. Every answer she's given me has been cryptic at best.

Everyone's seated at the bar, and when Emma and I approach, they all turn to greet us and their eyes land on her. I have no doubt that our whole group now knows that Vegas Emily is one and the same as runaway bride Emma Rothschild. I haven't spoken to everyone, but word travels fast.

Mia is the first to speak, and she slides off her barstool and opens her arms for Emma. "Hi, Em! Good to see you again!"

Emma gapes at her, but then shakes her head and accepts the hug, squeezing Mia back. "I'm sorry," I hear her whisper.

Arrow looks between us before settling his gaze on me. "If Mia likes her, I do too," he says so only I can hear.

When Mia releases her, Emma scans the faces of the rest of my friends, all pointed in her direction. "I'm sorry I lied about who I was." I love that she comes right out with it instead of skirting around the elephant in the room. "You all were very kind to me, and I should have trusted you with my identity. It was nice to have a weekend with amazing people without the baggage of being who I am, but you deserved better than that from me."

Grace perks up and seems to give Emma more consideration than she has before. "Consider yourself forgiven. We all have reasons for hiding who we are from time to time."

Chris turns to her and presses a kiss to her forehead, making me pretty sure Grace isn't just talking about Emma.

"Who's drinking?" Bailey asks from behind the bar.

Everyone raises their hands in unison. I'm not interested in getting shitfaced tonight, but after this week, a beer with my best friends in the world sounds pretty damn good.

Bailey rattles off the list of Indiana craft beers on tap—a constantly changing assortment I'm proud of—and everyone calls out their order. Grace and Mia opt for the sweet red wine that Bailey keeps behind her counter but doesn't put on the menu.

Emma stays quiet.

"Martini?" I ask with an arched brow.

She laughs. "No, I've made that mistake once already this

month. I'm not due again until next decade." She turns to Bailey. "Do you have any more of that wine?"

Bailey hesitates and looks at me. For her, sharing her sweet red wine is a badge of friendship she's not ready to offer Emma. As much as I'd like her to welcome Emma into our little group, I can't force that, so I wait, letting her make the decision.

"Sure," Bailey says finally, pouring Emma her glass. "But it's cheap as hell and comes in a screwcap bottle."

"Sounds perfect," Emma says, and swallows her first sip.

The TV plays overhead, and Bailey flips through the channels, looking for something more interesting than *Jeopardy*. She stops on one of those gossip entertainment shows and returns to her work behind the counter before I can signal her to change it again.

The lady on the screen rattles off about some pop star who's due to have twins in the next month, and then about a billion-dollar movie franchise that's falling apart, and I listen with one ear until I hear her segue into a discussion of the Rothschild-Dellaconte wedding.

I can't help it. My eyes flick to the screen, and I feel Emma go still beside me.

"The senator released a statement the day after the would-be wedding saying he hoped the press would give Emma privacy until she sorted out this personal matter," the woman on the screen says, "but the bride released her own statement yesterday in which she says, 'I let the pressure of such a public wedding get to me, and my decision to cancel was about the magnitude and spectacle of the wedding, not my commitment to Zachary. I'm still very much in love with him and grateful to have his patience until we can reschedule our vows.'" The woman smiles at the camera. "We here at *Hollywood Tonight* wish Emma and Zachary the very best."

Reschedule? When I turn to Emma, she's staring down into her untouched wine. Everyone else is staring at her too.

It shouldn't fucking matter. It. Shouldn't. Matter.

I slide off my chair and push through the swinging doors into the kitchen. I kick the bucket by the sink, and soapy water rushes out of it. I lean my forehead against the stainless-steel door of a walk-in freezer while I try to get a handle on my temper, because right now I want to break something. They're *postponing* the wedding? She's going through with her fake marriage?

"Keegan?" Emma says behind me, and I stiffen at the sound of her voice.

Water sloshes under her feet as she comes toward me, but I don't turn.

"What's wrong?"

"You're postponing it? You're still planning to marry him? To go through with it?"

She presses the palm of her hand against my back, and the innocent contact makes me want so much more I have to squeeze my eyes shut. "That was the statement my PR people came up with. We'll postpone it indefinitely before quietly splitting. It's less interesting to the press than a runaway bride story, and we need to keep this low profile. For Zachary's sake."

My racing heart slows, and I force myself to take a full breath.

Her hand trails down my back and then is gone. "Please look at me."

I spin around and grab her by the waist, switching our positions so her back is against the freezer. Her hat flies off and I pull off her sunglasses. Her eyes are wide with shock and her pink lips part. "I'm looking, Emma. God help me, I can't stop looking."

CHAPTER 26

EMMA

The stainless steel of the freezer door is cool against my back, a stark contrast to Keegan's heat leaning into me.

"I'm looking at you," he whispers, his gaze locked on my mouth. I lift my hand to his face and skim my thumb along the rough stubble of his jaw, and he swallows hard. "And do you know what I see? I see the woman who broke my heart when I was eighteen." He steps closer and bows his head, leaning his forehead against mine. "I see the woman who tore me apart because she planned to marry another man. When I look at you, I see the woman who walked into my bar in a soaking-wet wedding dress and made me feel whole again. I see the reason I've barely slept the last three nights." His voice is low and husky. "I see someone I want so much it scares me."

My heart is pounding so hard I'm surprised my body isn't vibrating with it. Emboldened by his words and the heat in his eyes, I graze my thumb across his lips, and he catches it and pulls it into his mouth, making my breath catch as he sucks and then releases.

His lips brush over mine lightly, once, twice, only lingering to suck on my bottom lip when I slide a hand into his hair. I'm trembling with a need I can barely contain. The man I've spent the last week dreaming about is right here against me.

He steps back, and I watch him intently. I don't know what this is or where it's going. Am I allowed to touch him? Does he want to touch me?

He skims his fingertips along my jaw and down my neck. He adds the pressure of his palm as he cups my breast through my dress. He brushes a thumb over one nipple then the other, and I gasp.

"Is this what you came here for?" he whispers in my ear. "Is this why you couldn't marry him? Are you here because no one can get you off like I can? Had you forgotten that this body is mine? Had you forgotten what it was like to come so hard you scream?"

The rawness of his words startles me, and I still.

He tugs my earlobe between his teeth. "Don't shut down. Don't do that. Be here with me right now and tell me something you want from me. It can be anything, but I need to know."

I love the feel of his mouth on my neck, his breath against my skin. I might just disintegrate under the heat of his touch, but I would do so happily.

"Right now," he says. "Tell me what you want from me right

in this moment, or I'm walking away."

I take his hand and guide it underneath my dress to where I'm already hot and wet between my legs from nothing more than my fantasies of him.

"Fuck," he murmurs. He rubs his fingers over me and lets his eyes float closed.

I arch into his touch, willing him to take it further, to make me *feel*, begging him with nothing more than the dance of my body under his touch.

He cups my ass with his big hand and lifts me enough to position one thick thigh between mine. His mouth skims over my neck, softly at first and then latching on and sucking as his fingers slide into me. I'm so close. I'm a live wire. All he has to do is stroke me just right, and I'll fall apart.

"I can't decide if you want me or if you're angry with me," I whisper, clinging to reason.

He drags a finger slowly in and out then plunges two back inside me, stretching me and filling me so completely it's almost too much. "You say it like those two things are mutually exclusive. I fucking hate that you lied to me. I'm furious that you almost married someone else a week after being in bed with me. I hate that you never told me about him and that you thought a fake marriage was the best you could do. But right now, I want to feel you come more than I want to be angry." He scrapes his teeth over my shoulder then soothes the spot with soft kisses. "Give this to me. Let me feel you come."

Keegan wanting me is enough. For now. I let the rest drain

away and focus on the heat of his hand between my legs. I focus on the way his touch makes it hard to focus on anything at all. His palm rubs my clit as his fingers stroke in and out, in and out, making my hips arch toward him as I whisper desperate little pleas. "Please, yes, please."

"Please what?"

"Keegan."

"Tell me you're not going back to him," he says into my ear. He steadies himself with one hand pressed against the freezer door by my head. "Fucking promise me that if I have to say goodbye to you again, it won't be so you can become his wife."

"It's over." I wrap my hand around his arm and cling to him. "I promise." And with those words, he presses his mouth against mine, my body squeezes around his fingers, and I come.

"Keegan?" a woman says.

When I open my eyes, I realize Keegan still has his closed; his breathing is rapid and shallow just like mine. He slowly opens his eyes as he pulls his hand out from between my legs.

Bailey's standing at the kitchen entrance, her back to us as if she knows she doesn't want to witness our compromising position. She clears her throat. "Mia's leaving and just wanted to confirm plans with you before she goes."

"Be there in a minute," Keegan says. His eyes search my face. "Are you okay?"

I nod. "Go ahead. I'm fine." But when he steps away and leaves me alone in the kitchen, my legs are wobbly, my hands are shaking, and I feel anything but *fine*.

I find the employee bathroom off the back hallway, and when I return to the kitchen, Bailey's pulling a rack of glasses from the dishwasher. She looks my way before quickly averting her gaze.

"You don't like me, do you?" I ask Bailey when her back is to me.

I can't see her expression, but her hands still where she was drying the top of the rack with a towel. "Should I?"

I draw back. "I know we didn't have the easiest start, what with the weekend in Vegas and everything, but I know you're important to Keegan and I think it'd be nice if we could be friends."

Now she does turn around, and I'm surprised to see her smirking at me. "You have no idea what it's like to have someone not like you, do you? You've never had this happen before."

I scoff. "Obviously, you don't read the papers. All sorts of people hate me."

She shakes her head. "But not in real life. Not someone you've had to deal with every day. You've spent your entire life surrounded by people who either worship you or kiss your ass because they want something from you. And yet here I am, someone you have to interact with if you want to be around Keegan, and I'm not willing to do either. That must be really hard."

I feel like I've been slapped. "You don't know anything about what my life's been like."

Bailey shrugs and sighs as she drops her shoulders. "You're right. I don't know. But here's what I do know: you were with my friend for one summer, and whatever happened between you two during that time was enough to screw him up, and you were with him in Vegas the weekend before you were supposed to get married to another man. Maybe I don't know what happened between you two, but to me that's irrelevant, because whatever it was screwed with his head. And I know that you're here now, and you're screwing with his head again."

"Are you in love with him?" I ask.

She closes her eyes and mutters something under her breath that I think might be *God grant me patience*. "No. I'm not in love with Keegan. I wish I were. Wouldn't it be nice to be with a guy that good? Good dad, good friend." She looks me over and shakes her head. "He's almost perfect if it weren't for his fucking shitty taste in women."

My eyes sting with tears. After all the things that have been said about me through the years, I don't know why this comment from this woman hurts so much. Is she right? Have I never had to deal with someone disliking me whom I actually saw face to face? Can that be true? People dislike me for all kinds of reasons—for the advantages I was born into, for the things my mother has said over the years, even for things said by the character I played on television. I've had people write vicious lies about me in magazines, tear me down on the internet, and critique every inch of my body in the most mean-spirited way possible. Once, I was heading into a charity event and had a woman spit on me from behind the police barricade because her daughter had wanted to see the *Lucy Matters* reunion movie, and since I backed out, that would never happen.

But have I ever had to have someone in my life who didn't like me and was willing to admit it to my face?

"You're right," I finally say.

Her attention is on the soapy water again, and when she turns to me, she's frowning. "About what?"

"About me not being good enough for Keegan. I'm not. And I know I'm not. And five years ago, how much I fell short was so painfully clear to me that I pushed him away. I knew then that he deserved better, and I know now. The only difference is that now I'm going to let him make the choice."

She dries her hands and studies me. The derision I saw on her face earlier fades away. "Okay," she says. "I can respect that."

CHAPTER 27
KEEGAN

"Emma!" Mia says.

When Em walks out of the kitchen, her lips are swollen and her cheeks are flushed. Anyone who looks at her could guess what we were doing back there. I have to take a deep breath, because she looks so fucking fine like that, and all I want to do right now is get her back to my place so we can finish what we started.

"I was just telling Keegan that we're having a pool party at Arrow's dad's tomorrow night. I hope you'll come."

Emma looks to me then back to Mia. "That would be fun. Thank you."

"And then my wedding planner just needs to know if you'll be joining us for the rehearsal Friday? I know the RSVP makes it sound formal, but I promise it's not. It'll be super fast. Easy breezy, I promise. We're going to go to dinner afterward and hanging out. It'll be a good time."

Emma shakes her head. "I don't want to intrude."

"The more the merrier," Bailey says, and I'm surprised when she smiles at Emma and adds, "Come."

Mia grins. "Exactly! Come hang with us. Arrow said we should have just gone to Scotland and gotten married in the mountains or something, and maybe he was right, but I just wanted to keep it casual and still have all my favorite people there."

Emma looks at me, and I nod. "She'll be with me," I say, and I realize that I hope it's true. We were supposed to spend today together, but it's been chaotic from start to finish. I want more time. I know this is temporary. I know we have too much unresolved shit for me to let my heart get involved. But for now, I just want to keep her close.

"I guess I'll see you tomorrow and Friday," Emma says to Mia.

EMMA

Five years ago…

I pin my last curl and slide my pearl earrings into place. When I look at my reflection, I see everything my mother will see: cheeks that are too full, arms that are too soft, a chest that makes me look bigger than I am. (*"Emmacakes, if you got a reduction, you might be able to pass for a twelve. Wouldn't that feel good?"*)

Tomorrow my mother is marrying the man who played my

father on television for ten years, and the media is calling the match *kismet* and droning on about life imitating art. Personally, I keep wondering if she'd go through with it if she knew about me and Harry. About all those years of secrecy and the things he "taught me" off set. I keep wondering if she'd even care if I told her everything or if she'd just tell me I was missing my father and blame my story on an "overactive imagination."

If I told her the truth, she might pull the jealousy card, but I feel nothing resembling jealousy. I just feel sick for her. Harry isn't a good man. A good man wouldn't have seduced a thirteen-year-old girl. He wouldn't have manipulated her into doing things she wasn't ready to do. He wouldn't have fed her insecurities until she felt powerless to end a relationship that had her taking three showers a day until her doctor put her on Prozac for "obsessive-compulsive tendencies"—a diagnosis scribbled onto a prescription pad as casually as someone handing over Tylenol for a headache.

I feel sad for my mother, but ultimately this marriage is her choice to make, so I don't let myself focus much on that. Every day it's been harder and harder to push away this gnawing anxiety about Harry remaining in my life because of this marriage. It's a reality I don't let myself think about much. When I do, I want to crawl out of my own skin and I feel the old compulsions coming back—my daily shower becomes twice as long, my skin red from too much scrubbing when I turn off the water.

My time with Keegan is the only thing keeping me grounded. When I'm with him, I feel pure and whole and *safe,* like Harry exists in another solar system.

Keegan invited me to go to Indiana. He wants me there with him. I don't know what terrifies me more: going with him, or staying here without him. I don't know if I can go through college like a normal student. I don't know if I can leave everything I know in LA behind. But I want to be with him more than I want anything else. I want this summer to be the beginning of something bigger with the first person whose love made me feel like *more* instead of *less*.

"What are you thinking about?" Keegan asks, stepping up behind me in the bathroom. He locks his gaze on mine in the mirror. "You're standing there, the most beautiful thing I've ever seen, but you're looking at your reflection like you're scared of it."

My hand flutters to my chest, and I blink as my reflection seems to transform before my eyes from a catalogue of my faults to a highlight reel of what Keegan loves about me. My dress for tonight is a classic satin black A-line that hits me mid-calf. I'm not petite enough to feel like Audrey Hepburn dressed like this, so I hated myself in it, but through Keegan's eyes I see a woman with curves that make him wild. I see the freckles he likes to trace with his rough fingertips when we have a lazy afternoon in bed. I see my bright blue eyes and the mouth he can't stop staring at.

"I know you don't want to go to this wedding tomorrow," he says. "Is it weddings you hate or this particular one?"

I shake my head. "I love weddings." *It's Harry I hate.* I gasp at the thought. I've never allowed myself to think those words. Maybe it seemed too scary to direct hatred toward the only person before Keegan who showed me affection, as if I should be grateful for his attention, even if it was twisted and manipulative. "I'm just thinking about how strange it is to see my mother marry a man who's not my father." That's true, even if it's not the whole truth.

"What do you think of Harry?" His eyes seem to be asking more from that question than its face value. Or am I reading too much into it?

"I think he's a flirt who loves women more than he loves keeping his promises." I force a smile. "And I hope he makes her happy, but I'm not holding my breath."

"It must be strange, having him as your stepfather when he played your father on television for so many years."

Only because it's a career I left to escape him. I shrug. "I suppose there are people who will remain in our lives no matter what."

"He'll be a fixture in yours now. I'm not sure how I feel about sharing you."

"Then by all means, don't." I smile, but beneath it I'm scared Keegan has seen too much or knows me too well and suspects something between me and Harry. I don't want him to know. I don't want him to see me differently or know that I was too weak when I needed to be strong. Guilt and shame tangle in my chest, wrapping their tentacles around my lungs.

He spins me in his arms and cups my face in his hands. "You know I don't deserve you, right?" He drags his gaze down my body and back up. "You're sexy and sweet. You're so fucking smart and you make me laugh." He brushes his knuckles down the side of my neck. The tentacles loosen their grip on my lungs, and I draw in a full breath. "I need you to know I'm not good enough, but you have me anyway." He dips his head to press a kiss to my bare shoulder. A flutter starts in my belly and radiates out through my fingertips. Air fills my lungs and washes away my fear. I love the way his touch makes me feel. "Have you thought any more about coming to Indiana with me?"

"I think we should talk about what that means." I meet his eyes and feel nothing but warmth and courage. "I don't want to do it if this isn't going somewhere, Keegan, but I don't want to make any assumptions, either. I know that's a crazy thing to say when we're so young, but as much as I love the idea of getting out of California, I do have a home here, and I don't want to leave if—"

He crushes his mouth to mine. Keegan can give the softest, sweetest kisses, but this isn't one. This kiss is him claiming me, and I want to give myself to him more than I want anything. I kiss him back hard—sucking on his bottom lip, twisting my hands into his hair.

When he draws back, he's breathless and so am I. He darts out his tongue as he drags a thumb over my swollen lips. "I don't want this to end," he says. His voice vibrates with the intensity in his words. "I think about you all the time. I know you don't want to leave your home and that the ocean is your favorite place, but that's what you are to me. You are the sea breeze on a hot day." He swallows hard. "You're the morning sun off the water and the promise of a fresh start. You're the closest thing I've ever had to *home* and the best thing that's ever happened to me. If you stay with me, I'll get you back to the sea after college. I promise you that. And I know that it's insane to think that a guy like me could have you—"

I hold my fingertips to his lips, and they're shaking, but not from fear. I'm trembling with joy. "Don't do that. Don't do that *guy like me* thing. Don't act like you're not worthy of me."

He shakes his head and pulls my hand away. "I'm *not*, Emma. I'm selfish and I'm greedy." He swallows. "But I'm working on it. For you, I want to be better."

"We both carry darkness in us. What if it drags us under?"

He brings my hand to his mouth and kisses my knuckles. "It's nearly as powerful as what I feel for you. I don't sit around thinking about weddings. But I do think about life with you and what that might look like. I've thought a time or two about you in a wedding dress with your blue stone in the hollow of your neck. If someday I get to be the man who unzips that dress, who leads you to his bed and gets to look at you wearing nothing but the sapphire that matches your eyes… So maybe I don't have wedding plans, but when I say I want you to come with me to Indiana, I mean that I want you in my life permanently. I mean that I'm in love with you."

I rise onto my toes and press my mouth to his. *God, I want this.* This man, this life he describes, the warmth I feel when I'm with him, so different from the twisted, used feeling I had with Harry that my mind rejects any comparison.

"I love you too," I whisper. "I'll go. I want to go."

He meets my eyes and draws in a shaky breath. "I want to get you naked and make a mess of your hair so badly right now." I grin. "Later. I promise." He groans, and I laugh. "But suddenly I'm in the mood to wear my sapphire. Would you go get it for me?"

His nostrils flare and he slides a hand under my skirt to cup my ass. "It's going to be a *long* night," he says, stroking the lace edge.

"Get my necklace and maybe I'll give you something to hold you over until later."

He arches a brow then rushes out of the bathroom. Five minutes ago, I was standing here filled with dread, but now I can't stop smiling. "Where is it?" he asks.

I follow him into the bedroom, where he has my jewelry box open. "It should be hanging on the left side."

He frowns and shakes his head. "I don't see it."

I join him. The hook where I keep my sapphire is empty, but everything else is hanging in its place. "Maybe I misplaced it." I pull open the other drawers and then search my bathroom. I'm never careless with that necklace, but I can't find it anywhere. Keegan looks panicked, and I squeeze his arm. "Don't worry. It'll show up." I hope I'm right, but if there was any magic in that necklace, it did its job by bringing me to Keegan.

CHAPTER 28
EMMA

Keegan doesn't speak on the drive home, and by the time he pulls his SUV into the garage, I'm convinced he regrets what we did at the bar.

I follow him silently into the house, and when he turns to close the door behind me, he doesn't move from his spot, blocking my path through the hallway.

"Do you regret it?" he asks softly. It's dark, but the light from his porch comes in the window and lets me see that his gaze is locked on my mouth.

"Regret what?" *I regret so much.*

He steps forward and lifts his hand but drops it before he touches my face. "Tonight. Letting me touch you."

I shake my head. "Only if it's going to make you pull away from me."

His neck moves as he swallows. "Do I look like I'm pulling

away?"

I don't have a chance to reply because he kisses me. As his mouth slants over mine, he slides one of those big hands into my hair, and I'm reminded how small he makes me feel. Not in the bad way, not small and powerless. His big hands, sweet touches, and tenderness paired with the way he's always been in awe of me. His hot eyes on my body and his groans of encouragement as he touches me. He can somehow make me feel small and powerful at the same time.

Someone clears her throat, and the sound pulls my attention down the hall where Olivia is standing with her arms crossed. She hits the wall, and the hallway floods with light. "Welcome home, lovebirds."

A man steps up behind her, and I hear his low, rich chuckle before I see his face. "Well, would you look at that."

Keegan's slower to turn, but when he does, the blood drains from his face. "Dad? When did you get here?"

KEEGAN

I instinctively step in front of Emma, as if she's naked and I need to shield her from their eyes. But the truth is, the damage has been done. My dad knows she's here.

"Olivia told me your actress friend was visiting," Dad says. "Honestly, I didn't believe it. I thought she dumped you for that old man years ago."

Behind me, Emma gasps, and I can practically hear her flinch. That's my dad for you, casually throwing someone's biggest secret into casual conversation at the first possible moment.

"Dad, why don't you grab a beer and go to the patio. I'll meet you out there in a minute."

My father smirks and nods to Emma before leaving the hallway. A few seconds later, I hear the patio door slide open then closed again.

Olivia shifts her gaze in the direction of the back door and me. "Should I not have said anything?"

"I told you I don't want him in my house." My jaw is tight. I turn to Emma. This day hasn't gone as I planned. Everything's been a mess. I fully intended to come home and finish what we started at the bar. I want so much more, but I have a house that's too fucking full, and I can't take her to my bed like I planned. It's time for triage. I squeeze her hand, barely keeping myself from pulling her whole body against mine. "Are you okay?"

"I'm…" She drags her bottom lip between her teeth and then grins at me. "All things considered, it wasn't a terrible night."

Jesus Christ. "It certainly had its high points." I cup her face and skim my thumb along her jaw. "You get some sleep, and we'll talk tomorrow."

She nods. "Okay. Goodnight."

I wait for her to retreat to her bedroom before I grab a beer for myself and follow my dad out onto the patio. He's sitting in one of the Adirondack chairs around the fire pit, gazing up at the stars.

"And here I thought you'd never talk to her again," he says. "I guess I'm the only one you hold grudges against, huh?"

"Dad, you can't tell anyone she's here. She…" What can I say? Not the truth, obviously. He can't have that. The information is too valuable, and I don't trust him with it.

"She's obviously not rescheduling like they're saying online." He arches a brow. "Unless she is and you were just kissing some other man's fiancé back there."

"What do you want from me?"

"A relationship," he says. "A chance."

"A chance for what?"

"I'm old. I'm lonely. I'm not running cons anymore, and life is a fucking bore. I want to spend time with my son and get to know my granddaughter. I'm not a bad man."

You kind of are, Dad. You're kind of the definition of a bad man. "Prove it. You handle this situation like someone who's not looking for easy money, you prove that you're out of the game, that you're living clean now, and you can be part of my life."

"Trips to Disney with my granddaughter?" he asks. "Sunday dinners? All that?"

"Sundays are a little rough for me, Dad."

"Oh, right. Because you're an NFL hotshot now." There's no bitterness in his words this time, and he smiles. "Goddamn, I still can't believe you lucked out on that one."

"That makes two of us."

He draws in a long breath. "Okay. I can prove it. I don't have anything against that girl, except for how she hurt you."

"We both know I wasn't innocent." I hold his gaze for a long beat. "Got a place to stay while you're in town?"

"Well, I was gonna stay here, but it looks like you're all full up. I can get a room."

"Do you have money?"

"Enough. I'll take care of it, and I'll prove to you I'm a changed man."

I want to believe him. I want to believe I won't be seeing pictures of me and Emma in the papers tomorrow morning or reading a story about how she's run to her old lover. I'm not sure I should believe him, but I want to, because other than hope, there's not much I can do about the fact that my dad saw Emma in my arms tonight. Not much other than say a little prayer of thanks that he doesn't know even more than he does.

KEEGAN

Five years ago...

I storm into my apartment and yank the door open to my father's bedroom. He's sitting in a chair watching TV. When he sees me, he flashes a dopey grin.

"Give it back," I say.

"Give what back?"

"You fucking know what I'm talking about. Her necklace.

Give it back. What the fuck, Dad? When did we become common criminals? I thought the point of what we do is that they gladly give us the money. We never take what they don't want to give. Isn't that what you told me?"

"She would've gladly given you the money." He shifts his gaze back to the TV as if he's grown bored with our conversation. "You just didn't take what you were owed."

"She doesn't owe me shit."

"Not now, she doesn't."

"Jesus Christ. How did you do it, anyway? I get that I was an idiot to believe you gave me your only key, but how did you bypass the security system? There's no fucking way you know the code."

He smirks and wags a finger at me. "See? Your problem is that you only see the most obvious solutions. Need into a house with a security system? You have to have the code. That's pretty basic thinking, but someone using the brain God gave them would get into the condo when the alarm wasn't activated."

"We *always* set the alarm when we leave. *Always.*"

He arches a brow, and I feel like I've been punched in the gut. Because we always set the alarm when we leave, but we don't always set it when we get home, especially when we're anxious to get in the door. Last night we came in from the beach, hands all over each other. We were both desperate to get inside, and I kicked the door shut behind me and we went straight to the shower. Anyone who had a key to the complex and was keeping tabs on us could have easily used that opportunity to walk straight into the condo, walk into the bedroom, and take whatever they wanted.

"You're a fucking bottom-feeding, simple thief," I spit. "After all that bullshit you've fed me all these years, this just proves you don't even buy your own lies."

"The only thing it proves is that I know how to finish a job."

"Where is it?" I'm gonna be sick. It's gone. He's taken it and it's gone, and it's all my fault. But this panic isn't just about the necklace. It's the sick reminder that I'm never going to be able to escape him. My father will always lurk in the background, waiting for his chance for a payday. If I refuse to be part of his schemes, he'll find a way to prove he's smarter, more conniving, and that he'll always win in the end.

"I already sold it," he mutters, flipping through a stack of mail. He takes an envelope from the middle, balls it up, and tosses it into the trash can. "Does this mean we can leave now? I'm so fucking over this town."

"Yeah. Leave anytime you want. What are you waiting for?"

He arches a brow. "Come on, then, pack your bags."

"I'm not going with you. Never again."

He leans his head back and stares at the ceiling in exasperation. "You sound like the little boy who wouldn't go with me because he still believed his mom was coming back."

I flinch, abs flexing as if his blow to the gut was physical. "I'm done. I'm out. I'm not playing your games anymore. I want to be better than that."

"Better than me, you mean. You think you're better than a guy who took a little boy in out of the kindness of his own heart? You think you're better than the man who raised you? The man who gave you food and shelter when your mom would've gladly turned you over to the foster system? You're better than the man who stayed in that stupid little town for three years just so you could play ball?" He pushes out of his chair and steps toward me, his eyes angrier than I've ever seen them. "But I'm a piece of trash, right? That what you're saying?"

I feel like I'm being torn in half. He did all that for me. He did more for me than my own damn mother and he didn't have to do shit. But I can't be the man he wants me to be and also be with Emma. "You do what you need to do. You get your money and lead your life how you want. But I'm *out*. I'm *done*."

He shakes his head. "You really think she's not playing you? I really hate to see it happen. You stand there and spit on me, but I still hate to see your heart break."

"She's not gonna hurt me." My voice breaks on the words, but I'm so fucking pissed at him, and I don't know what to do with all of this rage brewing inside me. Do I take it out on the only adult who ever bothered stepping up to be my parent?

"Okay. Just wait. Maybe you'll prove me wrong." But his smile is so big, I can tell he believes I'm the one who's wrong.

Turning away from the man who raised me, I rush out the door. My hands shaking with helpless anger, I text Emma to let her know something's come up and I won't be over tonight. Then

I go to the maps function on my phone and pull up every pawn shop in a fifty-mile radius. Tonight, I'll be looking for a blue sapphire necklace that I can't afford but am determined to return to Emma.

CHAPTER 29
EMMA

I take my time getting ready for bed. I brush my teeth, wash my face, and moisturize my arms and legs with the faintly scented lotion I picked up at the store. Back in my room, I hear Olivia get ready for bed then hear Keegan showing his dad to the front door. I wait for him to come to me, but I don't know if I'm waiting for him to say something about what happened earlier or hoping he'll pick up where he left off.

But he doesn't come, and I'm left alone in his guest bedroom, my body buzzing and my mind analyzing the events of the night from every angle. Did he not want to come in here because of Olivia, or did he change his mind? Is he still angry with me, and if he is, why is he bringing me to the wedding rehearsal as his date? Or did his dad say something to him about our arrangement?

I close my eyes and say a little prayer it isn't the last. I doubt I'll be able to sleep anytime soon, so I scroll through social media on my phone and jump in surprise when it rings.

I sigh in exasperation when I see my mom's number on the display. With a quick swipe on the screen, I hold the phone to my ear. "Mom, I'm sorry, but I told you I just need some time. I'm not ready to talk about it yet."

She doesn't reply.

"Hello?"

There's breathing on the other end of the line, and the hair stands up on the back of my neck. "Harry? Is that you?"

"I'm just worried about my girl," he says, his words curling in so hard on each other that I can practically smell the whiskey on his breath.

I climb out of bed as if movement could keep my skin from crawling. For five years, I've tried to stay off Harry's radar, and if I've been unsuccessful there, I've at least managed to keep him out of my life. I've changed my number a couple of times and avoided nights at my mom's at all costs. I've done what was necessary.

I squeeze my eyes shut, willing this to be a bad dream. "There's nothing to worry about. Don't call me again."

"Don't hang up. Let me hear your voice." His breathing sounds funny. A familiar funny from my nightmares that leaves me feeling thirteen again and makes bile surge from my belly.

I hang up my phone and throw it across the room. I back up until I hit a wall, then I sink to the floor, where I wrap my arms around my legs. I'm shivering.

I think Zachary knew that no matter how long it had been

since Harry touched me, part of the reason I wanted to get married was because I thought it would keep Harry that much further away.

As much as I've wanted to believe my fears were irrational, every time my life collided with Harry's, he'd do something to remind me that diligence isn't a choice. A man crazy enough to marry a woman to be closer to her daughter is a man crazy enough to break through any barrier to get what he wants.

Zachary always believed me. I think Keegan would have too. If I'd told him.

KEEGAN

I sit up straight at the sound of my bedroom door opening and see Emma's wild curls silhouetted against the hallway light. "Emma? Is everything okay?"

She steps into the room. "I'm sorry." The words come out too small, and if there was any part of me that thought she might be coming in here to finish what we started at the bar, the thought scatters the second I hear her voice.

"Come in here."

She closes the door behind her, shutting out the little light I had to see her by.

"Is everything okay?" I click on a lamp, and her eyes dart to the corners of the room as if she's waiting for the boogeyman to jump out and grab her.

When her eyes come to rest on me, her shoulders sag. "I don't want to sleep alone."

"So don't." I pull back the covers and pat the bed, and she slides in next to me and reaches to turn off the light. Only, once the room goes dark, she shivers so hard the whole bed shakes.

I roll to my side and wrap an arm around her, pulling her back against my front. Her hair tickles my nose, and her scent fills my head. I kiss her bare shoulder. "What can I do?"

"This," she says. I both hear and feel her fill her lungs and then feel her belly flatten as she presses the air out. "Just hold me."

I wish I could see her face. More than that, I wish I could get her to say something. Anything would be better than relying on this sense of doom that's too familiar. I remember getting this vibe from her five years ago, and the next day she left me a note full of apologies telling me she loved me enough to let me go. Is she leaving me again? Maybe, but I have to remember, this time she was never mine.

KEEGAN

Five years ago...

I found the necklace. I had to put down everything I saved from our last three cons to make the guy promise to hold it for me. This afternoon I'm going to the bank about taking out a small signature loan, but I found it and soon I'll be able to give it back to her, and in a couple weeks we'll head to Indiana. Maybe we can go sooner than planned. Maybe we'll head out after her mom's wedding. We'll leave this place as soon as we can and start over.

Normally, the idea of emptying my bank account would panic me—that's the way it works when you've been responsible for the bills since you were twelve—but I just know everything is going to fall into place as long as we're together.

"What are you daydreaming about?" Dad asks.

I'm sitting at the kitchen table with my laptop, trying to get everything in order to attend Blackhawk Hills University in the fall. I still haven't registered for classes or figured out where Em and I are going to live.

I bite back a smile at the idea of sharing an apartment with her. "Nothing," I say, shutting my computer. "What's up?"

He shakes his head and stares at me. I know he's been pissed at me since he learned I have no intention of taking money from Emma, but I never would have guessed him to be a common thief.

"Why are you looking at me like that?" I ask.

"I'm trying to decide if I should let you live in ignorance and have your heart broken later, or if I should go ahead and break your heart now."

My neck stiffens. I can feel him leeching my good mood from me, and I don't want any of it. I found the necklace, and she's coming with me. I don't need to focus on anything else. "Break my heart *how*?"

"It happens to the best of us. We go in for a simple con, and the next thing we know, our feelings are involved and we don't want to do it anymore. That would be one thing, but the sting comes when we find out we're the ones being conned. It happened to me with your mom." He shakes his head. "I fell hard for that woman and she got everything."

"Why are we talking about my mother?"

"Your mother was my Emma Rothschild."

I roll my eyes. "That doesn't make any sense. Emma and Mom are nothing alike."

"Wake up and see that she's conning you, son."

"Emma Rothschild, who has more money than God, is conning *me*. What exactly is she going to get out of that, Dad?"

"You're the perfect alibi. You're the perfect cover-up for the fact that she's fucking her mom's fiancé."

My irritated amusement washes away in a rush. *Harry.* I never liked the way he looked at her. And that time I walked in and he was standing closer to her than he should, closer than a man should stand to his future stepdaughter. The way she spun away from him quickly, as if she'd been caught doing something she shouldn't, even though they were just standing there. "Don't fuck with me," I warn Dad quietly.

"You can understand why I didn't want to tell you," he says. "I knew you'd think I was just after the money. But people like her have no use for people like us, not as long-term fixtures in our lives." He tosses a stack of glossy four-by-sixes on the table, turns around, and walks to the door. "You're my son, and I don't want you hurt."

The pictures are of Harry entering Emma's building, and the dates printed on the bottom range from the beginning of the summer to the end. The last one in the stack is from last night. While I was scraping together every last cent to get her grandmother's sapphire necklace back for her, Harry was going into her building.

"This doesn't prove anything," I say, my words too tight.

"It only proves that he 'visits' her a lot," he says, putting air quotes around the word. "Anything more is yours to find out, I guess." He sighs, as if it's all of no more consequence than a gallon of expired milk. "I'm heading out. I met a woman last night who seemed to like me."

I don't ask if he's going to see the woman for work or pleasure. I don't ask if he ever stayed long enough after taking these pictures of Harry to know how long the man stayed. I don't promise to see him later. I just listen for the door to click closed. I don't know how long I stare at the image of him going into her building from last night, a bouquet of daisies in his hand.

There has to be an explanation, but the seed of doubt has been planted. *"She's conning you, son."*

Extending my arm, I sweep it across the table, scattering the prints to the floor. "Fuck!" The word comes out as a guttural roar.

CHAPTER 30
EMMA

"You know, you can come out here," Olivia calls from the kitchen. "I don't bite."

Yes, but you remind me of why I shouldn't be here. And right now that's not a reminder that I want.

After waking up alone in Keegan's bed, I slipped into the bathroom, where I could hear Olivia and Keegan out in the kitchen feeding the baby breakfast. Unwilling to intrude on their family time, I went straight from the bathroom to the guest bedroom, where I've been reading—or pretending to read—ever since. Keegan said goodbye about thirty minutes ago. He stepped into my room dressed in well-worn jeans and a soft gray Gators T-shirt, baby Jazzy in his arms.

"Jazz and I are going to the Daddy and Me morning at the public library. Do you need anything before I go?"

I promised him I didn't and waved goodbye to the baby. She

smiled at me and waved back. It felt awesome, until I heard Olivia send them on their way and remembered again that I'm in the way.

Olivia pokes her head in. "I'm making cookies. Do you like to bake?"

Keegan just took their child to a Daddy and Me morning at the library, and she's *making cookies*. I shouldn't be here. I'm in the way of everything Keegan has wanted for the last two years. And why? He hasn't given me any indication that he wants to be with me or that he sees this going anywhere. He touched me at the bar and in the hallway last night, but he didn't seem to have any problem sharing his bed with me without it turning into anything more.

I lied in that letter I left him five years ago—the letter he returned to me on my wedding day. I didn't know I was lying, but I was. The truth is, I love him in a selfish way too. I love him because he makes me better and I feel better when I'm around him. I love him because it's easier to breathe when he's close. If the letter had been the truth, I wouldn't be here now, bringing my drama into his world. At the very least, I should have left when Olivia showed up.

"Thank you," I tell the sweet-faced brunette. "I'd love to help, but I'm kind of a disaster in the kitchen."

"Well, come keep me company, then." She turns and leaves the room as if she expects me to follow, so I do.

There's a mixer on the counter and what I imagine are the ingredients for cookies sitting by various bowls and measuring cups and spoons. I take a seat on one of the stools at the island and watch her as she gets to work.

"Keegan eats so healthy," she says, measuring out the flour. "And he's not tempted by much, but he loves my oatmeal chocolate chip cookies. He says they're the best thing he's ever tasted."

I swallow hard. She's so domestic. *She's his baby's mother.* "It's nice of you to make them for him."

"Oh, I have ulterior motives." She grins and dumps the flour into a bowl. "I'm trying to bake my way back into his heart."

Oh yeah, I definitely shouldn't be here. She wouldn't be telling me all of this if she didn't want me to know I'm in the way. Keegan's words in Vegas ring in my brain. *I'd bend over backwards if I thought I could make it work with Olivia.* "You're hoping for a second chance."

She snorts. "Second? This would be more like a sixth chance. Maybe eighth, depending how you count." She shakes her head. "I'm pretty sure I blew it with him. I wish I hadn't." She dips a measuring spoon into a box of baking soda. "Did you know that Keegan was a massive player in college?"

I bite my lip and shake my head, not trusting myself to speak. I don't want to admit that the only things I know about the last five years of Keegan's life came from social media.

"I'm not kidding. The boy had a way with the girls. They loved him. He knows what to say to make you feel good. He knows how to look at you and make you believe no other woman could ever measure up when, in reality, you're no more important to him than the last girl." She sighs. "It's a skill, for sure."

It's like she crawled into my memories and saw my first dates with Keegan. The only difference between how he made me feel and what she described is that I never stopped believing I was that special to him. I don't like thinking that he moved on from me and made every girl he came across feel the way I felt with him. It cheapens my fondest memories.

I prop my elbows on the counter, choosing to be hypnotized by the easy way she works rather than obsess over the implications of what she's telling me. There's something comforting about watching her work. It's as if she's made this recipe so many times she doesn't even have to think about what she's doing. "So, he had a lot of girlfriends?"

She laughs and tosses her dark hair over her shoulder. "Not girlfriends. He doesn't let people close enough for that. Here he is, this really easygoing player who doesn't have a care in the world. Nobody takes him seriously. They think he's all jokes and good times because he never lets anyone dig past the surface."

"I understand not wanting to share your past with everyone. Maybe he doesn't want sympathy. Keegan's had such a hard life."

Olivia grunts and sifts the dry ingredients together. "I guess I don't know. He's never been real big on sharing his past with me. I've gotten more information about his childhood from his father than from him."

That information is more satisfying than it should be. Keegan opened up to me on the very first date. We just clicked like that. And by the second date, he was sharing his tough memories. There did come a point where he seemed to stop talking about his past. If I brought up his mother or Blackhawk Valley, he'd change the subject. "He can be a little closed off, I guess."

"A little?" She taps the bowl of dry ingredients, settling everything into the bottom before moving to the empty bowl beside it and measuring out oil. "You, for example," she says, glancing up at me before looking back down to the bowl. "He never mentioned you. Not once."

"Really?" I snap my mouth shut, wishing I could take the word back. It's not like I want him to go around bragging about his summer with me, but to not even share it with the woman he desperately wanted a family with? Was I that insignificant?

I swallow hard. I can't let my old insecurities get to me now, but it would be so easy to question just how important I am to him.

"But now here you are." Her jaw hardens but she forces a smile. "Sleeping in his bed while I'm in the next room."

My phone rings, rattling against the stone of the island.

Olivia frowns at the display. "Is everything okay?"

The screen reads *Home*. I bite my bottom lip and nod. "I think so." I swipe the screen and put the phone to my ear. "Mom? Is that you?"

"Emma," he says softly. "I need you to hear me out."

I feel my body go hard from the inside out, flesh turning to stone to protect me from that voice. "I told you to stop calling me, Harry." I shake my head. "Stop. Calling. Me." Taking the phone from my ear, I tap the screen to end the call, and only then do I realize Olivia is staring at me with wide eyes.

KEEGAN

"Thank you for including me tonight," Emma says as I pull off the road and onto the long drive that leads up to the Woodison estate. She seems excited about coming tonight rather than nervous. "You didn't have to, but I'm glad you did, and I'm glad your friends don't hate me for lying to them in Vegas."

"They're good people," I say softly. "I'm lucky to call them my friends."

"Bailey said something to me last night," she says as I park the car in Arrow's drive.

"What's that?" I cut the engine and pull the key from the ignition.

Em drops her gaze to her hands. "She said I've never had to deal with someone who didn't either kiss my ass or worship me. She's wrong, of course. She obviously hasn't met my mother." She laughs, but it's a little forced. "But in a lot of ways, I'm thinking maybe she's right. I'm twenty-three years old and have no idea who I am. I almost married a man who doesn't love me just so I wouldn't have to be alone." She turns to me and holds my gaze, and the seconds stretch out between us. "What are you thinking?"

You wouldn't be alone if you hadn't pushed me away. If there was something specific that brought her to me last night, she hasn't told me what it was. All I know is that the tension so evident in her posture when she walked into my bedroom seemed to melt away when she was with me, and it felt damn good to sleep with her in my arms.

I woke up in the middle of the night rock hard, my hand already up her shirt absently stroking the underside of her breasts. She moaned softly in her sleep and rolled toward me.

It hurt to pull my hand away, to stop touching her and make myself take some slow, deep breaths and think of anything but her soft body and how naturally she responds to my touch. It's not that I don't think she would have wanted me to wake her up and touch her. I'm pretty sure she'd have happily gone along if that was where I'd taken our night in bed together. But our middle-of-the-night drunken decision in Vegas was hardly a decision at all. It was something we let happen and she might just regret. I'm not sure a vulnerable half-asleep decision made in the dark would be much better.

If we're going to sleep together again, I want lights, eye contact, and sobriety. I want her decision to come to my bed to be deliberate.

I want everything.

I slide one hand into her hair and study her perfect face. Blue eyes that remind me of the ocean she loves so much and soft pink lips that haunt my dreams. "Don't worry about Bailey. She means well but doesn't understand what's between us."

Her tongue darts out to wet her lips. "What is between us?" she whispers.

I trail my thumb along her cheek before sweeping it over her lips. "A lot of secrets, mistakes, lies." I drop my hand and force myself to take a deep breath, but that just fills my head with her scent, and that alone turns me on. This morning, I caught the smell of her shampoo when I was in the shower, and my head filled so completely with ideas of going back to my room and waking her up, of keeping her in my bed. I had to turn the water cold just to keep myself in check.

"That's all?" she asks. "Secrets, mistakes, and lies? That's all we have?"

I swallow hard. "And something that just keeps bringing us back together no matter how hard we try to fight it."

Her lips part and she drops her gaze to my mouth. "Are you going to kiss me?"

I tuck my keys into my pocket. "Not right now."

Her cheeks bloom red but she cocks her head and asks, "Why not?"

My pulse kicks up at that invitation. "Because my house is empty and my bed is waiting. Because this might be the last time the whole crew hangs out together here, and tasting you will tempt me to miss it. Because if I kiss you now, I'm going to want to take you home and keep kissing you." I smile at the sight of her pulse thrumming wildly at the base of her neck. "*Everywhere*."

"Oh."

I lean forward and let my lips brush her ear. "Because I want you to spend the next four hours thinking about me touching you." With that, I swing my door open and step out of the car and walk around to open her door.

"I really want you to kiss me right now," she says as she climbs out.

I grin and turn toward the back gate and the sounds of my friends' voices. "Then my work here is done."

CHAPTER 31

EMMA

*K*eegan's *going to make love to me tonight.* My skin hums in anticipation, and all night long, I've struggled to keep my mind on the conversation around me.

Arrow's father's place is beautiful, and the backyard is perfect for gatherings like these, complete with an outdoor kitchen, stone fire pit, and an elevated spa that circulates into the pool. The guys all seem at ease here, making themselves at home and going in and out of the house as they need to.

We goofed around in the pool a little before changing and having dinner, and now everyone's sitting around the fire pit. The guys are passing around some fancy whiskey Mason picked up in Europe over Christmas.

"Look who decided to join us!" Bailey says when another couple comes in through the gate.

The man is tall and has some serious artwork on his thickly

muscled arms. If I had to guess, I'd bet he's a football player too. The girl is beautiful, with dark hair and a constant smile.

"Emma," Keegan says, nodding to his friends. "This is Alex and Sebastian. You didn't get to meet them in Vegas because they were home with their new baby. You guys, this is Emma, an old friend of mine."

"I watched your show when I was a kid," Alex says, offering her hand. I shake it and notice that she's scarred from the side of her face down her neck.

"It's nice to meet you," Sebastian says. "Sorry we couldn't make it sooner. My sister's watching the baby for us tonight, but we didn't want to leave until Jazzy was asleep."

"Olivia's your sister?" I ask, looking between Keegan and Sebastian. I wonder how that works. Does Sebastian wish Keegan would make his sister settle down?

"That's what they tell me," Sebastian says, grinning, and he and Alex take seats around the fire.

The conversation turns to football and who got the best picks in the draft before circling back to how they all feel about leaving Blackhawk Valley.

Mason leans back in his chair and stretches his long legs out in front of him as he scans the scene before him. "It feels like the end of an era."

Sebastian sighs and nods, doing the same look-around Mason did. "Sure does. All those summer days at this pool amounted to something pretty amazing, though." He squeezes Alex's hand and they smile at each other.

"Only good things coming," Mia says.

"So, did you all grow up in Blackhawk Valley?" I ask. I love being surrounded by all their happy faces. These people have truly become lifelong friends.

Mia grins and points people out one by one. "Bailey, Sebastian, Alex, Arrow, and I did."

I shoot a glance in Keegan's direction. "That's it? No one else?"

The smile falls from her face and she locks eyes with Arrow before she says, "Brogan grew up here too."

Arrow bows his head. "I fucking miss that son of a bitch."

Bailey gives me a sad smile. "He died in an accident during his junior year at BHU. A drunk driver, hit and run."

I gasp. "That's terrible." Everyone is so solemn that I don't mention they forgot Keegan. Heck, maybe he didn't hang with them until college. Maybe they forget he lived here for a few years as a kid before coming back to play ball at BHU. "I'm sorry about your friend."

Bailey winces. "Yeah. Me too." She climbs out of her chair and heads into the house without another word.

"I'm so sorry," I say. "I had no idea. I didn't mean to bring up a bad memory."

Mason's jaw works as he watches her go. It's not until the door clicks closed behind her that he drags in a long, slow breath and turns to me. "How would you know?"

My gaze darts to the door and back to Mason. "So Bailey and Brogan were together, then?"

"No," Mia says. "My brother, Nic, also died in that accident."

She swirls her drink in her cup.

"Bailey was in love with him," Mason says, and the words seem to piss him off. He stands and gathers beer bottles and throws them into the recycling bin with more force than necessary.

The complicated dynamic between Mason and Bailey makes more sense now. She was in love with someone else, and he died, leaving Mason to compete with a dead man. "It's awful," I say. "I really am so sorry."

"Don't apologize," Arrow says. "I'm never sorry to talk about Brogan and Nic. We should remember how quickly it can all be yanked away."

Heads bob in agreement around the fire, and Keegan reaches for my hand and squeezes.

"Excuse me." I stand. "I'm going to use the restroom. Can I get anyone a drink while I'm in there?"

"You're a saint," Mia says, hoisting a bottle of wine into the air and flipping it upside down to show it's empty. "We need a new bottle, if you don't mind."

"It's my pleasure." I head into the house and to the guest bathroom Mia showed me shortly after we arrived. I'm still a little mortified that I brought up such a sad subject, and I can see my embarrassment in the mirror when I wash my hands. The thing is, even if it was something they didn't want to talk about, I don't think this group would hold it against me. That's just not how they are.

I shut off the light and step out of the bathroom, only to realize my path is blocked by a couple standing in the dark hall.

I look away quickly, but not before I see him kissing her. Bailey's back is against the wall, her arms around his neck.

"Please, Bailey." Mason's voice, low and deep. "Don't fucking do this anymore."

"What we did in Vegas…" She shakes her head and her voice trembles. "It was a mistake. If anyone finds out…"

He leans his forehead against hers. "I told you we'd talk about it after the wedding."

I don't think they have any idea that I'm here, so I turn back and clear my throat, embarrassed to catch them in such a private moment. "Excuse me."

They jump apart, as if I caught them doing something wrong.

"Sorry," Bailey mutters, and Mason steps aside to let me through.

I grab the wine and head out back to give it to Mia.

"Did you see Bailey in there?" she asks.

Swallowing, I nod. I don't want to betray anyone's secrets. "I think she's okay."

"I think we're going to head out," Keegan says before I can sit.

"Thank you so much for coming," Mia says, and everyone stands as we say our goodbyes.

Keegan's quiet as we climb into the car and on the way home. I feel like I ruined the vibe of the evening when my questions led to talk about their friend Brogan.

I don't know if I should say anything to Keegan about what I saw in the hall or if Bailey would be upset if I told him, so I decide I'll assume it's a secret unless Bailey tells me otherwise. "Do you think Bailey and Mason will figure it out and end up together?"

"I do," he says. "Maybe it's naïve, but there's not one couple in that group who hasn't had to work through some serious shit." He cuts his eyes to me before looking back to the road. "Everyone has secrets. Everyone has made mistakes they have to overcome." He reaches across the console and squeezes my thigh. "In the past I might not have believed that people could forgive some of the shit they have, but that crew makes me optimistic. They make me believe anything's possible."

"I like that. I mean, it means more, doesn't it? If you fought for the love you have?"

"Yeah, I guess so." His voice is thick. "Thank you for coming tonight."

"Are you kidding me? Every time I get to spend time around you and your friends, I feel like a different person." I bite my lip. "I mean that in a good way. It's nice to have a group like that. I don't take for granted that everyone's been so welcoming. Even Olivia took time to talk to me today."

His hand stills on my thigh. "What did you two talk about?"

I study him, wishing there were lights along this dark country road so I could see his face. "She told me you were a player in college. That you slept around a lot and had a way of making women feel important but never letting them in."

I hear him swallow. "I've never been very good at letting people get close. That was Olivia's biggest complaint about me." He turns to me briefly before putting his attention back on the road. "I came to BHU with a broken heart and I didn't ever want to go through that again."

I exhale slowly. "Does it make me a basic bitch that I want you to tell me I was different? That I wasn't just the first in a long line of girls you made feel special?"

His hand moves up my thigh and his fingertips slide under them hem of my dress. "Do you really doubt that?"

My hips lift off the seat, instinctively arching closer to his touch. "I don't want to, but the way she described it..."

"You left me, Emma. Not the other way around."

I close my eyes. I can't think when his hot hand is on my skin, moving ever so slightly. Making me want more.

"Did you do what I told you to do?"

"What?"

"I told you I wanted you to spend the night thinking about me touching you." His hand inches higher, and I exhale, my thighs clenching, my body aching for *more* and *now*.

"I did," I confess. "I thought about it a lot."

"Olivia's staying at Sebastian and Alex's place with Jazzy tonight." He pulls into the garage and turns off the car before turning to me. His eyes are hot and searching and his hand inches higher still, his fingers curling and his fingertips brushing against my panties. "Stay in my bed again tonight."

I gasp. "Yes."

Suddenly his hand, so close to where I wanted it a breath ago, is gone, and he's out of the car and opening my door. I climb out, and he closes the door behind me then presses me against it, kissing me hard and hungry, hands in my hair, tongue sliding and demanding. Gasping, I respond in kind, showing him this is what I want, what I've been thinking about, what I've been waiting for.

I cling to him and we stumble, kissing and touching as we make our way into the house.

He kicks the door closed behind us, and when his hands leave my hair, I moan in protest, but then I feel cool air against my back, and when he steps away, my dress falls to the floor. He flips a switch, and light floods the hallway.

The air in the house is cool, leaving trails of goosebumps over my skin, but his eyes are hot as he inspects every inch of me. It's as if I can feel each inch his eyes skim over, as if each moment that he looks is a promise of something he wants to do. He takes in my black lace bra and panties.

He cups one breast in his hand and skims a thumb over the lace. "Are these new?"

"Yes," I whisper. My breasts grow heavier under his inspection, my nipples hardening and aching for his touch. His gaze drifts down over my belly and over the triangle of lace between my legs.

"Were you hoping I'd see them?"

I feel like I'm tied together by a thin string and I'll scatter on the breeze with his slightest touch. "Yes."

"Take them off." His voice comes out rough and tight in a way I don't recognize. As if maybe, just maybe, he's spent as much time thinking about this as I have.

My hands tremble as I reach behind my back and unclasp my bra. It falls to the floor, and his nostrils flare, his eyes darkening. I peel my panties from my hips and step out of them, and suddenly this is all too scary—what I'm about to do and how vulnerable my heart feels. This isn't like Vegas. Then, I was drunk and lying to myself about my future. Tonight, I'm too sober to ignore the possibility that this might not mean anything to Keegan, that I lost my chance to be his, that all the talk about his friends fighting to make their relationships work wasn't code for us doing the same.

But then he's touching me. His mouth is on mine and his hands are everywhere at once, and all the panic in my mind drains away.

He slides his hands down my back as he leads me down the hall. In the next moment, we're in the kitchen and I'm pressed against the cool granite of the island, then he lifts me onto it as if I weigh nothing. "You're so fucking beautiful," he murmurs. "Do you know this is all I've thought about since you showed up here? Do you know how many times I had to stop myself from coming to you or how hard it was to be around everyone else tonight when I wanted to be here with you?" He dips his head and flicks my nipple with his tongue. "Doing this." My body shakes—loving the attention and needing more. He does it again, then treats the other to the same teasing torment. I arch my back, silently begging for his whole mouth, his tongue, for *more*.

"Patience, baby. I'm just getting started." With those words, he cups my face in his hands and kisses me so tenderly that I nearly melt. He takes that same tenderness as he moves his mouth down my neck, exploring the hollow of my collarbone with his soft lips.

When he cups my breasts in each hand, he's the one who

moans this time. He opens his mouth against my nipple and, with a suction that's neither gentle nor cautious, draws me into his mouth. My moan echoes off the vaulted ceilings, and he groans before treating the other side to the same torture.

"I've always loved your breasts," he says. "Not just because they're perfect, which they are, but because I love how much you get off on having them touched." He hesitates. "Or maybe you don't anymore." He pinches my nipple between his finger and thumb and tugs gently. "Maybe you've changed."

I gasp. I'm trying not to beg but hanging on by a thread. "You should find out."

He parts my legs, spreading my thighs to stand between them, then circles my nipple with his tongue, teasing and tasting in alternate measure, and when he finally draws me into his mouth again, I gasp and arch toward him. My thighs clench, my legs tightening around his waist. I roll my hips, giving my body the friction it needs. He squeezes my breasts in his hands, toys with me using lips and teeth and sometimes nothing more than the scruff on his jaw.

"Please, Keegan. Please." I don't know what I'm begging for. I'm not sure what I want. Forgiveness? A second chance? His mouth to never leave me?

"I'll give you everything you want, Em. You just have to give me the chance." He sinks lower and slides his hands under my ass, pulling forward as he presses his mouth between my legs. I prop myself up on my elbows and close my eyes. "Look at me," he demands. "Watch me."

I obey, fighting the urge to close my eyes as he kisses, sucks, and strokes. And when I come, it's with his words tied up in my mind with everything I could dream they might mean.

"I'll give you everything you want, Em. You just have to give me the chance."

CHAPTER 32
KEEGAN

She's so beautiful when she comes. I want to memorize every inch of her like this. The shape of her mouth, the arch of her neck, the flush on her skin.

She slides off the counter and unbuttons my shirt, tugging it down my arms. When she reaches for the hem of my tank, I lift my arms over my head and let her undress me. Next, she releases the button on my jeans and peels them off my hips so I'm standing before her in nothing but a pair of blue boxer briefs. She stares at my hard-on like she's a virgin who's never seen one before. But, of course, she's not. I know that personally. Our first night together in her condo in Laguna was a night I enjoyed more than I've ever enjoyed anything else in my life. Until tonight. Tonight trumps even that memory.

"What are you thinking about?" Her hand skims over my jaw, grazing the rough beard I've let grow since she showed up in my bar. "What's going on in that brain of yours?"

What happened five years ago? Why did you push me away?
"I'm thinking about how much I want to come in your mouth."
The words are meant to cover my thoughts, but as soon as I say
them, as soon as I see her eyes go dark and her mouth form that
sexy O of surprise, I want it.

She drops to her knees without hesitating, hooks her fingers
into the waistband of my boxer briefs, and pulls them down my
hips. She's fast, and her mouth is on me before I have the chance
to brace myself. Hot and wet, her lips and tongue slide over me,
testing the way I fit in her mouth.

My hands go to her hair, and I guide her back and forth
over my length. When she draws her cheeks in and sucks, I have
to squeeze my eyes shut and concentrate to keep myself from
jutting my hips and shoving my cock into the back of her throat.
Because *fuck,* this feels good. The heat, the wet, her sounds—
they're enough to make me lose my control.

But then she releases me without a word.

I open my eyes and see her on her knees before me, her lips
already swollen, her eyes questioning. She's so beautiful that my
gut knots with a need that's so much bigger than a blow job or
an orgasm.

"Are you okay?" I ask. "Did I hurt you?"

She shakes her head and licks her lips. "Was I doing something
wrong?"

"Why would you say that?"

"You stopped moving. Like it didn't feel good anymore." She

stands and drags her bottom lip between her teeth as she studies me.

Jesus. "I was trying not to fuck your mouth, Em."

The corner of her mouth hitches up in a nervous grin. "I thought that was what you wanted."

Lust surges through me so hard and hot that I'm consumed by the image of spinning her around and fucking her against the island without a condom. I narrowly resist. "I changed my mind."

I lead her to my room and guide her onto my bed, never taking my eyes off her as I find an unopened box of condoms in my bedside table and roll one on as she watches me. I want a picture of her like this—in my bed, stretched out and waiting for me, her skin flushed, her swollen lips parted, her body ready.

I climb onto the bed and settle over her, positioning myself between her legs, and she stills.

"Are you okay?"

She nods. "I don't remember Vegas." She searches my face, and I wonder what she's looking for. A promise from me? Details of a drunken night neither of us remembers? "I know what happened, but without the memory, it feels like it's been a long time."

I frame her face with my hands and look into her eyes. "We don't have to do this if you're not ready."

She swallows. "I want you." She lifts her hips and rubs herself along my length. "Please."

Fuck. I cannot deny this beautiful woman. Slowly, I slide into her, giving her the chance to adjust to me with even, steady strokes that leave me aching to drive fast and deep.

She draws up her knees and curls her nails into my shoulder blades, then whispers, "Please."

I thrust my hips, dragging out with all my restraint before driving back in, once, twice, and again until she's arching into me, her hips moving against mine and demanding more.

I lock my eyes on hers. This isn't like Vegas. This isn't a drunken search for release that even then I knew was a mistake. And perhaps tomorrow this decision will prove to be foolish, but it's not careless. This is the reunion of lovers. This is two people clinging to something precious they once had and lost.

I lower my mouth to hers and kiss her softly. And as she tightens around me, squeezing me tighter as she approaches her release, I suck on her bottom lip and trail kisses along her jaw and down her neck. There's too much I can't say, and I let my body do the talking. *I've missed you. I've never gotten over you.*

My heart will always be yours and yours alone.

EMMA

One night with Keegan could never be enough, and I selfishly hoped our night of greedy hands and bodies might pick up this morning. But when I wake up, the bed is empty and I can hear Keegan out in the kitchen.

I pull on his robe, tie it at the waist, and pad out to the kitchen, stopping when I see him with Olivia and Jazzy. They must have been here awhile, because I can see the remnants of breakfast in the sink. Keegan's already showered, his hair still wet at the temples.

"Good morning, sleepyhead," Olivia says. Her smile is forced, her jaw tight. "Must be nice to sleep the day away."

"Liv," Keegan says, warning in his tone. "Don't."

I look at the clock on the stove. It's nine thirty. She must think I'm some lazy, entitled rich bitch, but this isn't my typical life. Normally, I'm up by seven for a workout and breakfast before heading to the women's shelter in Savannah where I volunteer my mornings. My afternoons are typically spent on the phone, raising money and organizing fundraisers for any one of the not-for-profits for which I'm a board member. But Olivia doesn't know any of that. All she's seen is this out-of-character fragment of my life, and I can't blame her if the conclusions she's drawn about me are less than flattering.

"I'm just saying…" she mutters.

"I didn't want to wake you," Keegan says. "Jazzy and I are going to the park with my dad this morning."

His dad. I'd forgotten he was in town. Keegan seemed to shoo him out the door the other night and hasn't mentioned him since. For a beat, I wonder if his dad ever told him about our agreement, but then I push the thought away. Keegan would have said something to me. He wouldn't have liked knowing his dad cornered me into giving him money.

"Do you need anything while I'm out?"

"No, I'm fine. Thanks." I pour myself a cup of coffee and stay behind the island so as to not interrupt their family time at the table.

Keegan takes Jazzy from Olivia and comes into the kitchen. "Call me if you need anything." He kisses me softly, and Jazzy giggles. "Are you still up for joining us for the rehearsal tonight?"

I smile, but with Olivia looking on, my insecurities are back in full effect this morning. "Yeah, if you don't think I'll be in the way."

"I'm looking forward to it," he says. He presses another quick kiss to my lips then heads to the garage, leaving me here with his baby's mother, who's looking at me as if I'm somewhere between unwelcome houseguest and homewrecker.

"He's such a good dad," she says, forcing me to meet her gaze and stop studying my coffee. "The best."

"I can tell." I take a long drink. There's not enough caffeine in the world to prepare me for this conversation straight out of bed, but her comments left me feeling like a sloth and I really want to make a better impression.

"You'd never know he didn't have a stable home as a kid," she says, watching me. "But I think he's the exception, you know what I mean? Kids need stability. They need Mom and Dad. They need to know that family comes first."

I take another gulp of my coffee. Okay, so she's going with *Emma is a homewrecker* this morning. So be it. "It says a lot about his character," I say, not letting her bait me into a conversation about whether kids need both parents at home. "That had to have been hard—being just a kid when his mom died of cancer."

Olivia steps into the kitchen and frowns as she clears the breakfast plates from the counter. "His mom didn't die of cancer."

"Oh." Did I misremember her illness? For a beat, my cheeks heat and I feel like such an inconsiderate jerk, but the memory is there. Keegan walking beside me on the beach, telling me about his last memories of his mom healthy enough to cheer him on at a football game. *"That was before the chemo had her so sick she couldn't leave the house."* Olivia's frowning at me. "I thought it was some sort of cancer," I mumble, suddenly unsure.

She shakes her head. "Keegan's mom is alive. She lives in Texas and tours with some rock band. He might not like her, but she's not dead."

"Oh." The blood drains from my face, and I might be embarrassed if I weren't so confused. An old, familiar feeling creeps in around the edges of my thoughts. It's that raw anxiety from my acting days when I wasn't sure I could trust anyone, when it seemed like people were more interested in manipulating the truth for their benefit than in giving it to me straight. Why would he tell me his mother died of cancer if she's alive and living in Texas? Why did he tell me he grew up in Blackhawk Valley if none of his friends would think to include him when talking about who was raised here? And why would he lie to me?

The questions scatter in my mind when my phone rings and the display reads *Harry*. Every time I get a new phone and new number, I program his number into it so I'll know when not to pick up. I never take his calls, but it doesn't keep him from trying.

I reject the call with a swipe, and Olivia looks over at me from where she's washing dishes. "My mom is such a huge fan of his."

I wrap my arms around my waist. "Whose?"

She arches a brow. "Harry Evans? It would be amazing if you could get his autograph for her."

I give her a shaky smile. "Yeah. Sure. I'll see what I can do."

EMMA

Five years ago...

"This is what happens when you fight me."

Harry's words echo like a death knell in my brain as I survey my condo.

I didn't sleep last night. After Harry left, I took a long shower and waited for tears that didn't come. I turned the water as hot as it would go, sat on the tile floor, and let the water pour over me until it went cold, then I dried off and did my best to clean up the mess he left behind. *"This is what happens when you fight me."*

My condo was a disaster. The throw pillows were scattered across the floor, the coffee table was upended, and the glass of wine I was drinking before Harry arrived spilled and left a red stain on the living room rug that made the spot look like the scene of a crime.

Because it is.

I straightened everything carefully, scrubbed at the stain

until my hands hurt, balled up last night's clothes, and put them in the trash.

The scrape of a key in the lock makes me stiffen, and when Keegan steps inside, I want to run. I don't want him to see me like this. I don't want him to look at me.

"Good morning," he says softly. He closes the door behind himself and walks across the room to kiss my forehead.

I flinch at his touch. He notices.

He draws in a ragged breath. "Are you okay?"

"I'm fine." I sound like a robot. Feel like one, too. But robotic is better than the crazed alternative. Robotic beats feeling human and remembering last night and wanting to take a vegetable peeler to my skin.

"I'm sorry I couldn't come over last night like we planned."

"It's fine." But what if he had? What if he'd seen? Panic claws at the mask I'm wearing, threatening to tear it to shreds.

"How'd the rehearsal go last night?"

"Fine." I want him to leave. Last night when Harry showed up at my door and pushed inside before I could send him away, I kept wishing for Keegan to show up. Now my amazing, tender Keegan is here and I just want him to leave because I don't know how to explain or if I should or could.

His eyes scan the living room as if he's looking for something. They land on the red stain and he frowns.

"I spilled my wine."

He nods and tucks his hands into his pockets as he walks into the kitchen. His eyes land on the daisies Harry brought. They're on the counter, forgotten, their soft white petals wilting.

Is it my imagination, or does Keegan sneer at them? For a wild minute, I think that they're me, that I'm the wilted petal and Keegan just knows, that he's disgusted by me. *I'm* disgusted by me.

"Nice flowers," he says.

No they're not. They're a child's flower. Harry always loved giving me daisies. I always hated them.

I grab them from the counter and step around the island to shove them into the trash bin under the sink—another piece of evidence from last night discarded, and yet I feel no closer to being free of it.

When I shut the cabinet door, Keegan's staring at me. "Is there something going on between you and Harry?"

I freeze and goosebumps zip up my arms. "What?"

"I think you heard what I said."

"He's marrying my mom." Does my voice sound hysterical, or is that just how I feel? "That's ridiculous."

He sets his jaw and folds his arms. "Is it? I don't want to be *that guy,* the jealous boyfriend who can't handle his girl having male friends. But I don't like him and I don't like the way he looks at you." His gaze drops to the cabinet with the trash can. "A man doesn't visit his stepdaughter at night and bring flowers."

I remind myself to breathe. *Inhale. Exhale.* This is Keegan. I can tell Keegan anything. "We're…friends." God, how awful it feels to lie. But the truth? The truth makes me somehow feel like a dirty tramp and a vulnerable child all at the same time. It makes me feel like my life is something that's happening to me, something that's never been in my control. I don't want Keegan to see me that way.

I don't want to tell him the truth, because if I say it out loud, it might be real.

He searches my face. "You're going to come to Indiana with me? We're going to get away from here?"

"Yeah." I force a smile. I am a robot. "Of course."

He steps forward and reaches out to touch my face, but I flinch, and he drops his hand. "What's wrong today?"

"Nothing. I'm fine." The words come out too fast.

"Why do I feel like you're pulling away? Is that just me?"

I shake my head and mentally chant, *It's fine, it's fine, it's fine, it's fine, it's fine, it's fine.* But it's not fine. I don't want Keegan to touch me. I don't want his fingers where Harry's were last night. I don't want Keegan's touch to make me think of Harry, but I'm afraid right now it will.

"You have a bruise." He sets his jaw and nods to the bite mark on the side of my neck.

"This is what happens when you fight me."

"I ran into something." I hate myself for lying to him. But more than that, I hate myself for not being able to stop Harry. I hate myself for letting him do whatever he wanted to me until I was sixteen, because that's why he thought he could do whatever he wanted to me last night.

It's my fault. It's my fault. It's my fault.

"I should get going," I blurt, because if he stays close much longer, I'm going to lose it. I'm going to stop being a robot. I'm going to become flesh and blood and then I'm going to melt into a puddle of grief at his feet and beg him to forgive me.

Forgive me? Why do I need forgiveness when I said no? Why do I need forgiveness when I begged him to stop?

"Emma?"

"Yeah?"

His gaze drops to my neck and then shifts to the cabinet before returning to my eyes. "We all have secrets. We all have dark parts of ourselves. But if you and I are going to get through this…if we're going to do this life together, maybe we should both…" He looks away.

Don't make me talk about it. Don't make me make it real. "I should go." The tears are too close to the surface now.

"Do you want me to come? To the wedding?"

Yes. I want you to stay by my side. I want you to keep me safe from him. I want you to hold me and tell me it wasn't my fault. I want you to love me when I don't deserve to be loved. "No. I'll see you tomorrow. It's…with the wedding and everything…it's just easier this way."

He searches my face. I wonder what he sees there. Does he see a chubby little girl who desperately wanted to be *enough*? Does he see a young woman who left Hollywood only to realize she has no idea who she is without it? Or does he see a coward who, for too many years, turned her head to the side and pretended she was a statue just because when she told him no, he got angry and mocked her on set—or worse, ignored her—and she was so fucking lonely, did it really hurt to let him make himself feel good?

"You could tell me anything," he whispers.

I nod, too afraid my voice might betray me if I speak. He leans forward and kisses my forehead. I close my eyes, because it hurts too much to watch him walk away.

When the door clicks, I walk slowly to my room and pack a bag with shockingly steady hands. My car arrives to take me to the church. I'm supposed to help my mother dress for her wedding. I'm supposed to watch her marry the man who pinned me down and bit my neck.

"This is what happens when you fight me."

"Straight to the church?" the driver asks.

I shake my head. "LAX, please." I see his frown in the rearview mirror, but he nods. I hesitate, then ask, "If I give you a note, will you take it somewhere for me after you drop me at the airport?"

"Of course."

I pull a piece of paper and pen from the notebook in my bag.

Dear Keegan, I begin, marveling at how my handwriting doesn't betray the storm brewing inside me. It's not until I finish and reread the letter that I see the ink smudge where a teardrop landed.

CHAPTER 33
KEEGAN

The woman I've loved since I met her five years ago is at home waiting for me, and the mother of my child is sitting in my storeroom throwing long looks my way. If this isn't screwed up, I'm not sure what is.

This morning with Dad went all right. He seemed truly excited to be spending time with Jazzy, and since he didn't start teaching her how to spot a mark, I suppose it can't hurt anything. He's been true to his word and hasn't told anyone that Emma's here or tried to use the information to get money from either of us. Maybe he has changed.

"Do you have plans tonight?" Olivia asks. "Want to hang with me at the house? Maybe watch old movies and make popcorn after we get the baby down?"

"I can't. Emma and I have the wedding rehearsal. We could get a sitter for Jazz if you wanted to come?"

She shakes her head. "We'll be fine. Don't worry about us. My brother and Alex invited us for dinner again, so we can just do that." Olivia looks up at me through her lashes. "I bet it will be a beautiful wedding."

She holds my gaze for a bit too long, and I look away when it feels uncomfortable. "I'm sure it will be nice."

"Are you excited?" Her voice is almost wistful.

"I guess." More than excited about the wedding, I'm anxious to spend more time with Emma, happy to have an excuse to dance with her, to hold her. "Are you coming?"

"I don't know. Maybe I shouldn't get in the way of you and your new woman." She folds her arms. "I'm beginning to feel like an unneeded accessory."

"Olivia, you know that's not true. You should come. Arrow and Mia want you there."

She hums. "We'll see." She saunters over to the sink, where I've been cleaning the tubing for one of the kegs. She pulls on my arm until I turn to face her. "For the record, I wish we were the ones getting married this weekend. I wish I had done better before so I wouldn't have to watch my family slip from my fingers now."

I flinch and shake my head. "You only care to keep me when you think you might be losing me."

"Keegan, I mean it. I miss you. I miss us." She takes my face in her hands. She rises onto her toes and presses her lips to mine. I feel nothing.

I take her wrists and pull her hands from my face as I step

back. "Don't." I shake my head. "I can't do this with you. Not now. Not anymore."

"You're the father of my child. We'll always have that bond, and no Hollywood bitch can take that away."

"Don't you ever call her that again." My voice is low, the warning simmering under the words.

"Fine. But did you ever wonder why she was willing to marry a gay man?"

"Who told you that?"

She sighs. "I was in the nursery when she told you. I heard the whole conversation."

"You can't tell anyone."

She rolls her eyes. "Your dad and I had a good laugh about it, but I promise I won't tell anyone else about your precious friend's secret."

"You told my *dad*?" I shake my head. *Fuck, fuck, fuck.* "I told you we can't trust him. What the fuck did you think you were doing?"

"I thought I was putting together a story that didn't make sense to me. But he helped me understand. Did you know she gets regular calls from Harry Evans? Her stepfather? Her former costar? But I'm sure there's nothing to that, just like there was nothing to it five years ago, am I right?" She lifts her chin and stares me down for a long beat before turning around and storming out of the storeroom. The back door clangs closed, and before I can figure out what the hell just happened or start to wrap my brain around what Olivia just said, Bailey comes in.

"You pissed off somebody this afternoon."

My head is swimming, and I shake it to try to clear it. "I gave up trying to please Olivia months ago."

"Hmm." She lifts the tube from the sink and shakes her head as she studies it. "Can't say I blame you there." She looks up at me. "You didn't tell Emma, did you? About your past?"

My jaw hardens and I look away. *Harry is still calling her?*

"You don't owe her any explanation. That's not what I'm saying here. I'm saying that whether you decide to tell her or not, your past will always be between you. People like that don't know what it's like to be people like us, Keegan. She won't understand a life where your best choice is to take the money."

I lift my chin. "Are you sure you're talking about me and Em and not you and Mason?"

She shrugs. "I'm talking about both, and you know it. I'm talking about how you and I are the whores the rich people entertained themselves with for a while. I like Em. I do. But I'm saying that you're kidding yourself if you think the life you had once isn't going to affect the life you want. You have to tell her."

"I will. She's just having a fucking tough week, and I don't want to pile on." Five minutes ago, I was sure we were on our way to a better week, a better month, a better year. I was sure Emma and I had a life stretching out before us where we could make right everything that we got wrong the first time. *Both of us.* But if Harry's calling her, maybe nothing really changes.

Bailey shrugs. "Just be careful where you put those expectations. When this falls apart, it's going to hurt, and I don't care to see either one of you so hurt you can't come back from it."

I haven't been able to look her in the eye since I picked her up to take her to the rehearsal. Olivia's words echo in my head. Why is Harry calling her?

"I should probably keep my mouth shut," Em says, jerking me from my thoughts. "But I want to ask you something." She's looking out the passenger window, watching the rolling horse farms of Blackhawk Valley pass her by.

I shake off my earlier thoughts, taking a beat or two longer than necessary to process her words. "What?"

"Why did you tell me your mom died?" She turns to me, and my stomach plummets. "You told me she died of cancer, and today Olivia said that your mom is alive and living in Texas."

Fuck. I turn onto the main stretch through downtown and circle around the block to park behind the bar. Easing the car into a space, I throw it in park and cut the engine. I've spent my entire afternoon thinking about what Olivia told me, and meanwhile, Emma's been quietly stewing about an old lie I'd forgotten I told her.

Aren't we a pair of lying fools? Maybe we deserve each other.

When I turn to face her, she's frowning at me. "Don't say you didn't tell me that. I remember you telling me. I remember you describing what it was like to watch her waste away." She grimaces. "Can you please explain?"

I swallow hard, but my shame leaves a bad taste in my mouth.

"You want me to explain that I lied to you?"

She flinches and looks away. "I want you to explain why you'd tell me you grew up in Blackhawk Valley and lost your mom when neither is true."

"I'll explain." I feel my jaw harden. "And then you can explain why Harry still calls you."

She turns back to me with wide eyes and gapes. "How did you know that?"

It's like a knife twisting in my gut. I didn't want it to be true. I wanted Olivia to be grasping at straws, but she was only reporting the facts. "Was that why you were going to marry the senator?" I force myself to say the words. "Were you going to marry a gay man so you could keep sleeping with your mother's husband?"

She shakes her head violently. "Don't. Don't act like you know anything. Don't act like you understand."

"I would if you'd tell me. But when I asked you about him five years ago, I got pushed away. I got a fucking Dear John letter." I drag a hand over my face. I don't want to do this. I'm such an idiot. I believed we could get through it this time, that we were strong enough to get past the secrets, but I feel it all falling apart.

"Can you just take me home? I don't think I want to be around people tonight."

I jam the key back into the ignition and drive home in silence, the roar of panic so loud in my head that I couldn't talk over it if I wanted to. As soon as the car slows in the drive, she opens her door.

"Emma."

She stops and turns to me.

"I have to go to the rehearsal, but I need you to promise me something."

She bites down on her trembling bottom lip, and I want to pull her into my arms so badly. This is killing me. "What?"

"Don't run. Don't leave me this time. We need to talk. We all have secrets. I lied to you about where I was from. I lied to you about my mother. And you kept secrets from me too." I reach out and drop my hand before I can touch her face. "Promise me you'll be here when I get home. If you want to leave after we talk, then I'll respect that."

"I'll be here."

CHAPTER 34
EMMA

The moon shines bright over the oak tree in Keegan's back yard. It's the perfect evening, the air is cool and clear, and frogs sing their summertime song in the distance. Sitting in the house and waiting for Keegan to come home was making me want to run away, so I came out here where the walls aren't closing in on me, where I can breathe and tell myself nothing good will come of leaving. It's time to talk. It's time to tell my secrets. Even Zachary never got the whole story. I've only ever told the details to my mother—and she thinks I'm a liar.

What if Keegan doesn't believe you either?

The voice in the back of my mind echoes my greatest fear, and I gulp in the cool night air in an attempt to wash it away. Once, Keegan told me we all carry secrets. Once, he promised that if we opened up about ours, we could make a life together.

"Emma!" The deep voice entering my sanctuary makes my whole body stiffen. I hear the gate click, the soft swish of grass under feet as he walks toward me.

Standing from my chair on the patio, I squeeze my eyes shut and clench my fists at my sides. How did he know to find me here?

I turn slowly to meet my stepfather's eyes and wrap my arms around my chest as if I could retroactively protect myself from him. I want to protect the little girl I was. I want to tell her not to believe his lies, that she's good enough without him and doesn't need his approval. I want to squeeze her hand and promise her she can say *no* and still be loved.

Harry smiles at me, that slow grin that stretches across his face and makes women, young and old alike, swoon in the seats of their local movie theater. But not me. To me, that smile is a reminder of years of confusion, shame, and guilt. It's a reminder of secrets that made me first feel older than I was and then later smaller and more helpless than I was. It's a reminder of his voice whispering for me to *hush, just a little longer,* of his body pinning me down, of his gentle reminder that *this has to be our secret.*

I left my career to escape him, and he found his way back into my life. I took on a fake engagement and almost a fake marriage to escape him. And now I'm here. Was I running to Keegan or away from Harry?

"You did it for me," he says, stepping forward. "You left your wedding for me."

I flinch. Only Harry would make the ordeal of my canceled

wedding about *him*. "I didn't."

He takes another step and reaches out to brush his fingertips across my cheek. My stomach heaves in revulsion, and I scramble backward but he continues forward. "I've missed you."

Tears burn my eyes because somehow just his presence here has me feeling like a little girl all over again—helpless, confused about right and wrong, unsure about what to think of this man I held such affection for doing things I was pretty sure he shouldn't do. Then I'm eighteen again, scrabbling from the smell of whiskey on his breath and begging him to leave. *"This is what happens when you fight me."*

"I'm going to leave your mother," he says. When he steps closer, I take another step back, only to realize that I'm against the back of the house and he's too close.

"I don't care what you do." I force myself to meet his eyes as I lift my chin. "Whatever you do, it has nothing to do with me. I don't want you anywhere near me."

He sighs. "I know I put you in a bad position that summer. I'm sorry you felt like I pushed myself on you. You were running around with that boy to punish me for marrying your mother. You just make me crazy. Don't you see that? Can you blame me for loving you?"

I turn my head. "Will you please leave? You're trespassing on private property."

"I'm divorcing your mother. You and I can be together again. You're not a kid anymore, and who cares what people think anyway? You know there was a reason you didn't marry Zachary.

Don't fight it. This connection we have is never going to go away."

"I feel no connection to you," I say. "Only disgust."

He presses his body against me, pinning me between him and the brick as he grabs a handful of my hair. "Did you forget what happens when you fight me?" He yanks on my hair and I take a deep breath, remind myself I'm not a child, that I'm not helpless. I shove, hard. He's strong and only moves back a step before regaining his footing and pressing against me again.

"The lady asked you to leave." Keegan's voice is like cool water on a burn—a jarring relief that stings as much as it soothes. I hate him seeing me here like this with Harry. I hate knowing what he must think, and I hate that I wasn't brave enough to tell him the truth before.

Harry looks over his shoulder and arches a brow at Keegan. "You again?"

Keegan grabs the back of Harry's shirt and yanks him off me, releasing him in time to swing and connect his right fist with Harry's jaw. "Me again," Keegan says, swinging again. This time there's a *crack* when his fist makes contact, and Harry's nose seems to explode.

"Fuck!" Harry screeches, grabbing his nose. Blood covers his hands and drips from between his fingers. "My face!"

"Get off my fucking property, asshole." Keegan's voice is so firm, so strong, that I want to wrap myself up in it.

Harry turns and sneers at Keegan. "You're nothing more than trash, and someday she's going to open her eyes and see you for what you really are—an enterprising cheat who's only in the NFL because his old girlfriend called in a few favors."

KEEGAN

I might never be able to forget the look of terror on her face when Harry had her pressed against the wall. That wasn't a girl talking to her former lover. That was a victim curling into herself at the nearness of her abuser. And I was so wrapped up in my jealousy that I never saw him for what he was.

Fuck.

He's gone, and I watch with trembling hands as Emma steadies her breathing, her chest rising and falling with each deliberate breath.

"Are you okay?"

"Yeah." She forces a smile. And maybe we have a lot of secrets between us, but I know this woman. I know that's not her real smile, and I know she's not okay.

I open my arms. "Come here."

Her smile falls and her composure crumbles as she shakes her head. "I'm sorry. I'm so sorry. I didn't want to involve you like that."

"Jesus, Emma." Stepping forward, I fold her into my arms. She leans her forehead against my chest and pulls in big, panicky gulps of air. "Hey, shh. I've got you." I slide my fingers into her hair and kiss her forehead. I can feel her trembling, as if her fear has to exit her body in the form of physical energy. "I've got you. You're with me now."

"I don't know how he knew to come here. I'm so sorry. I shouldn't be here. What if Jasmine had been home? What if—"

"Don't worry about any of that. Just breathe." I hold her for a long time in the moonlight, reminding her to breathe, reminding her she's safe. Later, when it seems like she's calmed down, I take her into the house and have her sit at the counter while I pour her a shot of whiskey. "There you go."

She looks at the amber liquid then at me. "Seriously?"

I arch a brow. "It won't change that he showed up here or fix all the things he's done to you, but neither will shaking as hard as you are right now."

She takes the shot quickly and grimaces as she swallows. I slide onto the stool next to her and straddle it, propping my arms on the back as I study her. "You never told me about your relationship with him." I swallow. "I'm afraid I never gave you the chance."

She looks away, and watching the emotions pass over her face in quick succession is like flipping through a stack of snapshots. Confusion, grief, anger, sadness. It's all there, and I hate myself for not seeing this before, for not seeing him for the creep he was before.

"Start at the beginning," I say softly.

"It started when I was thirteen," she says.

"Son of a bitch." Anger flares in my chest—hot and renewed. I grip the back of the chair to keep myself planted so I don't go after him. The black eye and broken nose I sent him away with are way too small a punishment. The man deserves prison time. Worse.

"Had anyone found out about it then, I would have argued that it was consensual, but in retrospect and after a lot of fucking therapy, I can tell you that even though I never told him no back then, those were *not* the makings of a healthy, consensual relationship."

"How old was he then? His forties?"

She nods then lifts her eyes to meet mine. "Forty-three."

"The sick fuck."

"Yeah. But I was an idiot little girl, and he convinced me he wouldn't want me so much, that he wouldn't risk everything to be with me, if I wasn't special. He said no one would approve of our relationship because I was young, but he said I was so mature for my age. That year was the start of when I was feeling self-conscious about my weight. The press had started to notice that the chubby little girl was turning into a fat preteen, and the chubby cheeks everyone loved on me as a kid were suddenly the subject of public ridicule." She lifts her eyes to mine and holds my gaze. "I've had to work really hard to forgive myself for not telling him no ten years ago. I've had to work really hard to place the blame on his shoulders where it belongs. He manipulated me, but I never thought of it that way then. I just thought…" She shakes her head.

"He was a father figure," I say softly. "And you were still a child."

"I had such a messed-up idea of what love was, of how it worked. I didn't have any healthy relationships. Everything was *quid pro quo*, even with my mother. And so when he'd pull out his dick and tell me to get on my knees, when he'd make extravagant promises in exchange for sexual favors—a gift from Tiffany's, or a word with the director of a film I wanted to be considered for—I didn't think he was a creepy pedophile. I thought he was my secret boyfriend and he was trying to be *nice* to me."

I reach for her hand and hold it in mine. I'm nauseated, and every word of her story literally hurts, but I know she needs to tell it. I just wish I had found a way to convince her to tell it sooner. I'm not sure I'll be able to forgive myself for that mistake.

She squeezes my hand. "He's the reason I quit acting and the reason I pulled out of the *Lucy Matters* reunion movie. I wanted it to stop, and I felt like as long as I was on that show with him, I'd never be free of it. Then, less than two years later, he took up with my mom. What kind of man does that? He said he wanted to be close to me. That he missed me."

"That was the summer we were together?"

She nods. "He didn't like me being with you. He could handle it when I was alone—and I was *always* alone before you—but when he realized I was with you, it made him crazy." Her eyes fill with tears. "I was so happy during our months together. I loved you. I didn't care that you weren't part of my world—maybe that was part of the appeal. I didn't care that you had nothing. It was the first time I'd felt real love." She studies our entwined fingers before lifting her gaze to mine again. "It was real, wasn't it?"

My chest aches from the guilt that's eating at me. "Yes. So real it never went away."

She squeezes her eyes shut and draws in a ragged breath. "The night of the wedding rehearsal, after, he came to my condo with flowers. He was drunk. Before that, when he'd come to me earlier in the summer, he'd seemed kind of pathetic to me— begging me to take him back even as he was planning to marry my mother. But that night he wasn't pathetic at all. He was drunk and angry. I told him to leave, and he smacked me. It was the first time I told him no. Maybe I always believed that if I could just find the courage to say no, to push him away despite his bullshit manipulations, if I could just make him understand that I didn't want him to touch me, he'd be out of my life for good. He'd done such a good job making me believe everything we'd done was my fault that I believed I was in control. But that night I did push him away. I did tell him no. I fought back, and it didn't matter to him."

I stare at the door, wondering where he went, wondering if I can catch up to him and let my fist finish what it started. Because *God fucking damn.* He raped her, and when she was acting strange the next morning, I thought it was because she was cheating on me. My father was there taking a *picture* when the asshole went into her building. I need to punch something really fucking soon or I'm going to lose my shit.

Emma's not looking at me anymore. She's staring through the island as if she's watching her nightmare of a past unfold in the pattern on the stone. "I ran. I couldn't go to the wedding. I went to France for two weeks, but when I got home, I went to my mom," she says. "I didn't want to go to the police. I knew they'd ask questions. I knew the fact that I'd had a sexual relationship with him for years before that night would hurt my case. I knew no one would believe that a girl like me wouldn't *want* a man like that to touch her. I was too ashamed to go to you, felt too dirty and used, and so I went to my mom. I told her everything. I told her about my first time with him when I was thirteen. I told her about trying to end it and how he always found a way to pull me back in, a way to make me feel guilty if I wanted to stop. I told her that he'd slapped me that night, knocked me down, bit me when I tried to fight. That he held me down, and that it didn't take long for me to turn my head to the side, close my eyes, and tell myself I was a statue, to disconnect from my body like I'd done so many times before. She cried with me. She held me and rocked me in her arms." She blinks, as if coming back to herself. "It was the closest I've ever felt to my mother."

She was too ashamed to come to me. Too fucking ashamed, and I fed that by implying she had an inappropriate relationship with him. "What happened?"

She draws in a ragged breath. "Well, he told her *his* side. He'd gone over to check on me because he knew I was taking their engagement hard and I'd been acting funny at the rehearsal. He said I'd begged him not to marry her and then threw myself at him. He described me taking off his shirt and seducing him. He said one thing led to another and that afterward he told me he still wanted to marry my mom if she'd forgive him for what we'd done. He told her that when he said that, I lost my mind. That I started screaming and threatening to yell rape." Her eyes are dry and her cheeks pale when she adds, "She believed every bit of it."

The motherfucker stole her mother from her too. "How did he explain sleeping with a thirteen-year-old?"

"He denied that part. He told her I'd always had a crush on him and he'd always discouraged it, but since he didn't think anything would come of it, he didn't see the harm."

"She believed it all. Just like that?"

"In her defense, I'd never said a word before that day, and she was fresh off her honeymoon with the man I was accusing. I think his story was easier for her to believe than the truth. It upset her life less."

I pour us each another shot of whiskey. She swirls hers in the glass, and I down mine, focusing on the heat in my chest instead of my anger. "If I'd had any idea, I never would have walked away. I never would have let you push me out. I was supposed to be with you that night. I should have been there. I should have protected you." But instead I was searching for something my father stole from her.

She gives a sad smile as she draws her feet onto the stool, wrapping her arms around her knees. "He wouldn't have come up if you'd been there. It would have happened after you left or a different time. You can't blame yourself."

"Why'd you push me away?" I gulp in air, swallowing hard as if I can suck the question back into my chest where I've held it for five years. "Why did you give up on us?"

"Because he made me believe it was my fault. I'm not broken

anymore, Keegan, but I was then. I was ashamed. He made me blame myself just enough that I couldn't bear telling you."

"I wouldn't have blamed you." I close my eyes, guilt lashing through me as I realize my accusations were a kind of blame. "I wish I'd known the truth."

"You wouldn't have blamed me. I knew that, and I couldn't bear the thought of it. Because what if I told you and you reacted as I thought you would and blamed him completely? What if you believed in me but it turned out he was right and it was partially my fault? I pushed you away because I wasn't prepared to believe that I deserved to be forgiven. I pushed you away because I hated myself so much after that night that it felt deceptive and ugly to let you love me, with or without the truth. I had to let you think the worst because inside I *believed* the worst."

I slide off the stool and take her hands to guide her to the floor to stand in front of me. I cup her face in my hands and look her in the eye. "I would have done anything for you. I would have loved you until you forgave yourself. I would have reminded you that I believed you until *you* believed it was never your fault."

CHAPTER 35
EMMA

Early morning sun slants into the room between the drapes as Keegan climbs into bed with me and pulls me into his arms. He's freshly showered and fully clothed in jeans and a polo shirt, while I'm in nothing but one of his soft, well-worn T-shirts.

"Hey there, early bird," I whisper. "Let me guess, you already worked out, had a healthy, made-from-scratch breakfast, showered, and conquered a small country while I slept in?"

He leans his forehead against mine and grins. "You forgot the part where I rescued damsels in distress."

I hum, fighting my eyes to open. "Right. I always forget that part because you make it look so easy. How many damsels did you rescue this morning?"

He skims his thumb over my bottom lip. "There was only one I was interested in rescuing, and it turned out she'd already rescued herself."

I catch his thumb between my teeth and bite down lightly before releasing it. "I remember it differently. Did you ever consider you saved her by just being there?"

He groans as he snakes a hand up my shirt and cups my breast. His thumb, wet from my mouth, skims across my nipple.

Last night after I spilled my guts to Keegan, he drew me a bath with bubbles and lit candles and insisted that I take a long soak. When I told him I didn't want to be alone, he stripped out of his clothes and climbed in behind me. From the tub to the bed, the night was all gentle touches and reassurances. It was Keegan holding me until I fell asleep and his hands in my hair when I woke him up with my mouth in the middle of the night.

"I have to go do the groomsman thing," he says now, his hand still up my shirt. "Keep the door locked, and if you see any sign of Harry, call the police. We'll go tomorrow and get a protective order filed."

I nod. We talked about the protective order last night, and I agreed it was past due. "I don't think he's coming back. His face means everything to him, and if you see him again, you might ruin it permanently."

"I'd at least like the opportunity to try," he mutters.

"Everything will be fine, and I'll meet you at the wedding."

"You remember how to get there?"

"That's what GPS is for," I say, smiling.

He rolls me over, and I part my legs so he can settle between them. He props himself up on his elbows as he looks down at me.

"He said something last night…" He swallows and searches my face. "About you being the only reason I got to play in the NFL. Is that true?"

My chest feels tight. He doesn't look angry or hurt, but tender. "The Gators are owned by good family friends of the Dellacontes. When their defensive end got hurt, I knew they were going to have to put someone new on their roster."

He shakes his head in wonder. "You hadn't talked to me in four years. Do you know getting me on the team completely changed my life? Changed Jazzy's?"

"All I did was make a phone call." I slide my fingers through his hair. "I asked them to watch your tapes. I put you on their radar. Everything else was you."

"No one has ever done anything like that for me. Thank you." He dips his head and skims his lips over mine. "I love you, Emma Rothschild."

My breath catches at his words. "Yeah?"

"Fuck yes." He shakes his head as he studies my face. "So much that it scares me."

"I love you too."

His nostrils flare and he lowers his mouth to mine, kissing me in a long, searching sweep of lips and tongue. "I can never pay you back for something that big, but tell me how I can try."

I slide a hand up his shirt and run my nails down his back. "I have a couple ideas." I arch my hips off the bed and scrape my nails along the edge of his waistband.

"You're going to make me late," he says, circling his hips against mine.

"Then you'd better be quick about it," I whisper, unbuttoning his jeans.

I'm in the kitchen when I hear the front door open. My whole body tenses as I force myself to turn, and even though I know the door was locked and know it's illogical, I expect to see Harry there.

I breathe easier when I see it's just Olivia.

"Thank God you're here," she says. "Everyone's busy and I have an appointment at the spa." She sighs heavily and reaches her arms out as if she's trying to hand the baby to me.

"I'm sorry. What?"

"Take her, I have to go!"

I look around. Surely this woman isn't trying to hand her baby off to *me*, a virtual stranger, so she can go to the spa?

She rolls her eyes. "Oh my God! If you're going to date him, this is part of the deal. He's a dad. He has a little girl. I need you to take her because I have to go. Tell him I'll come get her at the reception." She shoves the baby against my chest, tosses a bag to the floor, then turns around and rushes out the door.

I can only race after her, and I don't find my voice until she's climbing into her car. "Wait! Keegan's not here!" When that doesn't slow her down, I frantically add, "I burn eggs!"

But she must not understand that the eggs are a metaphor for just how unfit I am to take care of her baby, because she just waves and repeats, "I'll meet you at the reception!" She starts the car, and the engine turns over with a grumble before she backs out of the drive.

The chubby-cheeked baby grins at me, showing four of what are probably the cutest damn teeth this world has ever seen, then she grabs a fistful of my hair and yanks.

"Hi," I whisper. I need to call Keegan. Except Keegan's busy, and she's right. If I want Keegan, Jazzy's going to be in my life too.

The baby buzzes her lips and makes a face. Under my hand, her diaper vibrates and then there's a distinct...odor.

"Oh boy." I take a deep breath and take her into the nursery to change her diaper. I've done this with Becky's baby. No reason this should be any different.

Two hours later, I've called Keegan, updated him on the situation, and promised I have it under control. He answered my four hundred questions and told me where to find the extra car seat in the garage so I can bring her to the wedding. Since then, I've determined that Jasmine is the cutest baby in the history of the world and fallen in love with the happy girl. She's full of smiles, and when I put her down for a nap, as Keegan suggested, she flips over to her belly and closes her eyes.

"I'm pretty sure you're more angel than child," I whisper, smoothing her curls before I turn off the light and leave the room. As I dress for Arrow and Mia's wedding, I'm smiling, high on my pseudo-parenting skills and baby snuggles.

EMMA
Five years ago...

The sand is soft under my thighs, and the sound of the water makes me breathe easy. It's not the beach I'm used to, and the voices around me chatter in French, but it's still the ocean and it calms me. I let the waves roll in to touch my toes when a man sits next to me, *right* next to me. As if I invited him there. As if we know each other.

He looks out at the water, silent, contemplative, as if he didn't just invade a stranger's space. I open my mouth to say something, then decide against it and stand.

"I wouldn't go yet if I were you." His English has just a hint of a Southern accent.

"I don't know you." My voice trembles on the words, because there's something about this man. Something about the way he holds himself and the lift of his chin and the smile starting to curl his lips that makes me feel unsafe.

"You're in love with my son," he says. "Why shouldn't I be here?"

I blink at him, unsure if I should believe him and unwilling to give him any information if he's lying. "Who's your son?"

His slick smile turns to a Cheshire grin. "Funny you wouldn't know which man I'm referring to. That kind of proves my point."

"I don't know what you're talking about." I turn and walk away, only stopping when he speaks again.

"Keegan's my boy. You've been seeing him this summer, haven't you? Until you brushed him off like so much lint."

I close my eyes and tell myself to relax, but my chest aches at the mention of Keegan's name. I miss him so much, but even after a week in France and away from my problems at home, I know I did what I needed to do when I wrote him that letter. I force myself to turn and wrap my arms around my chest. "It's nice to meet you," I say, but my voice betrays me, and we both know I'm lying.

I don't like this at all. I don't like the way he approached me, or the fact that he tracked me down here, or the condescending "I have something on you" tone in his voice.

"You know," he says, "most fathers would be glad to see their son shack up with a rich celebrity. I mean, if he stayed with you, he'd pretty much have it made, wouldn't he? But I'm not most fathers, and my son has no idea what he's gotten himself into with you."

Goosebumps break out all over my hot skin. It's like when you have a fever that makes you hot and cold all at once.

"I told him he was being played," he says. "I told him he was wrong about you, but the fool was blinded by love, and then it turned out I was right and you were a liar."

"I've never lied to him."

"A lie by omission is still a lie, sweetheart."

I swallow hard and look away, determined to bite my tongue

and not give anything away to this man I don't trust. Maybe I don't have a reason for that, but down to my bones, I *can't* trust him. "What do you want from me?"

"I'm just looking out for my boy. I haven't been the best father, but I want to give him a shot at a better life—a life that he can be proud of. Something real."

"I want what's best for Keegan."

He nods. "Good. Then we can agree on what you need to do for him next."

CHAPTER 36
KEEGAN

Arrow and Mia's wedding ceremony is on the lake on his father's property just outside of Blackhawk Valley. Doing a ceremony outside this time of year, they risked thunderstorms, humidity, and high temps. But somehow they ended up getting a wedding day that's seventy-five degrees and partly cloudy.

Whoever they hired to make this place ready for a wedding did a great job. There's a flower-covered arbor in front of the lake, and white chairs fill the lawn beyond.

I keep looking at Emma, thinking this must be weird for her. Here she is, only a week out from her would-be wedding, and she's watching another couple get married.

As promised, the ceremony is short and sweet, but includes the bride and groom speaking vows they wrote themselves. My throat goes thick as I watch them, knowing what they had to fight through to get here and the ugly secrets they had to overcome to find their way to this moment. Is it too much to want that for myself too?

My eyes lock on Emma, where she sits holding Jazzy in the front row. She's so beautiful. Today she's here as Emma Rothschild and isn't making any attempt to hide her identity with a wig or ball cap. She's in a peach dress that came in the box of belongings Becky sent for her. Her hair is down around her shoulders, the wispy curls flying around her face in the breeze.

Arrow and Mia are pronounced husband and wife, and he kisses her long and hard before they walk down the aisle and lead the rest of us to the reception tent.

I've looked forward to this wedding most of the year just because it meant I got to see my friends. Chances are we won't get to be together like this until the next one of us gets married, but tonight, despite all those months of anticipation about having my college friends in one place, I just want to be close to Emma.

When she called me earlier to let me know that Liv dropped Jazzy off, I offered to come get her, but she promised me she had it handled, and from all appearances, she's a pro. Watching her hold my baby girl does something to me. It's a sight that makes me have hopes for the future. It makes me want this to be just the beginning.

EMMA

The ceremony was beautiful, and the reception is just as breathtaking. The tent is bustling with servers circulating with trays of hors d'oeuvres and drinks. As we wait for the bride and groom to finish pictures, the band plays softly in the background.

Keegan's whole crew is here, and Olivia is supposed to join us for the reception, but Jazzy and I are getting along just fine, *thankyouverymuch.*

Seeing Arrow and Mia get married today made me that much more confident that I did the right thing by walking away from my wedding. These two love each other so much that it just feels good to see them be together. This is what marriage should be. Two people who aren't just friends or just lovers, but who are both and who will fight for each other.

I don't know what my future holds. Before last night, my secrets were so weighed down by shame and guilt, I didn't think I'd ever be strong enough to drag them from the darkness to the light. Maybe Keegan's secrets aren't so different, but the lies have put a pin of doubt in our relationship that I'm ready to be rid of. Tonight, after the reception, we can talk. He's already admitted he lied, but I'm ready for the explanation.

"Nice reception," someone says behind me.

"It's beautiful," I say, turning toward Olivia's voice.

She reaches her arms out for Jazzy, but I just stare at her stupidly.

"My baby?" she says, arching a brow. She's wearing a sapphire necklace.

She clears her throat. "Are you okay?"

"Where'd you get that necklace?"

"From Keegan," she says. She tilts her head to the side and brushes my grandmother's stone with her fingertips. "It's simple, but I think that's what makes it so pretty."

Keegan. Keegan, who fed me so many lies the summer we met. Keegan, who told me his mother was dead and that he lived in Blackhawk Valley as a child. Keegan, who once warned me that a guy like him could take anything he wanted from someone like me.

But of all the things he could have taken, to take my grandmother's necklace just seems cruel.

"You look like you've seen a ghost," Olivia says, taking Jazzy from my arms. "Why don't you go sit down for a while?"

"That's my necklace," I blurt.

Her cheeks turn red and she reaches to get it off with one hand while holding Jazzy in the other. "Oh my God, that's so embarrassing. I had no idea." She shakes her head and exhales a long breath. "Not that I should be surprised. I mean, he got everything else from you, am I right?"

I swallow hard and stare at the white gold chain and blue stone, and she deposits it in my hand. "What do you mean?"

She laughs. "Come on, I'm not new around here. I talked to Keegan's dad. I know you worked it out so you'd pay for his college. Lucky him. The rest of us had to take out loans."

"That was my decision to make," I whisper. *Why did she have my grandmother's necklace?* "It was something I wanted to do for him."

"Yeah, right. As if that wasn't exactly what he was after when he hired that guy to follow you with the camera."

The hair stands up on the back of my neck. "Excuse me?"

"Remember, you two first met because some creepy man kept taking pictures of you and this sweet guy swept in to save the day?" She wiggles her brows. "His dad told me the whole story, how Keegan set it all up to look like he was a hero, and you fell, hook, line, and sinker. He had the whole story about needing money for school, and he got it."

I blink at her as suddenly the memory falls into place—the day on the beach, the day in front of the ice cream store, the man with the camera. No. It was a coincidence that Keegan was there. He was working in Laguna. He never asked for money. His dad did, but Keegan didn't know about that.

"His dad said Keegan knew how to spot an easy mark," she says. She bounces the baby in her arms as she cocks her head to the side. "You were lonely. You were insecure. All you needed was a good-looking guy paying you some attention, and he had you eating out of his hand. He picked you, too. It wasn't his dad's idea that time. After he spotted you walking your dog one day, he started watching your schedule, getting to know your habits. He could read you and see how lonely you were."

I want to scream at her, to slap her and ask how dare she tell such terrible lies. But my stomach is sick because I already know she's telling me the truth. Keegan's carefully crafted stories that he never bothered to tell me were complete works of fiction. I had to figure out on my own which pieces were lies, and I still don't know if there are parts of him I believe to be true that aren't.

When someone has stolen your heart while lying to you, how can you trust yourself to sort the truth from the fiction?

"You're still lonely, aren't you? And you think you're going to come to town and take my family away from me," Olivia says, "but maybe he doesn't want you. Maybe he just feels guilty for getting exactly what he set out to get from you. He wants to be a better man, but I hate to see him sacrifice his family to make that happen."

I feel sick, and I make a fist around the necklace and rush from the reception.

KEEGAN

Five years ago…

"Keegan, my name is Amanda, and I'm an admissions counselor at Blackhawk Hills University. I noticed you weren't enrolled in classes yet, and I wondered if I could help you with that."

I sit up in bed and drag a hand over my face. "I'm sorry. I'm not sure I'm coming anymore."

"Oh." She's silent for a long beat. "May I ask why?"

Because I don't know if I can live a straight life without Emma guiding me. Because I'm fucking empty and broken, and I don't know if I can be the man she believed I was. "Money, I guess," I mutter. "I'm not comfortable taking out the loans."

"There's no need for loans," the woman on the phone says. "There's a trust set up in your name. Your tuition and room and board are paid for, and there will be a small stipend, too. Didn't you get the letter?"

The letter would have been mailed to my mom's house in Texas. That was the address I used on the application when I had no intention of going to BHU, when it was all just part of the cover story to get money from Emma. I haven't been there in years. "I didn't. Who set up the trust?"

"It's a program through the university. We have donors who go through the applicants and choose a student or students to sponsor anonymously. You should consider yourself very lucky for being the beneficiary of someone's generosity."

A trust? A donor? "Can I find out who my donor is before I accept?"

"I'm sorry. It doesn't work that way."

"And what happens if I decide not to enroll?"

"Well, that'll be up to the donor, of course. Perhaps they'll give the gift to another student, or perhaps they won't. Either way, I'm sure that after the time they've invested in you, they'd be very disappointed if you walked away from this opportunity."

I drag a hand through my hair and pace my bedroom. Did Emma do this? Is this her way of apologizing for pushing me away? I don't want her money, and the idea of her finding some way to give it to me makes me sick.

The woman clears her throat. "Is there a change in your life and you need to postpone your start date? We could have the trust lawyer contact your donor and find out if you can accept the gift in the spring or even next fall."

"No, I—" I sink onto the couch and lean my head back. What if the money's not from Emma? What if I'm being given a chance to change my life? What if the best chance I have at getting Emma back is going to BHU and being who I pretended to be with her?

CHAPTER 37
KEEGAN

When we're finally released from picture duty, I search the reception tent for Emma and can't find her. I find her back at the house, sitting by the fire pit, her arms folded as she stares off into the distance. "Hey, what's wrong?"

She licks her lips as she turns to me, and I can tell by the way she holds herself and the pain on her face that she has something to tell me. Is she leaving? Is this over now? "You'd tell me, wouldn't you? If you needed money?"

Oh, damn. "I'm okay." It's almost true. I'm on my way to *okay*. I'll get there. I'll sell the bar and maybe think about selling my house in Blackhawk Valley to make ends meet until I can get into a cheaper condo lease. "What's going on?"

She tilts her head to the side then reaches toward me with a closed fist and slowly opens her fingers to reveal a sapphire necklace. "I told you there was nothing you could take from me that I didn't want to give. I meant it."

The necklace. "Where did you get this?"

"Olivia was wearing it."

I search her face, and my heart falls to the pit of my stomach. Hurt twists her features, as if someone is cutting into her chest with no anesthesia.

"I'm leaving now."

"Leaving?" I shake my head. Why did Olivia have the necklace? "Wait. Emma, I didn't give it to her. She must have found it in my drawer and borrowed it."

"Found it *in your drawer.*" She closes her eyes and swallows. "Do you even hear yourself? You had it, Keegan."

"And I can explain."

She shrugs. "I don't think I want to hear your explanations anymore."

"What's going on? Why are you leaving? Mia and Arrow will wonder where you went, and I want—"

"I'm leaving *you,* Keegan. I'm not just leaving the wedding. I'm driving home tonight."

I shake my head. "No. What happened?"

"All you had to do was ask. For the money for college, for the necklace. I would have given you anything. But you knew that, didn't you? That's why you fed me lies. Olivia told me everything." She swallows thickly, and I hear it. It's the sound of a closing door, the sound of her drawing in truth I don't want her to have. "How I was the perfect mark. How you set out to get the money to pay for BHU."

I frown. "But I didn't take money from you."

"No, you were too clever for that. I made sure it was anonymous."

I shake my head again. None of this makes any sense, and my confusion is turning into panic. "What did Olivia say to you? Don't go without talking to me."

"I don't even know what to believe anymore."

"Believe in *us*. This is real." My whisper is jagged with my own desperation. I drop my drink on the bench and walk toward her. She inches backward but doesn't turn away. I cup her face in my hands and look into her eyes as they fill with tears. "You and me. Right here. Right now."

"How can I live with someone I don't trust?"

I flinch from that blow. "But you *can* trust me. Olivia's right. I was in the game. I was after money, but I'm not the same man I was then. I wasn't even the same man by the end of the summer. I was—" I look away. It hurts too much to see the truth in her eyes, to see clear as day that it doesn't matter what I say right now. She's been poisoned, and everything I say is tainted.

"Will you just tell me something?" she says.

"Anything."

"The first time we made love. The way you kissed me and touched me. You said you got carried away, that I did something to you. Was that real, or was it part of the plan? Was any of it real."

"It was real. Completely real. I went in with a plan and I fell *hard*."

"But you wouldn't have approached me if you didn't want my money."

I pull her closer because I can feel her slipping away. "Does it matter?"

She squeezes her eyes shut and tears roll out the corners. "Yes, Keegan. It matters. The fact that your mom is alive and living in Texas when you told me she'd died of cancer matters. The fact that you're not from where you said matters. The fact that you've never shared details—*true* details—about your childhood, that matters."

"I *love* you."

"I love you too." Her voice hitches with a sob. "But I don't even know you." She steps back, and it feels like she's taking my heart with her. "I have to leave."

"I'll take care of you." My hands fall to my sides. I'm a shell. "I'll give you anything. Don't do this. Don't give up on us."

"You can't give me what I need."

If there was anything left in me, it would ache with those words. Because that's what I've always feared. I can't give her what she needs because I'm not enough. Because I don't know how to love like that. "What do you need? I'll try. Please."

"I need to know that the man I love has always wanted me for the right reasons. I need to know that all the things he said to me, the words that made me feel cherished for the first time in my life, I need to know those things were true." A tear rolls down her cheek. "You can't give me that."

"What are you doing all the way over here?" Bailey asks. Her dress swishes around her feet as she makes her way toward me. She motions in the direction of the reception tent and the setting sun. "The party is *that way*." She grins, but the smile falls from her face when she sees mine. She takes off her sunglasses. "What's wrong?"

"Emma left." The words don't feel right. Somehow, even though it's not the first time, even though I knew we still had shit between us, *somehow* I was a sucker and believed we could do it. I believed I could have *more*.

"Oh. Is she okay? She was in such a good mood earlier. Is she sick? Oh my God, is she *pregnant*?"

I shake my head. I feel sick. I feel hollow.

The first time she left me, I honestly never wanted to fall in love again. It hurt so fucking much. It's like I was the Tin Man who only wanted a heart, and she gave me one and then stabbed a knife into it. And here we are again, and I have no one to blame but myself.

"Keegan? What happened?"

Opening my hand, I stare at the sapphire necklace she gave me before walking away.

"Holy shit," Bailey says. "That's beautiful."

"I screwed up. Olivia... I don't know how she knew... My dad must've... *Fuck*. Why would he tell her all that? Except she told him dirt too..." I drag a hand over my face.

"Olivia's been hanging out with your dad at The End Zone a lot when you're not there. They're best buddies. My guess is she's been plying him with beer and savoring the details she could use to get you back. She's a fucking bitch."

I narrow my eyes at her. "She's still the mother of my child, Bail."

"Right. That." She sighs. "Sorrynotsorry. She's still a bitch."

"I don't know what I'm supposed to do."

She turns toward the reception before turning back to me. "Go after her. I'll cover for you." When I don't move, she says, "I'm serious, Keegan. You want her, you go after her."

"What happened to 'people like us are only entertainment to people like them'?"

"I'm a jaded bitch. Go. After. Her." She sinks onto the bench beside me. "Come on. Give a trailer park girl a reason to believe in happily-ever-after. Please?"

CHAPTER 38
KEEGAN

"I was raised in Texas." The few words are only the first of many I need to say tonight, but they feel like they were superglued into my chest, and pushing them out rips me apart. I step into the guest bedroom in time to see Emma zipping a suitcase, but I don't let that stop me. "I only went to Blackhawk Valley once as a child. I was there because Dad was working a con on an old widow who lived here. But the place reminded me of something out of a movie, and I thought if I ever had kids, I didn't want to drag them from town to town like Dad dragged me around. I wanted them to be raised in a place like this."

She slides the suitcase off the bed and onto the floor, picks up her phone, and taps into the web browser.

I might as well be invisible, and that hurts so much I want to stop. To protect myself from more pain. But I push on. "My mom never had cancer, but I spent my childhood watching her shave her head and walk around looking as weak as possible so people would think she did. The sick woman was her con of choice, and maybe she didn't die of cancer, but when she left us—when she left *me* after conning the man I call my father—it felt like she died. She barely knew him, but she had no trouble walking away and letting him raise me. It was easier to tell the story she'd claimed so many times than it was to tell people the truth about where I came from."

She squeezes her eyes shut, and when she opens them, her fingers fly across the screen of her phone as she books a hotel. I want to look and see how far she plans to get tonight and where she's driving—back to Savannah or to LA? But I don't let myself. I have to focus on saying all the things I should have said five years ago.

"Before I met you, I never intended to go to college. I never had any designs to play college or pro ball, because I was exactly who my father raised me to be. I was a guy who knew how to get by without ever having to work. A guy who'd spent so much of his life blurring the lines between truth and lies that some days I didn't even remember what was real."

I think about closing the bedroom door and blocking her way out, but I can't do that to her, so I stay to the side, keeping the path clear and praying she won't use it. "I'll never forget the day I saw you walking on that beach. I wasn't supposed to be there, but it was the most beautiful place I'd ever seen and I couldn't stay away. I saw you walking that little dog, and I just…" I look at her. She hasn't spoken a word, and I can't decide if that's good or bad. I can't decide if I want to know what she's thinking or if I just want to get through this. "I wanted you. I knew who you were immediately. I always thought you were pretty when I saw you on TV, but in person… Fuck, Em. In person, you *glow.* I knew that you were untouchable and I could never have anything as beautiful as you."

She shakes her head—the first indication she's given me that she's even listening, and that gives me the courage to continue.

"I knew I couldn't have you, and that pissed me off. There are a lot of things in my life I've wanted and couldn't have. I'd made my peace with that. But you? God, it ate me up inside to look at you and know you'd never be mine. I was sick of settling. So when you say that you can't trust that I was attracted to you, *fuck that.* Attraction was the easy part. What I wasn't prepared for was what you did to me"—I tap my chest—"in here. You had so much. You had *everything,* and I wanted a piece. And along the way, just to say *fuck you* to the universe, I wanted to pretend for a minute that I could have you too. It didn't go like I planned, and by the time I slept with you, I didn't want your money anymore. I just wanted *you.*"

"You should have told me." A tear rolls down her cheek. "You had so many opportunities."

"I didn't know how to tell you the truth without losing you. How could I tell you I used you and I conned you? I set you up with a plan to take everything I could from you, and then when you believed I was better than that, I wanted to believe it too. I won't ask you to forgive me for what I did—for what I set out to do—because I know how ugly it is. But what I need you to do is consider what happened to me along the way. You changed what I was after. You changed who I was and what I believed I could have. By the time it ended, all I wanted was a chance to be the man you believed I was."

She shakes her head. "It was all a lie."

I feel her slipping through my fingers, and reach out to grab her but then force my hands back to my sides. I need her to stay because she wants to. I need her to want me enough that it's worth finding the courage to stay. "But the lie became the truth. That's who I've become. You didn't just make me want to be a better man, you turned me into one. It was as if your love reached into me and changed the structure of my cells, the very essence of who I was. You gave me the strength to be someone better. I know you don't need me, and I know you can leave me today and carry on just fine without me, but you will always, *always* be the very best thing that ever happened to me."

"Thank you," she whispers. She tucks her phone in her purse and slings it over her shoulder before rolling her suitcase to the front door.

"I couldn't go back to the guy who used everyone. I'm not him anymore." I follow her, fists clenched at my sides, stomach in knots. "Emma. Don't leave me again. *Please.*"

She steps outside and unlocks the car that brought her here. "I need to think, Keegan," she says as she walks to the trunk. She loads her suitcase and avoids my gaze. "I need to step away and process everything."

"You're *running*."

She pauses with her hand on the driver's-side door. "Yeah. I guess that's what I do." Then she ducks her head and climbs into the car, and I'm just standing there in my tux, helpless to do anything but watch as she drives away.

CHAPTER 39
KEEGAN

"You took money from Emma. You conned her out of money I told you I didn't want."

Dad spins around on his barstool and gapes at me. "What?"

After Emma left, I came straight to the bar and found my father right where I thought I would. "You had no right." My voice shakes, and I can tell by his pale face he knows I'm telling the truth. I want to blame this all on him—my decision not to tell Emma the truth sooner, her decision to climb into that car and drive away. I drag a hand over my face and collapse onto the stool beside him. "Olivia told Emma everything." I swallow. "She left me. I don't think she's coming back. I love her and I've lost her."

He picks up his half-empty beer and drains the rest. "That's my fault," he says softly. "I thought you'd choose Olivia after you were done rescuing Emma from her canceled wedding, and I was trying to get close to her, hoping you wouldn't push me out anymore if your girl wanted me around." He shakes his head. "It was careless, telling her all that, but I swear I wouldn't have done it if I'd realized…"

I wave to Patsy, the server who's running The End Zone while the rest of us are supposed to be at Mia and Arrow's wedding. She pours me a shot of whiskey and slides it down the bar. I stare at it. "You shouldn't have had her pay for BHU. I never would have taken the money if I'd known it was from her."

He stares at his empty glass. "I know, but it was the closest I could come to paying for it myself. I wanted that for you, and I thought she owed it to you—sneaking around with that old man while she was supposed to be with you."

I shake my head. "It wasn't like that. You were wrong about her. We both were." The truth settles into my gut like lead. "But we'd made our lives out of deception and couldn't believe everyone else wasn't as crooked as we were."

He waves at Patsy and she shakes her head. "You've about had enough tonight, don't you think?"

Dad sighs. "But you weren't crooked. You were the worst conman I'd ever met. Too good deep down to do a job right." He studies me for a beat. "Too good deep down to be stuck in the life I'd made for us. You deserved at least one chance at something better, and I gave it to you in the only way I knew how. But don't you see why? Look at you now. Look what you've become."

I throw back my shot, letting the heat fill the cracks around my aching heart. "I wouldn't be anything if it hadn't been for her."

EMMA

The rolling waves of the Gulf of Mexico roll into shore just beyond my balcony and help me breathe a little easier. Breathing hasn't felt right since I left Keegan. I understand the metaphor of a breaking heart, because my chest literally aches, and I don't want to take a full breath, because it hurts as if the shards sitting in there are poking into the tender tissue of my lungs.

He called a couple of times the day after I left. I didn't answer. He's texted a dozen times since. I haven't replied.

The sliding glass door slides open and closed again.

"I owe you an apology," Mom says. Becky met me here shortly after I arrived, telling me friends don't let friends nurse broken hearts alone. Mom arrived not long after that, and Becky refused to let her in the door until she listened to how Harry showed up at Keegan's and tried to force himself on me again. "You know I'm not good at apologizing, and I'm sorry for that too. I should have listened to you five years ago. I should have believed you, because mothers should believe their daughters, but I didn't want to. I wanted it all to be a terrible lie, because the truth was too horrible. I told myself, if she's telling the truth, she'll fight me and insist that I listen. But you didn't, and I wanted to choose his story over yours so badly that I gave myself permission to think yours was all some jealous lie."

I cut my gaze away from her and focus on the steady rhythm of the waves rolling onto the shore, one after the next. This is life—moving on and continuing at its steady pace, no matter how much we might hurt inside and wish it all would *stop*.

"A mother doesn't want to think she's put her daughter into the path of a predator over and over and over again. I chose what was easier. His bullshit was easier, and I'm sorry."

The words themselves cut something open inside me—an unhealed wound I've had wrapped up tight for five years. "Mom..." I shake my head. I don't know what to say. Words tangle on my tongue, confused and contradictory. *How could you? Thank you. You're selfish. I know this is hard for you.*

"I told him I wanted a divorce a few months ago. He's broke and wanted my money more than he ever wanted me. He swore he'd make a public spectacle if I went through with the divorce. I've been waiting because I didn't want to take the attention off you and Zachary. And that marriage...there's another place I failed you."

I turn away from the waves and look at her. She looks decades older today. Has she aged so suddenly, or did I stop looking her in the eyes so long ago that I never noticed the wrinkles that have formed there?

"I should have known it wasn't what you wanted," she says. "There was something off about you two together. You and Zach are clearly good friends, but it didn't compare to you and Keegan together. Something was missing, and instead of telling you to wait, instead of advising my *daughter* not to settle for a marriage where something important is missing, I chose what was easier. I told myself the marriage was going to make my daughter happy, and I needed to do everything I could to make that happen because I was never able to give her happiness before." She gives a shaky smile, but her eyes remain sad. "I know an apology isn't enough. I know I don't deserve your forgiveness. But if you're going to keep hating me the way you have for the last five years, then I want you to do it knowing that I *know* I screwed up."

"I don't hate you," I whisper.

"Maybe you should. I think I would." She lifts her eyes to the clear sky. "If I could go back in time, I'd do it all differently. I would never marry Harry. I'd listen when my little girl told me she felt like she spent too much time on the set and she wanted to quit the show. I'd have asked more questions instead of pushing her to keep going. I can't change any of that, but if I could..."

"I forgive you, Mom. You believed what you needed to believe to stay sane. We all do that."

She shakes her head. "Don't do that. Don't be so easy on me. Yell at me or something. Make me feel terrible, because I deserve worse."

"You're still my mom. You're not perfect, but neither am I." I take a breath. "You were just protecting yourself."

"And is that why you ran from Keegan? To protect yourself?"

I shake my head. "It's not the same."

She rubs my back with her open palm, and the physical

affection is so out of character that it takes me by surprise. "I can tell you from experience: it's not worth it. Better to be cut open and be true to your heart than to protect yourself and live half a life."

CHAPTER 40
KEEGAN

"Keegan, there you are!" Bailey and I both turn to Olivia as she walks into the bar with Jazzy on her hip and a grin on her face. "You're a tough man to track down lately." She looks back and forth between me and Bailey. "Damn. Who died?"

I shake my head. "Don't. Not now."

She rolls her eyes. "Come on. You can't be serious about that girl. She's not even..."

"What?" I ask through clenched teeth.

"She's in the way, okay? Dre dumped me, and suddenly you weren't interested, and I'm alone with no job, and the second you decide you're not paying my bills anymore, I'm screwed. I have student loans but no degree, a baby but no husband." She shakes her head. "All I have to show for anything is this beautiful girl and her daddy, a guy who loved me once."

Bailey nods at me before turning back to tending bar. "We'll talk later."

I've spent the last week avoiding Olivia and refusing to talk to her about anything that didn't directly affect Jazzy, but it's time to talk. "My dad told you?" I ask.

"Yeah. It took some time, but I got the old man to spill the beans. He's sweet. He admires you, ya know. You changed, turned over a new leaf, became the better man. He wants to be like you someday. I found his story real interesting, though, and I figured it couldn't hurt to tell her. You two couldn't have anything like that between you anyway. Am I right?"

I thought I was too tired to feel angry anymore, but she's bringing it back full force. "You knew exactly what you were doing."

Olivia sinks down onto the stool next to me. "I'm sorry I was immature before. I'm sorry I couldn't see that we should be together. Just give me a chance. We had fun together."

"Liv, you were always holding out for something better."

"I'm not anymore. I was stupid. But Jazzy..." She shakes her head. "That kid is so awesome that I'd do anything to give her a good family."

"Including being with a man you don't really love and living a life you don't really want?"

Her smile falls away. "I didn't know the necklace was hers. I saw it in your drawer one day and borrowed it. I forgot I had it until I was looking for something to wear with my dress that night. I figured it was something of your mom's or something.

Did you steal it from her?"

I shake my head. "No. Dad did. I tracked it down and emptied out my savings to buy it back for her. It belonged to her grandmother."

She cocks her head to the side and studies me. "Then why was it in your drawer, Keegan?"

"I meant to give it back a long time ago. I kept thinking that I'd get around to shipping it. But that's the necklace she always said she couldn't imagine getting married without. I think part of me didn't want her to have it."

Her face falls and her words go soft. "Because you didn't want her marrying someone other than you."

I meet her eyes. "Liv, I love her. She is the reason I'm worth a shit today. She's the reason Dad and I aren't still wandering around the country screwing one woman after another out of her money."

"Sounds exciting," she says, propping her chin on her fists.

"Don't glamorize it. It's not like the movies. It's pathetic—seducing women, getting them to give me money for this or that fake problem. I might as well have been whoring myself out. At least that would have been more honest, but it was the life I knew. It felt normal. And then I fell in love with Emma, and it was like seeing the world in a whole new way. She made me believe in myself like I never had before."

"Is she the reason you never let me in?" she asks, a resigned sadness to her features now.

"It wasn't intentional. With other girls, I wasn't interested in getting emotional. I didn't want to fall in love—I'd been there, done that, and it fucking killed me. But once I knew you were pregnant, I wanted to let you in. I really did. I do love you, Liv, but the thing that was missing between us? I think Em already had it."

She swallows and rubs her bare arms. "I'm sorry if I screwed everything up."

"I wish she hadn't found out like she did, but she needed to find out, and if she can't forgive me, that's just something I'm going to have to come to terms with."

"Well, if she never comes to her senses, maybe someday you and I—"

I shake my head. "Don't do that to yourself. Don't settle for half my heart just because you're scared you can't do any better."

Her eyes fill with tears. "Keegan Keller, any girl would be lucky to have you and half your heart. I'm sorry it took me so long to realize that."

EMMA

"Are you about done yet?" Becky asks from behind me.

I push myself up off the sand and wipe my sandy hands on my shorts. She's been patient with me all week, and I couldn't ask for a better friend. "Done with what?" I ask.

"Punishing him for what he did? Are you done so you can

quit punishing yourself?"

"I don't know what you mean." I shake my head. "I'm not punishing myself."

She folds her arms and leans her shoulder into the jamb of the open sliding glass door. "You're miserable. This can't go on."

"I don't know what to do. My relationship with Harry was so bad because it was entirely built on his ability to manipulate me to get what he wanted. And to find out that Keegan was the same?"

"Your relationship with Harry was so bad because he's a pedophile. He liked that he could control you," she says. "Don't do that to Keegan. He's made mistakes, but he doesn't deserve that. Don't put your relationship with him in the same category."

"He just wanted money from me."

"Did he? Is that why he asked you to come to Indiana with him? Is that why he wanted you to leave behind the city where you could have made millions more if you'd been willing to keep acting?"

I swallow hard. I know what she's saying makes sense, but my pride is so damn battered I don't want to hear it. "He *played* me."

"Five years ago," she says. "And then you pushed him away and he had no idea that you had anything to do with sending him to college. Then, when you ran away from your wedding, he took you in without hesitating. He's *not* Harry."

"I know he's not. Of course he's not."

"You know what the real problem is here, don't you?"

I fold my arms and shake my head. "I'm guessing you're

going to tell me."

"The real problem, sweet girl, is that you don't believe that anyone could love you if there's nothing in it for them. Your problem is that what Olivia told you confirmed what you already believed, and it was easier for you to hold on to that and run away than it was for you to accept that he truly loves you and you deserve to be happy."

"What about him? What if me being there means he doesn't get to have the family he wants? I did find my way back to him," I say, then I stop for a beat to marvel at that. Sometimes it seems like the world brings us back together with the people we need most. "But I ran away because I got scared that I'm not enough for him."

"Isn't that his choice to make?"

I still, realizing her words echo what I promised Bailey that night at the bar. I told her I still didn't believe I was good enough for Keegan, but I was going to let him make that choice. But then Olivia's words got in my head and I wondered if it was true, if maybe Keegan just felt guilty for the lies and was sacrificing more than he should to make it up to me.

"What if he's already back with Olivia?"

She gives me a sad smile. "Then I guess you have your answer."

"He's not with her," a man says.

Gasping, I spin around to see Keegan's father approaching us on the beach.

"He can't be with Olivia when he's in love with you."

Becky darts her gaze between us, and I put my hand on her

arm. "It's okay. He's Keegan's dad."

She draws in a breath. "Want me to stay?"

I shake my head. "No. Let us talk."

"Call for me if you need me. I won't be far."

Keegan's dad watches her go, and when she reaches the stairs that lead back to the condo, he pulls a small thumb drive from his pocket. "This is for you."

I stare at it as he places it into my open palm. "What is it?"

"It's Harry Evans's private collection of photos of you—plenty of evidence there to prove you two had a relationship ten years ago." Pain sweeps over his face, and he squeezes his eyes shut for a beat before looking at me again. "I only regret that I can't go back in time. I wouldn't have let him bring you those flowers if I'd known what he would do. I thought you wanted him there. I believed…" He clenches his fists and his nostrils flare. "I don't know if you want to do anything with it, but I hope you'll take it to the police. I hope that son of a bitch will get the punishment he deserves."

"How did you…?"

"I just had to get close enough to him to get to his laptop. After that, it wasn't hard. I'm good at getting people to let me in." He shrugs and shifts his gaze out to the water. "It's how I got by for most of my life, but I'm not using my gifts for greed anymore. I need to prove it to my son, but that's going to take some time."

I curl my fingers around the thumb drive. The girl I once was didn't have the courage to tell anyone about Harry, and then I became a woman who didn't have any evidence even if she wanted to tell. "Thank you."

When he turns back to me, there are tears in his eyes. "Don't make Keegan pay for my mistakes. I should have raised him better. I should have cleaned up my act the second his mother walked away, but instead I saw an opportunity to use a kid to get ahead. But he's good deep down, that one. I always knew it. He's too good for the con and I was always afraid he'd end up hurt because of it. That's why when I thought you were sneaking around with Harry, I assumed the worst." He shakes his head and swallows thickly. "I failed you both."

"Does he know you're here? That you're giving me this?"

"No. I was afraid he might tell me not to come, and I wanted the chance to apologize in person." He drags a hand through his gray hair. "I wanted a chance to do what Keegan would do."

CHAPTER 41
KEEGAN

"Can you fill the bucket with water for Daddy?" I ask Jazzy, handing her a tiny blue pail.

She takes it from my hands and toddles toward the ocean, scooping up a couple of milliliters before shrieking when the cold water washes over her toes and she rushes back to me.

Back in Seaside, the only thing I can do is put my head down and train hard for next season. Emma still hasn't been in touch and that burns like hell, but I'm giving her the space she said she needed.

"Dump it here," I tell Jazzy, pointing to the moat we've scooped out around our sand castle. "There you go."

She plops onto her bottom and uses a shovel to dig a new hole. I press my hand against my chest as I watch her. I wouldn't change any of it. Emma made me want to be a better man, but if she'd never left me, I wouldn't have Jazzy. I have to believe this time will result in something incredible too.

"Do you know what fish love is?"

My head snaps up at the sound of Emma's voice. She's on the beach in front of my condo and walking toward me.

This stretch of beach along the Gulf of Mexico is considered by many as the most beautiful beach in the world. The sand is soft and white, and the water displays colors of blue and green and everything in between.

When I moved down here last year to train with the Gators, I couldn't believe my luck. To get to live in such a beautiful place, to get to wake up and look at the ocean every day. But right now, the ocean isn't the beauty that's stolen my attention. Instead, I can't get my eyes off Emma.

She's wearing a simple light pink sundress that moves in the wind, molding around her curves. Her red curls fly in the breeze of the ocean. She sighs and plops down onto the sand beside me, tucking her legs beneath her.

"What's fish love?" I ask, and my voice is shaking.

"It's some old parable. The man eats the fish and he says he loves the fish, but he only loves the fish because the fish tastes good and makes him feel good. He loves the fish because of what it can do for him."

Jazzy toddles up to Em and hands her a shovel. "Dig."

Emma obeys, digging a small hole in the sand between us as she continues. "It's a selfish love, fish love. And the point of the parable is that we shouldn't seek fish love. We should seek to give and receive selfless love." She pulls a folded piece of paper from the pocket in her dress and puts down her shovel so she can unfold it with both hands.

When I see her loopy handwriting and my squared note on top of it, I realize it's the note she wrote me five years ago. It's the note I gave back to her the night before her wedding.

She skims her fingers over her old words—*Please know this: As much as I want you for myself, I want more for you to be happy. Do that for me.* Then she traces over my *ditto*.

"Selfless love is confusing," she says, lifting her eyes to mine. "I wanted to let you go then because I thought you deserved better than some screwed-up girl. But maybe I was being selfish because I was scared for you to know my secrets. I wanted to be who you thought I was, and if I told you about Harry, I couldn't be that anymore."

It hurts to think that she hid part of herself because she didn't think I could love her if I knew her secrets, and the pain is so acute because I did the same. I'm not sure what to say, so I just wait, listening.

"You wanted to be who I thought you were, so you didn't tell me the truth."

Jazzy plops down in front of Emma and uses her hands to push sand back into the hole.

"Selfless love is hard to figure out because we're all kind of selfish at our core, so I thought, maybe, screw the parable." She grins at me and swallows. "I want selfish love. I want to be with you because you make me feel safe. That's selfish. I want to wake up in your arms because you make me feel beautiful. Selfish. I want to be by your side as you raise this beautiful baby because it makes me believe that life has more goodness in it than I ever realized."

"That's really selfish," I say. "Kind of like how I want you in my life because you remind me why I want to be a better man?"

She nods. "Yeah. Selfish."

I draw in a deep breath and slide my sandy hand over hers. "Or how I want to go to sleep with you in my arms because you're so insanely beautiful that I need to touch you to convince myself you're here and that I'm lucky enough to have you."

She blinks and tears roll from the corners of her eyes, and I'm filled with relief and hope and love and adoration so intense I wish she could simply see herself as I see her. "So selfish."

I nod. "I could do selfish. The other way seems to drive us apart too much, and I don't care for that—selfishly, of course."

"Of course."

"So we try loving each other and making each other happy for a while. I think you'll find that I can be pretty good at this fish-love thing." I bite back laughter and shake my head.

"What?" she asks.

I cut my eyes to Jazzy then back to Emma. "I'm pretty sure there's a dirty joke opportunity there, but I'm going to let it pass me by. Little ears and all."

She laughs. "Fair enough." She scans the beach before meeting my eyes again. "Do you like living here?"

"It's been good to me," I say. "I never expected to end up here, but here I am."

"Here you are," she says. She sighs and tucks her arm under mine, leaning her head on my shoulder. "You think I'd like it?"

"I know you would." I dip down to kiss her forehead and breathe in her scent. "Does that mean you're staying?"

"If you'll have me."

"One second, okay?" I pull out my phone and send a quick text. Two minutes later, the nanny is scooping Jazzy into her arms and carrying her into the house for a bath.

"I like your daughter," Emma says, watching them go.

"She's amazing." I wait until she looks at me again. I'm not sure I really deserve this—the moment, the woman, the forgiveness— but I'm going to take it and I'm going to earn it by giving her the best life I can. "I can't believe you're really here."

"I can't believe you know my secrets and still want to be with me," she says.

"I want to be the person you can tell anything. I want to be the one you always know will love you regardless." I cup her face in my hands and lower my mouth to hers.

She whispers, "Ditto."

EPILOGUE
EMMA

"Do you know how long it's been since I've taken my clothes off for anybody but Keegan?" I ask as I pull my jeans back on.

Bailey wiggles her eyebrows. "Was is it as good for you as it was for me?"

"Somehow it wasn't as awkward as I expected." I laugh. "Is it weird for you?"

Bailey snorts. "You forget I used to be a stripper. Body parts are body parts." She shrugs then scrolls through the images on her digital camera. "Not that I think Keegan will feel that way. Damn, girl. You look hot in these. I think he will particularly like the one of you in his jersey."

I bite my lip. "I hope." I've been staying with Keegan for a month, and it's been a rollercoaster of emotions in that short time. I went to the police with the pictures Keegan's dad gave me, and they arrested Harry for statutory rape. When the police found more pictures on his computer, Harry took a plea deal so he wouldn't have to go through the public humiliation of a trial.

Closing that chapter in my life has been exhausting and freeing, and Keegan has been by my side through every step. When I found out Bailey was coming to town, I asked if she'd do some boudoir shots for me. She'd mentioned she'd done them for a couple of friends, and I decided I should do it, even if I missed our fifth "anniversary" by a few weeks.

"Emma?" Keegan calls from the front door. "Are you home?"

"She's in the bedroom with me," Bailey says. "Just getting her clothes back on."

I cover my mouth, but a giggle-snort slips through my fingers as Keegan joins us in the bedroom. He must have showered after practice, because his hair's wet and he smells like soap and not sweaty football player—though, to be honest, I enjoy him both ways.

He steps behind me and wraps his arms around my front before pressing a kiss to the top of my head. "Why do I feel like you two were up to no good in here?"

"Because you know me well?" Bailey asks, smirking.

"True story," he mutters. "Why are you in town, anyway? Patsy said she's going to run the bar for a couple days?"

"Aren't I allowed?"

I can feel his shrug. "It's fine with me, but don't you normally hate to take time off?"

"Yeah, well, Mason's avoiding my calls, so I decided to come talk some sense into him in person."

I feel Keegan tense behind me. "Is everything okay, Bail? You two never told me what happened in Vegas, but if you're pregnant…"

"I'm not pregnant." She tucks her camera into her bag and looks him in the eye. "And everything will be fine once he gives me a divorce."

Keegan and I gasp in unison, but he's the first to speak. "When did he give you a wedding?"

She frowns at her bare ring finger. "You two weren't the only ones to get drunk and make poor decisions in Vegas. The only difference is your bad decision ended up with an unsigned marriage certificate, whereas ours… Well, he promised me we could deal with it after Mia and Arrow's wedding, so it won't matter long anyway." She hoists her backpack on her shoulder and meets my eyes. "I will get back to you with the results of our little project. Wish me luck with Mason."

"Good…luck?" Keegan says, and Bailey walks out the door before I can recover my shock.

When we hear the front door close, I spin in Keegan's arms and gape. "They got *married*?"

He shrugs and drags his hands down my body to settle on my hips. "I guess Vegas makes you do crazy things."

I slide my hands under his T-shirt and find the button on his jeans. "Things you desperately wanted to do anyway."

"Exactly," he whispers. "Want to tell me what you and Bailey were doing in the bedroom with the camera she uses for boudoir shoots?"

"Nope." I unzip his jeans and shove them from his hips. "It's supposed to be a surprise."

He pulls his T-shirt off over his head and then goes for mine. "Will I like it?"

"I hope so."

He throws my T-shirt to the floor and unbuttons my jeans. "Maybe you should show me what I should expect?"

I grin. "You're awfully confident in your assumptions."

"You missed the fifth anniversary of our first date," he says. He pushes my jeans down and leads me to step out of them. "You owe me something."

I prop my hands on my bare hips. "And what did you get me?" I frown, remembering our first date and how he said he'd be just as nervous about his gift for me.

He trails kisses along my shoulder. "Do you want it now or later?"

I step back. "You're distracting me." I laugh, but my stomach is a bundle of nerves. "I want it now, Keegan. What did you get me?"

He scans my face and looks almost nervous. "It's in the top drawer."

I open his dresser and find a black velvet box in the front. My heart hammers wildly, and when I turn to ask if I can open it, he's down on one knee. He takes the box from my hands and opens it. Before I can catch my breath, he pulls out the ring inside and lifts it up.

"Emma Rothschild, I never intended to propose in my boxers." He grins and I laugh, nerves and elation making the sound ring through the room. "I have reservations for this beautiful dinner on the beach where you'd get to listen to the waves and feel the breeze on your face as I asked you to be my wife. But that just goes to show you how crazy you make me, and how nothing has ever gone as planned with you."

I press a hand to my chest as if that might calm my wild heart. "I like this better than the plan."

"I've been hoping for a family since I was a little boy, and I've only recently realized that family isn't how it looks on TV. It's not the people we were born related to or the ones we live with. Family is who you choose along the way. I spent two years hoping Jazzy and Olivia and I could be family without realizing we already were. My friends are part of my family too. They picked up where you left off in making me a better man, and they do what family should—being there for me even when I don't deserve it. I want you to be my family too. But I want you to be the kind of family I come home to every night. I want you to carry my babies and help raise Jasmine." He takes my hand and his is shaking as he slides the sapphire engagement ring on my finger. "Please say yes."

"I knew I wanted to say yes the night of our first date." I sink to my knees in front of him so we're kneeling together. "I saw you then for who you really are, and I think you saw me too."

He kisses me hard, one hand in my hair and the other pulling my body against his until we're tumbling onto the floor and he's lowering himself onto me. "I don't ever want to see you wearing nothing but your sapphire necklace again," he whispers. "From now on, I want you wearing my ring too."

"It's a deal."

THE END

Thank you for reading *Falling Hard,* the fourth book in The Blackhawk Boys series. If you'd like to receive an email when I release Mason's story in book five, *In Too Deep*, please sign up for my newsletter. If you enjoyed this book, please consider leaving a review. Thank you for reading. It's an honor!

FALLING HARD
Playlist

"How Long Will I Love You?" by Ellie Goulding
"Starving" by Hailee Steinfeld
"Dive" by Ed Sheeran
"To Build a Home" by The Cinematic Orchestra
"L.S.D." by Jax
"Stay" by Zedd feat. Alessia Cara
"Perfect" by Ed Sheeran
"Issues" by Julia Michaels
"New Man" by Ed Sheeran
"Paris" by The Chainsmokers
"Adore You" by Miley Cyrus
"Deep the Water" by Lewis Watson
"Find My Way Back" by Cody Fry

Other Books
by LEXI RYAN

The Blackhawk Boys
Spinning Out (Arrow's story)
Rushing In (Chris's story)
Going Under (Sebastian's story)
Falling Hard (Keegan's story)
In Too Deep (Mason's story – coming September 2017)

Love Unbound
by LEXI RYAN

If you enjoy the Blackhawk Boys, you may also enjoy the books in Love Unbound, the linked series of books set in New Hope and about the characters readers have come to love.

Splintered Hearts (A Love Unbound Series)
Unbreak Me (Maggie's story)
Stolen Wishes: A Wish I May Prequel Novella (Will and Cally's prequel)
Wish I May (Will and Cally's novel)

Or read them together in the omnibus edition,
Splintered Hearts: The New Hope Trilogy

Here and Now (A Love Unbound Series)

Lost in Me (Hanna's story begins)

Fall to You (Hanna's story continues)

All for This (Hanna's story concludes)

Or read them together in the omnibus edition,

Here and Now: The Complete Series

Reckless and Real (A Love Unbound Series)

Something Wild (Liz and Sam's story begins)

Something Reckless (Liz and Sam's story continues)

Something Real (Liz and Sam's story concludes)

Or read them together in the omnibus edition,

Reckless and Real: The Complete Series

Mended Hearts (A Love Unbound Series)

Playing with Fire (Nix's story)

Holding Her Close (Janelle and Cade's story)

ACKNOWLEDGMENTS

I always thank my husband first, mostly because he's freaking awesome and I'm a big believer in acknowledging that. He understands me and my process, and he picks up the slack when getting a book revised to my standards means working on vacation—as it did this time—or a weekend (or three) away from the family. Thank you for everything, Brian. Thank you for believing in me and encouraging me when I need it most. You're truly my favorite.

In addition to my rock-star husband, I'm surrounded by a family who supports me every day. To my kids, Jack and Mary, thank you for making me laugh and giving me a reason to work hard. I am so proud to be your mommy. To my mom, dad, brothers, and sisters, thank you for cheering me on—each in your own way. I'm so grateful to have been born into this crazy crew of seven kids.

I'm lucky enough to have a life full of amazing friends, too. Mira is not only my bestie, she's half life coach and half therapist. This girl knows all about my daily challenges—from my career woes to my mothering mishaps. She is the bringer of laughter, the giver of pep talks, and the holder of all my (terribly boring) secrets. Thank you for the chatty time, sister. Thanks also to my workout friends and the entire CrossFit Terre Haute crew, especially Robin, who checks up on me when I disappear too long into the writing cave. I've been blessed with so many amazing people in my life—from my lifelong friends to my newfound buddies. You encourage me, you believe in me, and you know how to make me laugh.

To everyone who provided me feedback on Keegan and Emma's story along the way—especially Heather Carver, Janice Owen, Lisa Kuhne, Mira Lyn Kelly, and Samantha Leighton—you're all awesome. Thank you to attorney Claire Carter who provided me with information about some legal issues I touch on in this book. Any errors in the interpretation of the law are my own. As always, I owe thanks to many people for helping to make this idea in my head into something worth reading.

Thank you to the team that helped me package this book and promote it. Sarah Hansen at Okay Creations designed my beautiful cover and did a lovely job branding the series. Rhonda Stapleton, thank you for the insightful line and content edits and for being understanding when I can't meet a deadline to save my life. Thanks to Arran McNicol at Editing720 for proofreading. A shout-out to my assistant Lisa Kuhne for trying to keep me in line. (It's a losing battle, but she gives it her all.) To all of the bloggers and reviewers who help spread the word about my books, I am humbled by the time you take out of your busy lives for my stories. I can't thank you enough. You're the best.

To my agent, Dan Mandel, for believing in me and staying by my side. Thanks to you and Stefanie Diaz for getting my books into the hands of readers all over the world. Thank you for being part of my team.

To all my writer friends on Facebook, Instagram, and my various writer loops, thank you for being my friends, my squad, and my sounding board. Thank you for sharing your wisdom. I'm so proud to call you friends.

And last but certainly not least, a big thank-you to my fans. I've said it before and I'll continue to say it every chance I get—you're the coolest, smartest, best readers in the world. I wouldn't get to do this job without you, and appreciate each and every one of you!

~Lexi

CONTACT

I love hearing from readers. Find me on my Facebook page at facebook.com/lexiryanauthor, follow me on Twitter and Instagram @writerlexiryan, shoot me an email at writerlexiryan@gmail.com, or find me on my website: www.lexiryan.com